FOR MY MOM & DAD

Published in Canada and the USA in 2015 by Groundwood Books

Groundwood Books / House of Anansi Press
110 Spadina Avenue, Suite 801, Toronto, Ontario M5V 2K4
or c/o Publishers Group West
1700 Fourth Street, Berkeley CA 94710

We acknowledge for their financial support of our publishing program the Government of Canada through the Canada Book Fund (CBF).

Library and Archives Canada Cataloguing in Publication
Tolstikova, Dasha, author, illustrator
A year without mom / written and illustrated
by Dasha Tolstikova.
Issued in print and electronic formats.
ISBN 978-1-55498-692-7 (bound). — ISBN 978-1-55498-693-4 (ebook fxl). — ISBN 978-1-55498-828-0 (kindle kf8)
1. Tolstikova, Dasha — Childhood and youth — Comic books, strips, etc. 2. Tolstikova, Dasha — Childhood and youth — Juvenile literature. 3. Girls — Russia (Federation) — Moscow — Comic books, strips, etc. 4. Girls — Russia (Federation) —Moscow — Juvenile literature. 5. Mothers and daughters — Comic books, strips, etc. 6. Mothers and daughters — Juvenile literature. 7. Moscow (Russia) — Comic books, strips, etc. 8. Moscow (Russia) — Juvenile literature. 9. Graphic novels.
I. Title.
DK593.T65 2015 j947'.31086092 C2015-900038-6
C2015-900039-4

The illustrations were done in pencil and ink wash on Arches hot press paper and edited in Photoshop.
Design by Michael Solomon
Printed and bound in Singapore

FSC
www.fsc.org
MIX
Paper from responsible sources
FSC® C019704

A YEAR
WITHOUT MOM

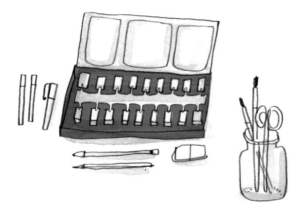

DASHA TOLSTIKOVA

YA GN FIC Year

GROUNDWOOD BOOKS
HOUSE OF ANANSI PRESS
TORONTO   BERKELEY

Once, when I was very small,
I bit my mom's finger.

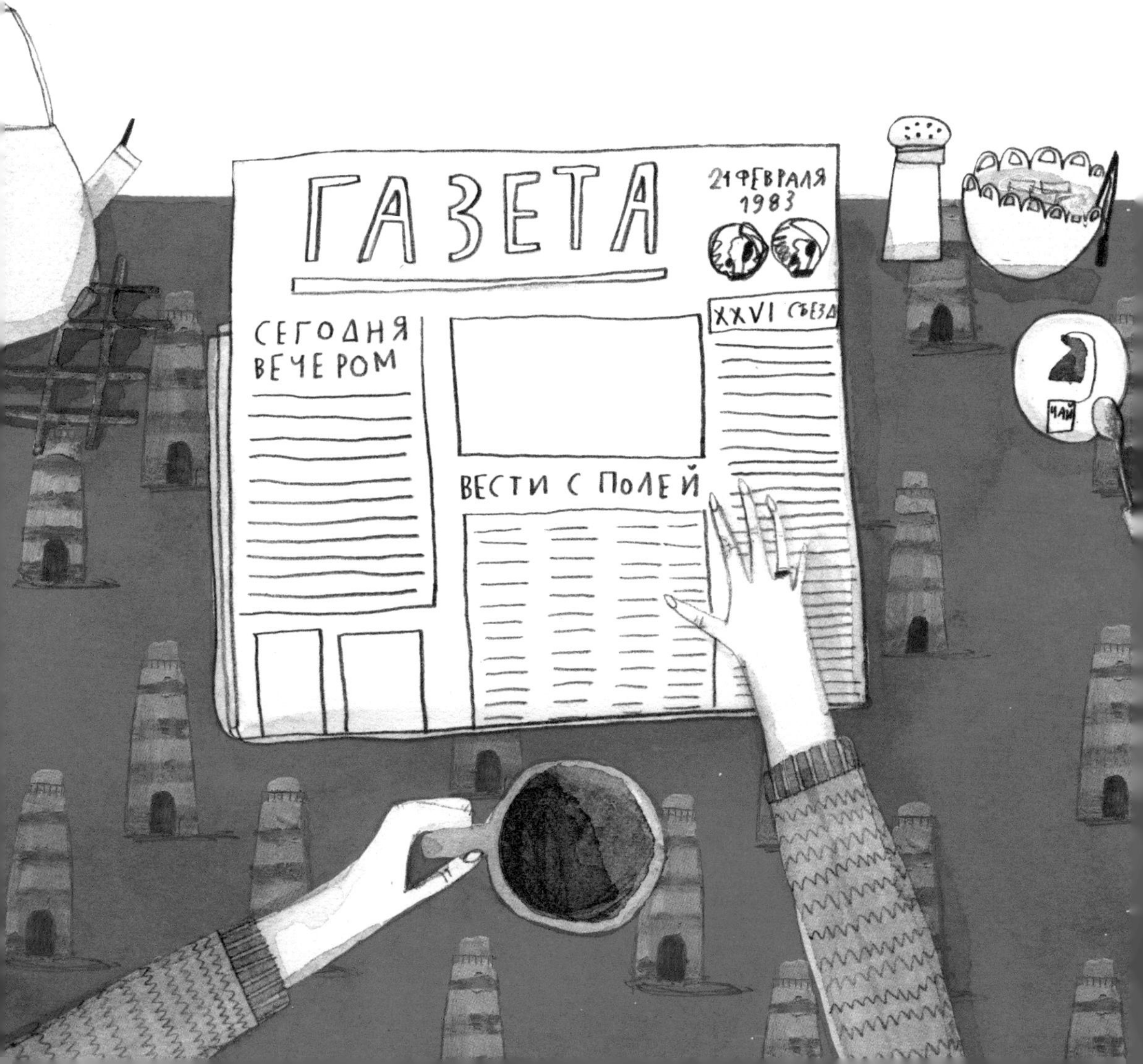
ГАЗЕТА
21 ФЕВРАЛЯ 1983
XXVI СЪЕЗД
СЕГОДНЯ ВЕЧЕРОМ
ВЕСТИ С ПОЛЕЙ
ЧАЙ

THE WORLD

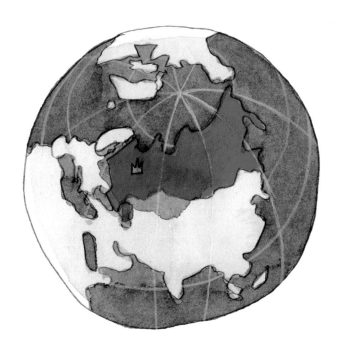

THE COUNTRY

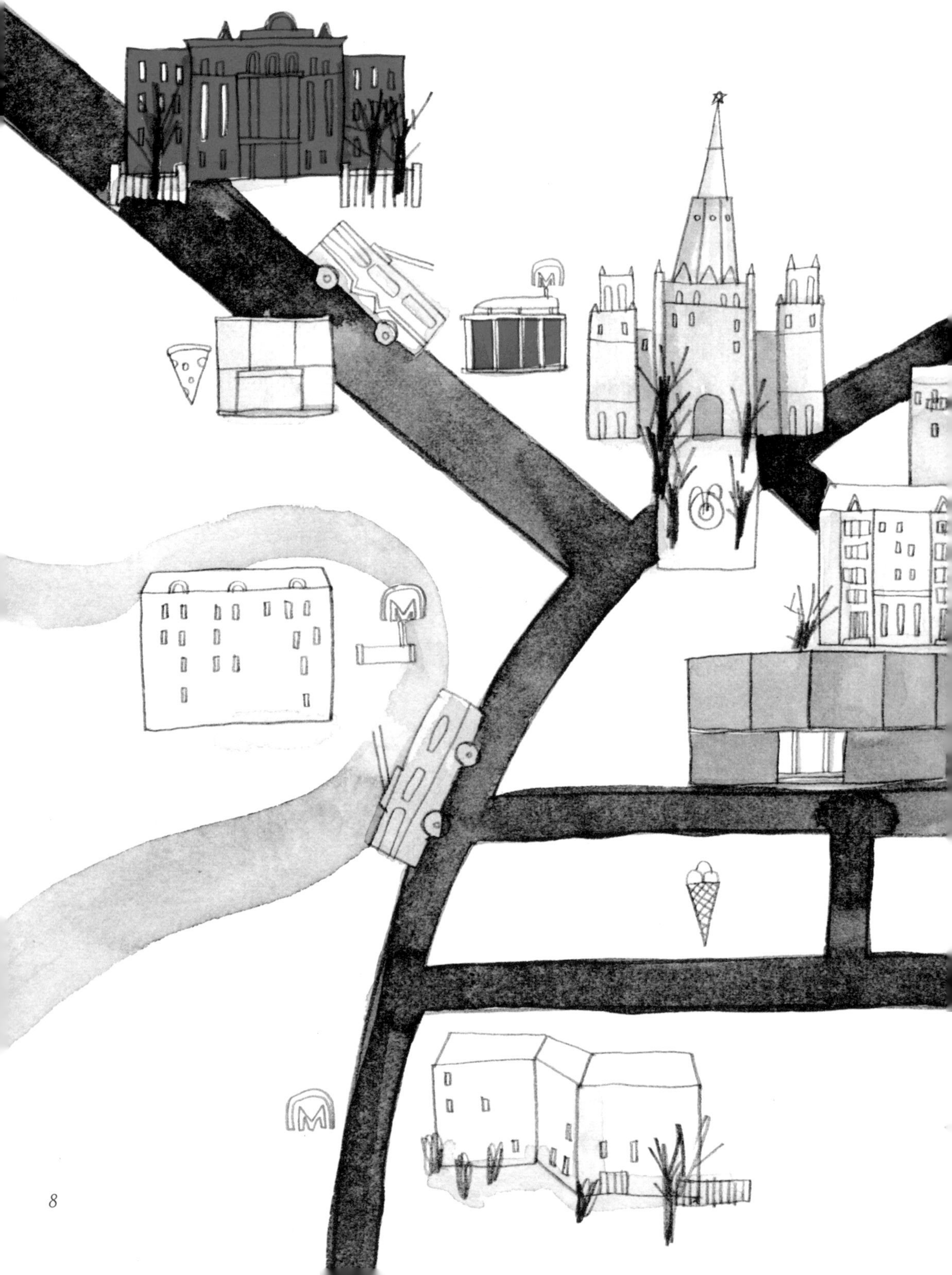
M
M
M

THE CITY

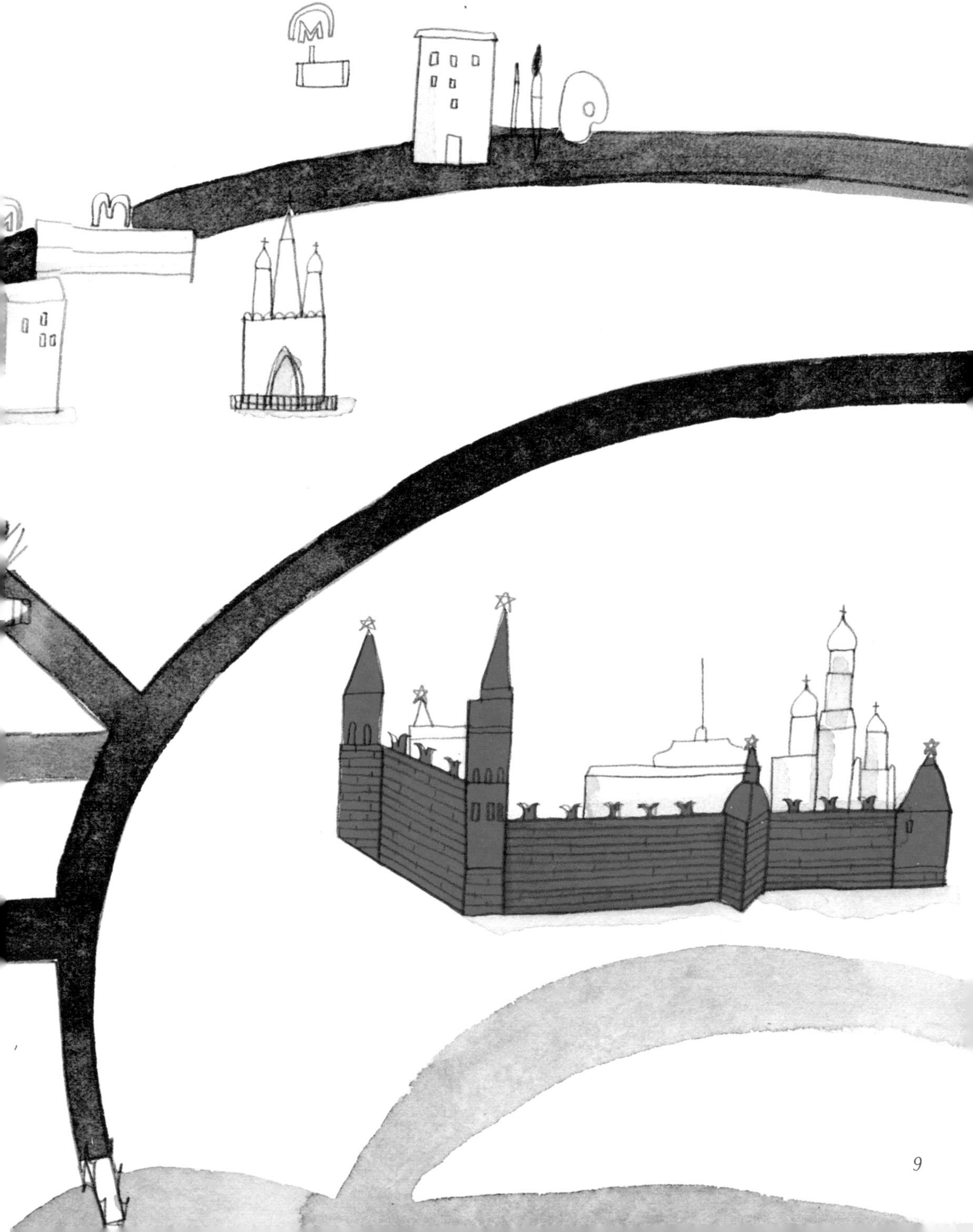
M

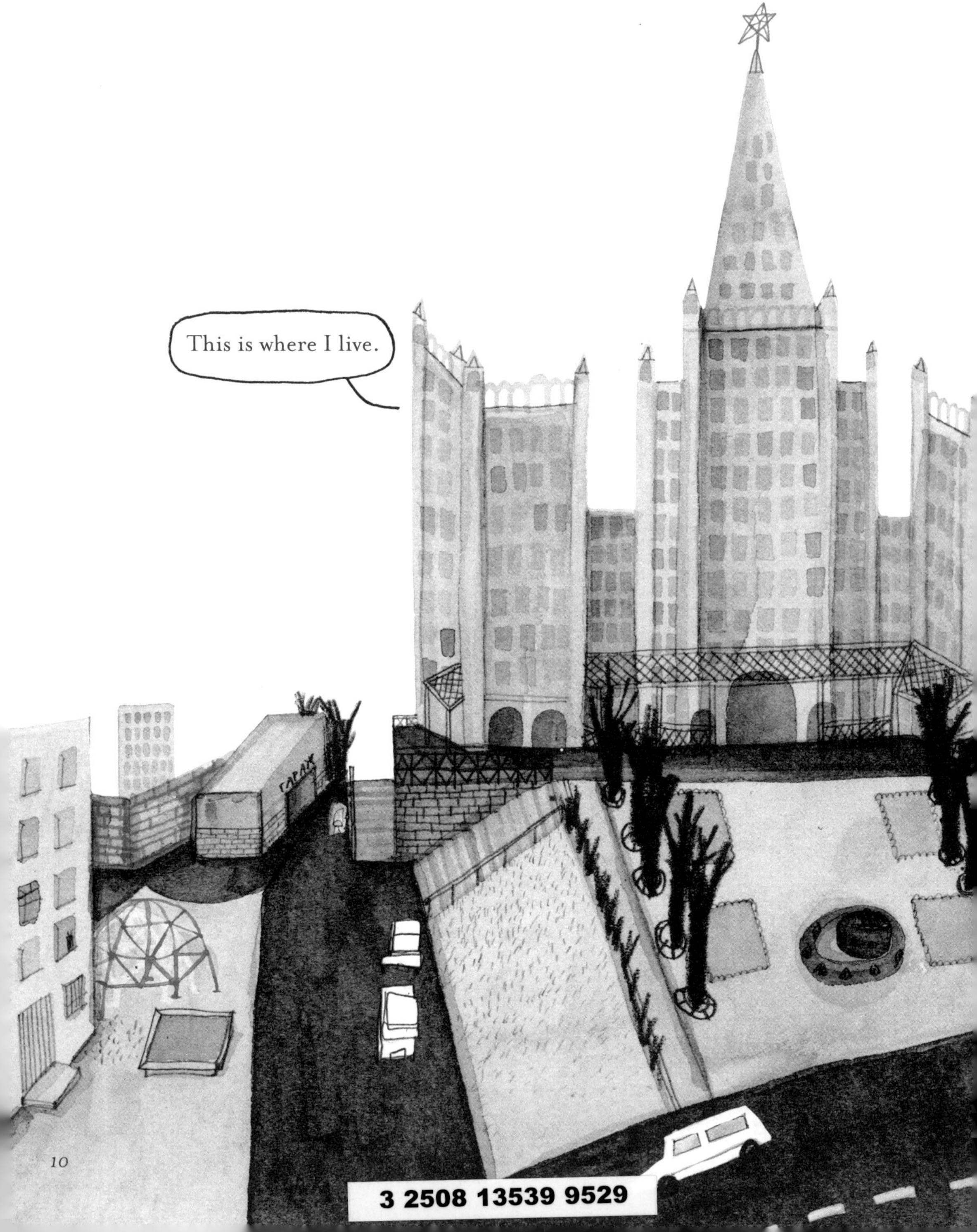
This is where I live.

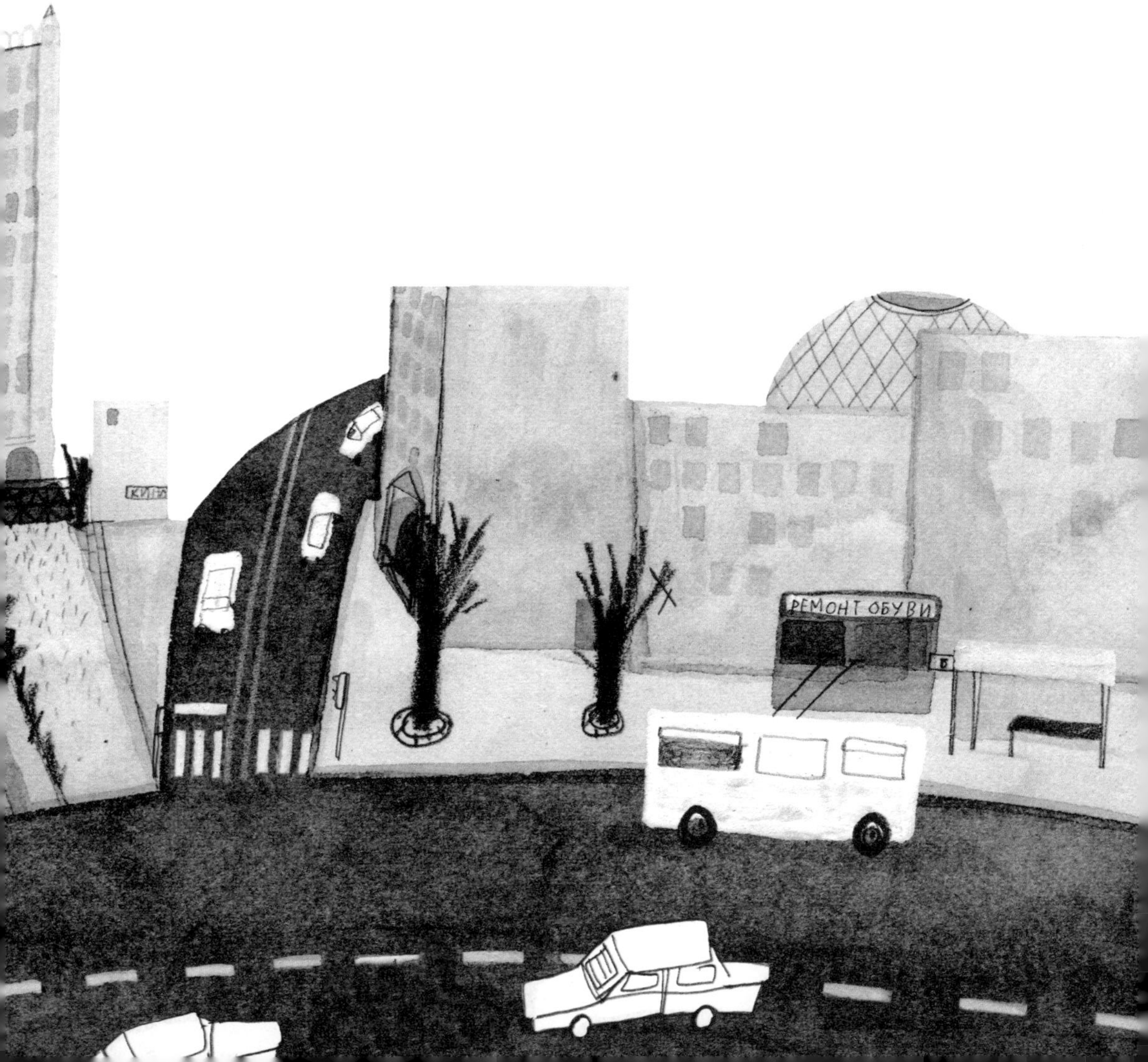
РЕМОНТ ОБУВИ

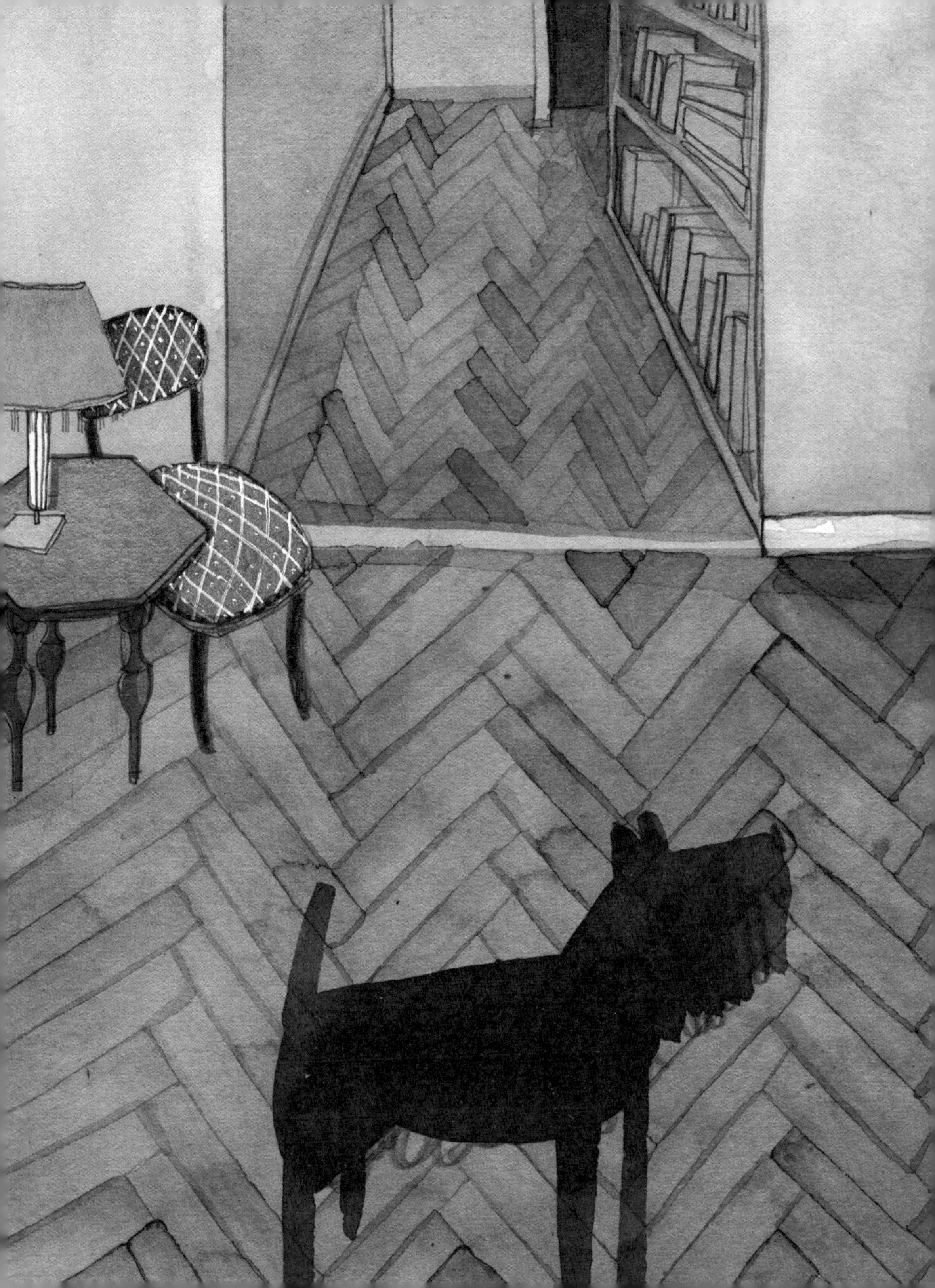

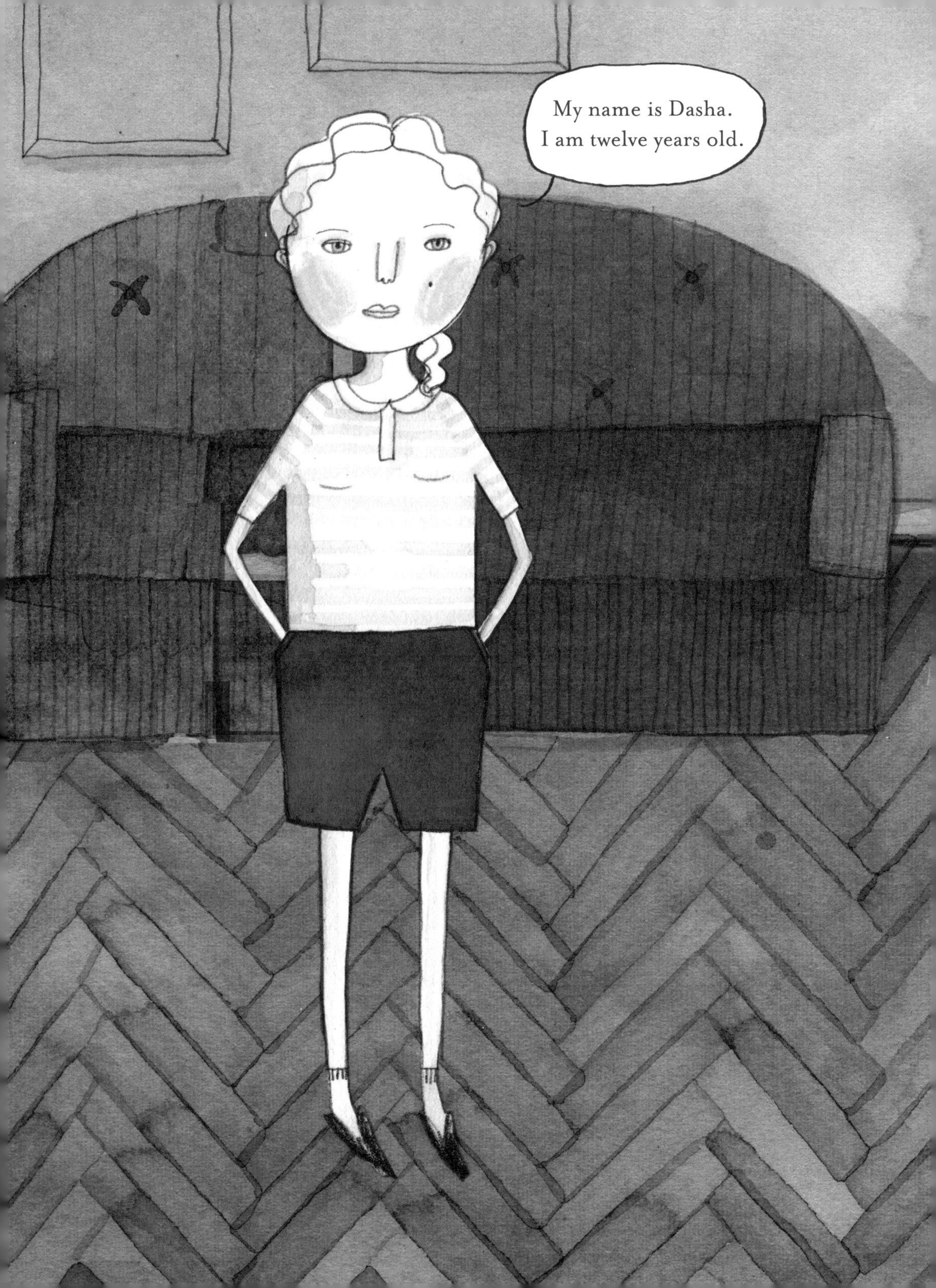
My name is Dasha.
I am twelve years old.

My mom and I live with my grandparents — my mom's mom and her stepdad — and our dog in a four-room apartment. I want a cat, but I am allergic, so we can only have the dog. We have always lived with my grandparents, even when my parents were still married. When my father moved to LA, I started sleeping in my mom's room.

When I was a baby I was sick a lot, and my mom stayed home with me — she was writing her dissertation on absurdist Russian poets of the early twentieth century anyway.

I like the absurdist Russian poets — they are funny.

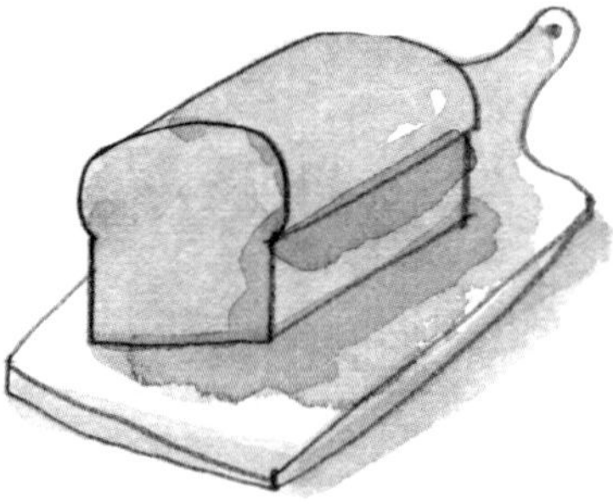

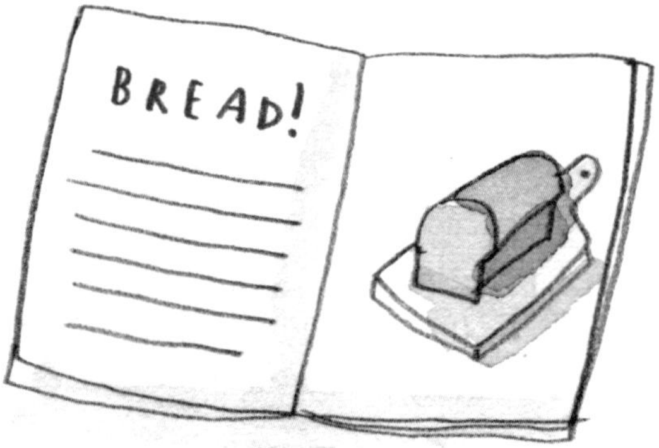
BREAD!

After she finished her dissertation, my mom went to work as a copywriter at an advertising agency. She writes ads for places like Bread Factory #8. They give her fresh bread and she brings it home so we can all try it and say things like,

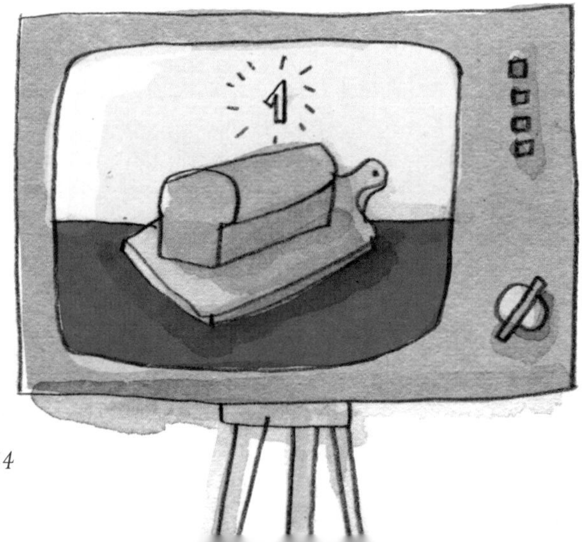
1

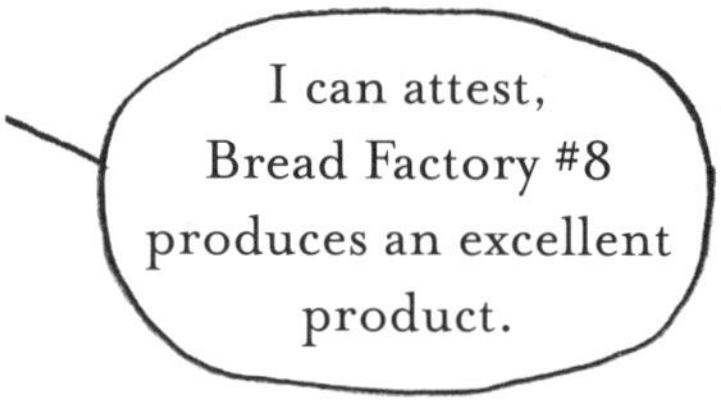
I can attest,
Bread Factory #8
produces an excellent
product.

My mom really loves her job, but she always talks about how advertising in Russia isn't so good.

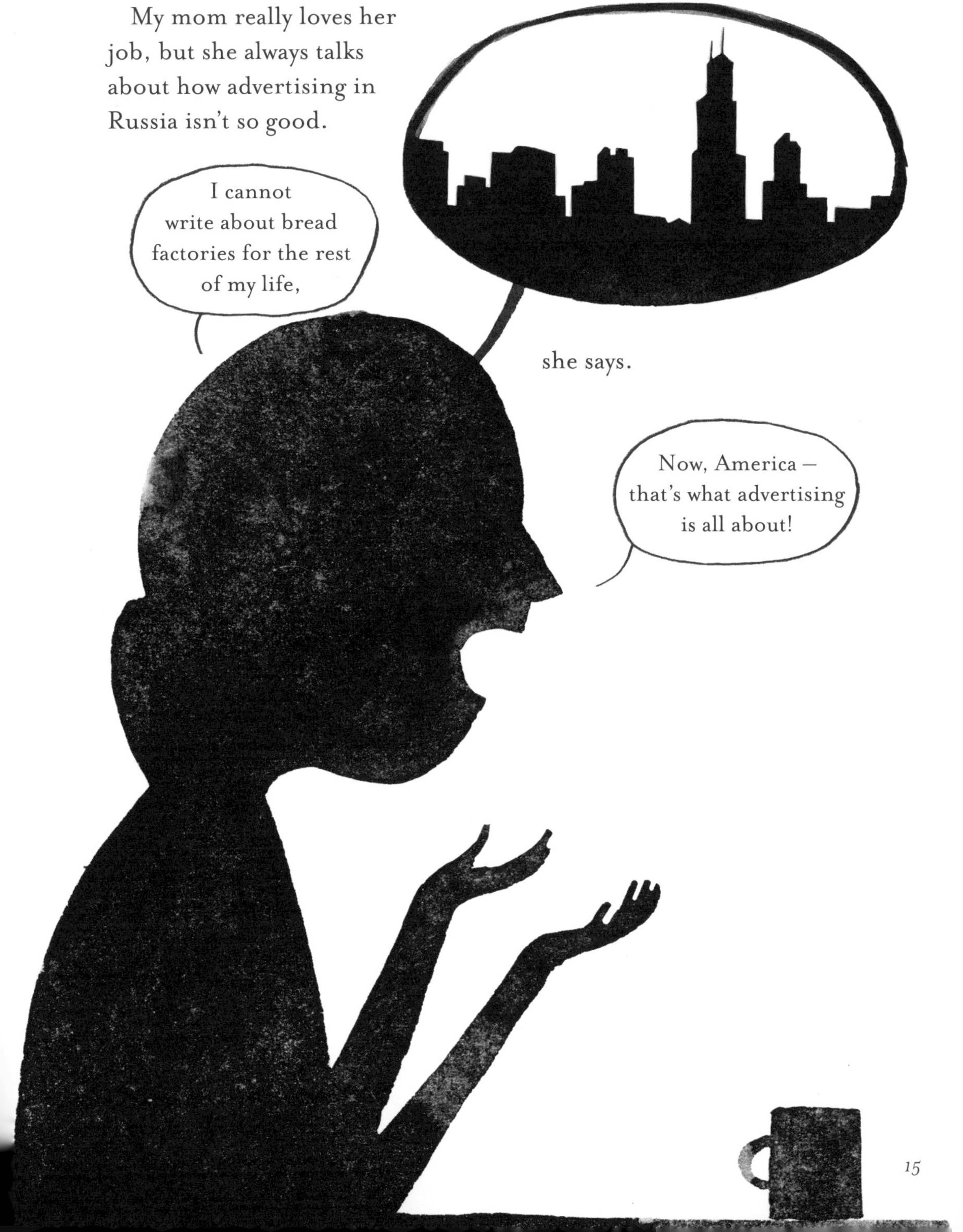
I cannot write about bread factories for the rest of my life,
Now, America – that's what advertising is all about!

she says.

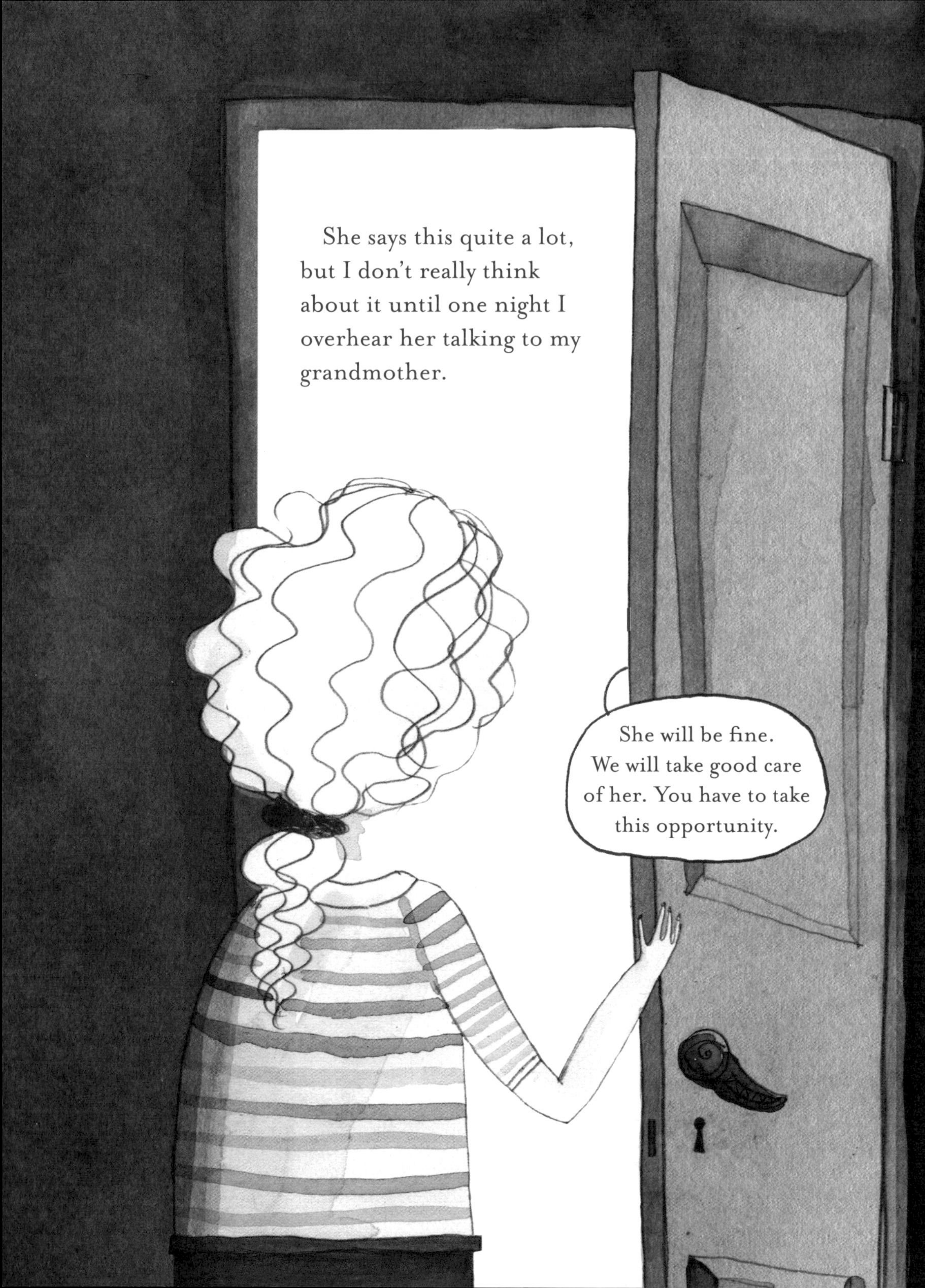
She says this quite a lot, but I don't really think about it until one night I overhear her talking to my grandmother.
She will be fine. We will take good care of her. You have to take this opportunity.

WHAT'S GOING ON?
ARE THEY TALKING ABOUT ME?
WHY DO I NEED TO BE TAKEN CARE OF?

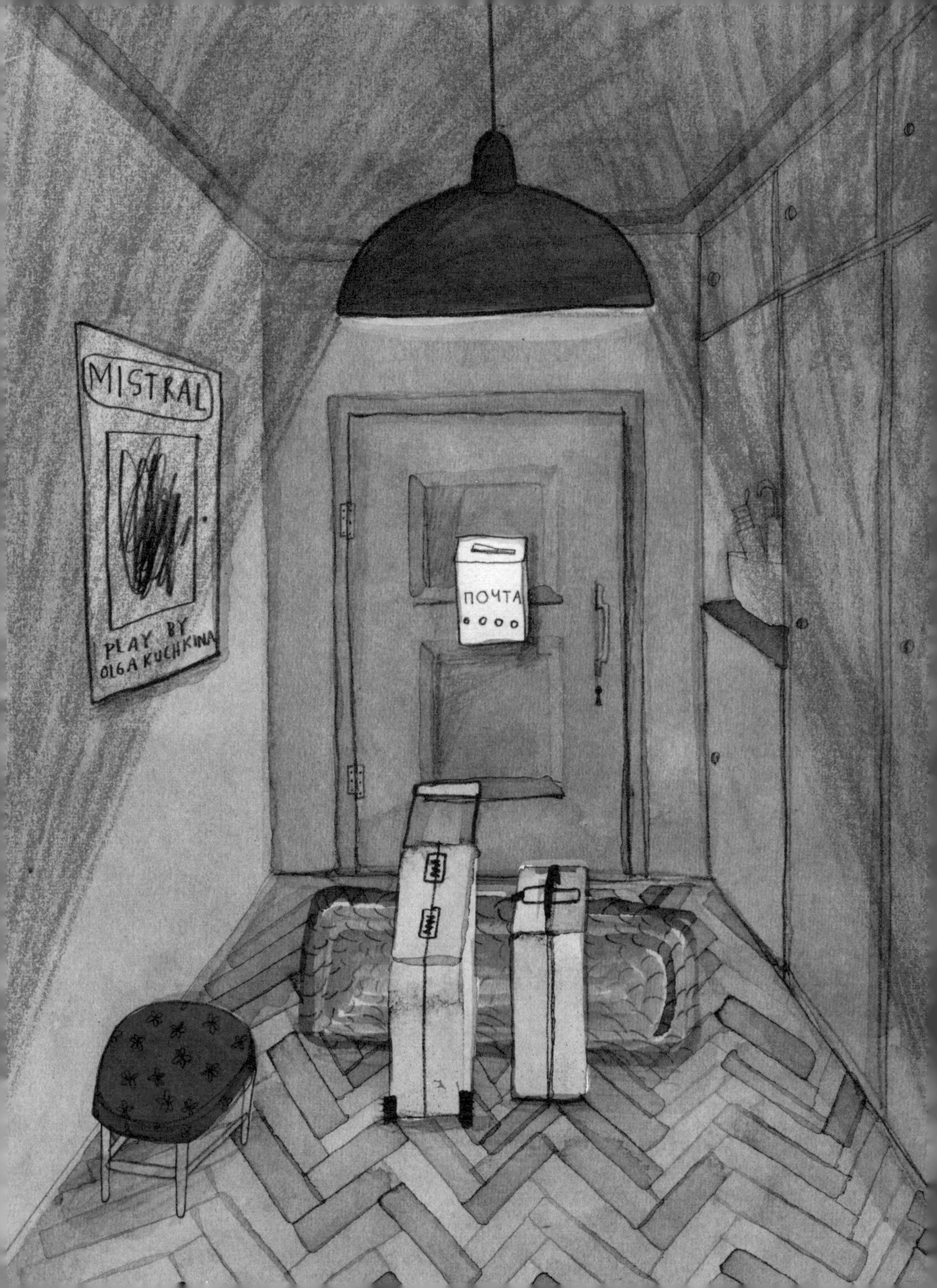
MISTRAL
PLAY BY
OLGA KUCHKINA
ПОЧТА

A few days later, my mom packs up her bags and my grandparents get ready to drive her to the airport. My mom has been accepted into a master's program in advertising at an American university. I will be staying in Moscow with my grandmother and grandfather.

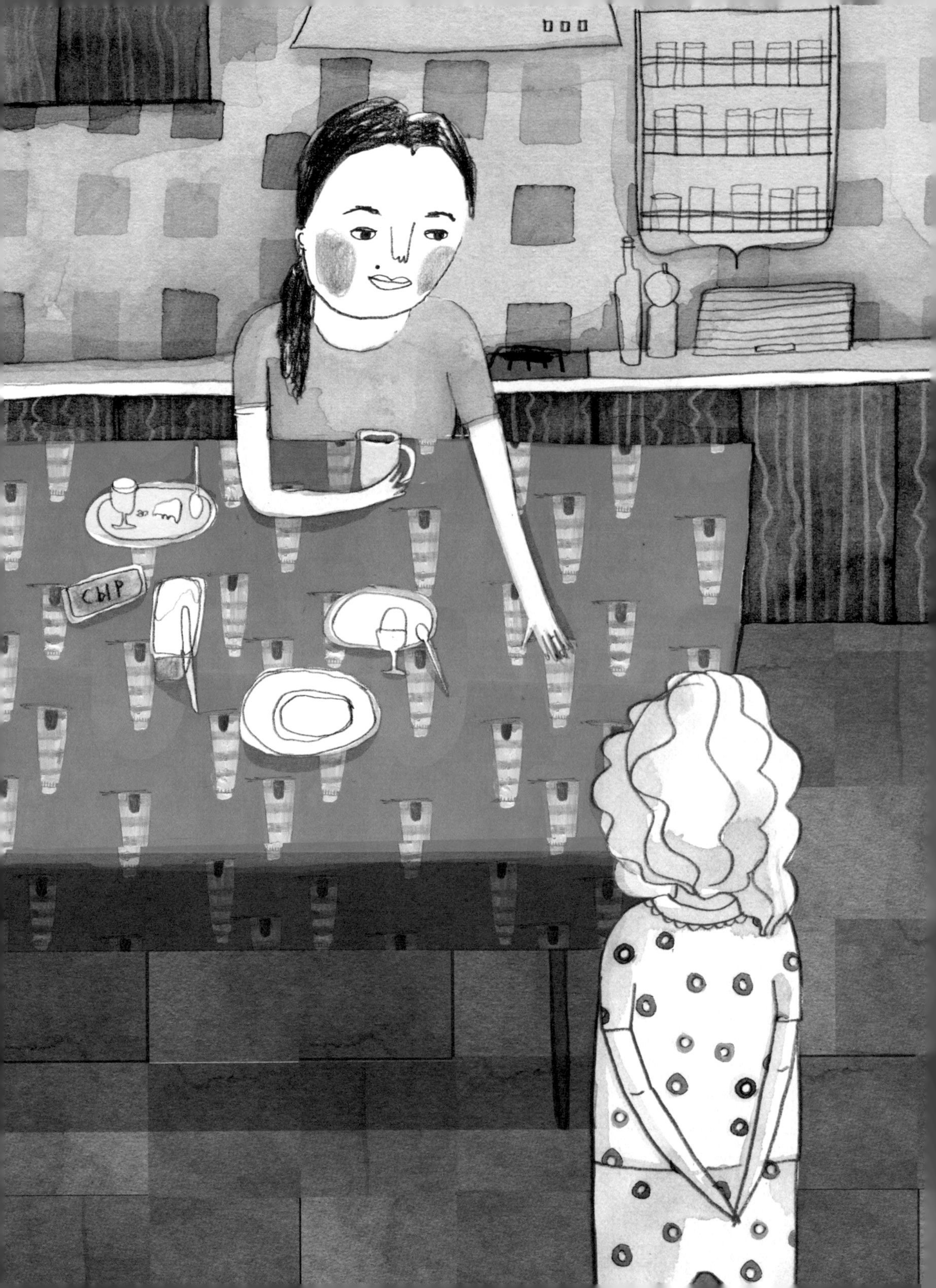
СЫР

It's an early-morning flight, and I am not going to the airport with them. My mom is sad to leave, and my grandmother thinks it will be easier to say good-bye at home. I slink around the kitchen while she eats breakfast. I am being brave.

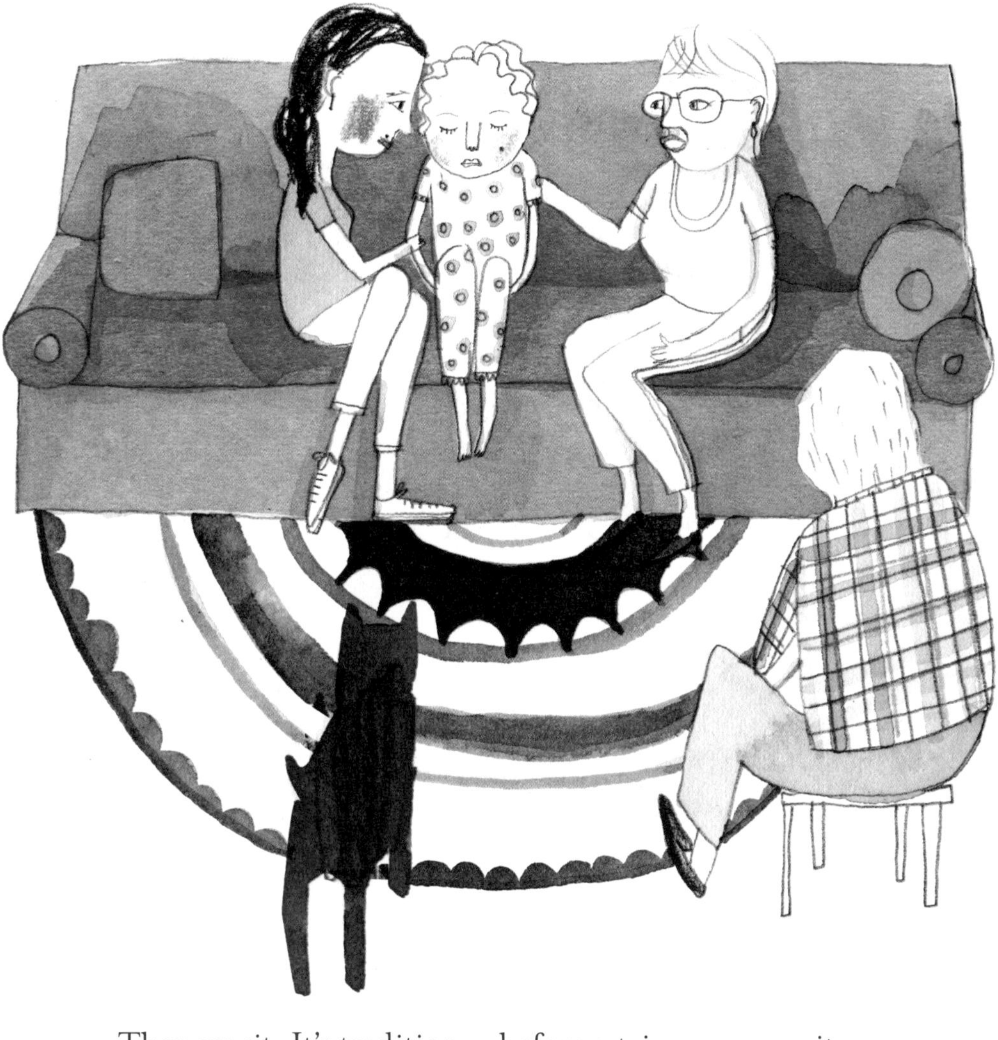

Then we sit. It's tradition — before a trip everyone sits down quietly and silently wishes the traveler well. Then the oldest or the youngest person gets up and the trip begins. I don't want to get up, so my grandmother has to.

All of a sudden, they are running late
and it's all rush, rush — checking on the
bags? Passport? Tickets? My grandfather
goes to call the elevator. It's old and slow
and takes five minutes to get up to our
eleventh floor. My mom and I hold hands,
and I think about how cool her hands
always are, and then I bite her finger.

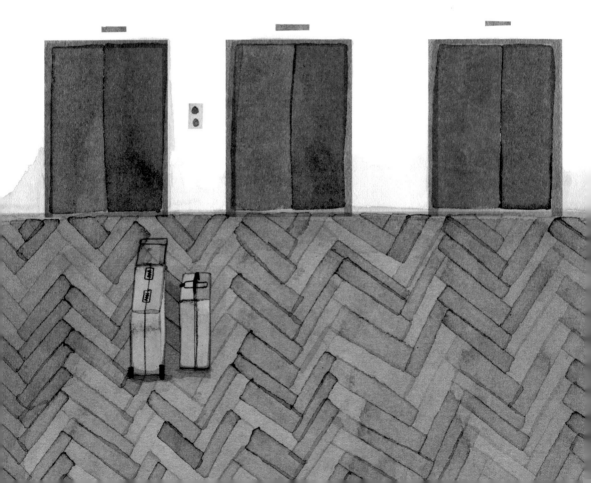

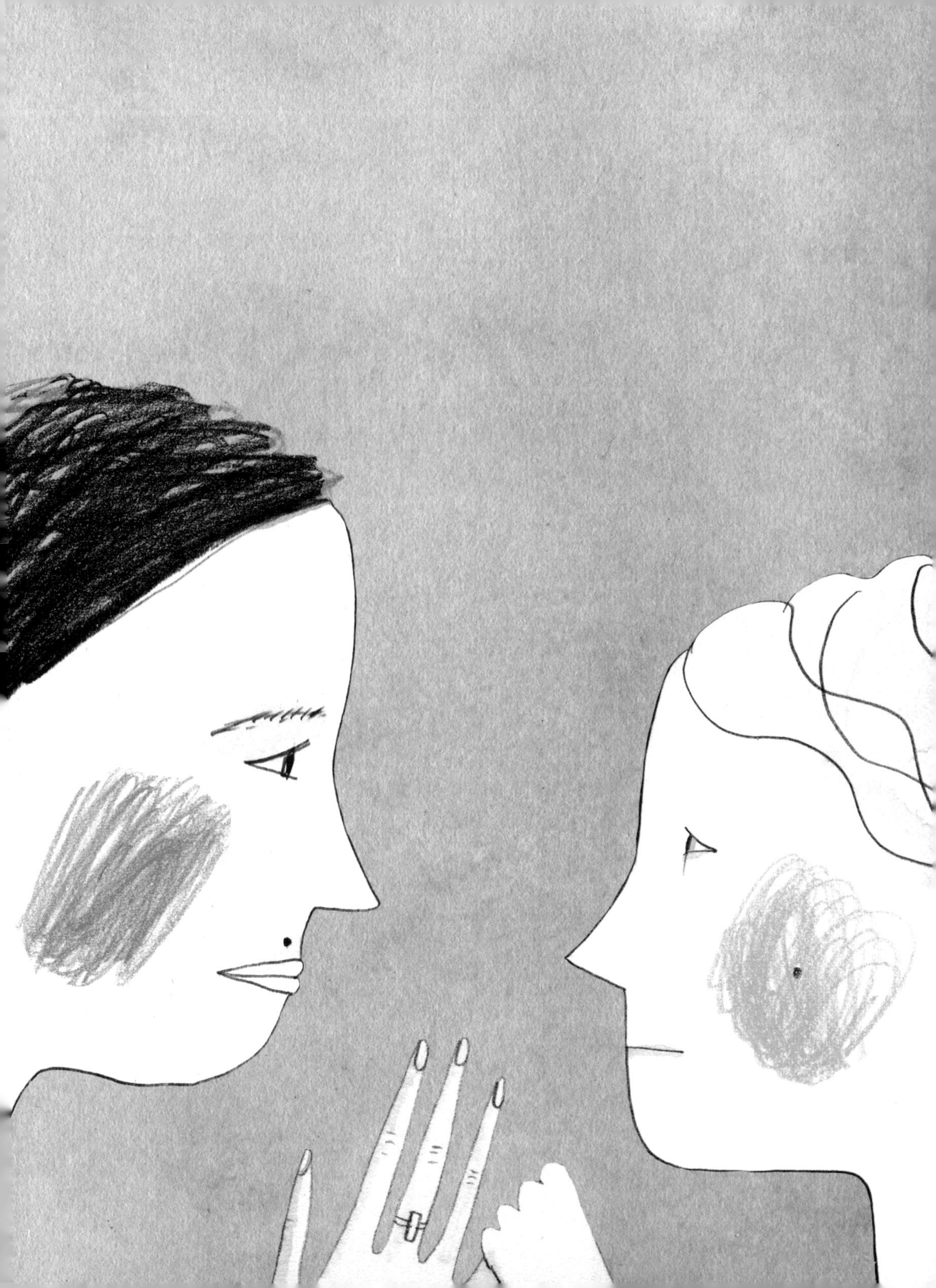

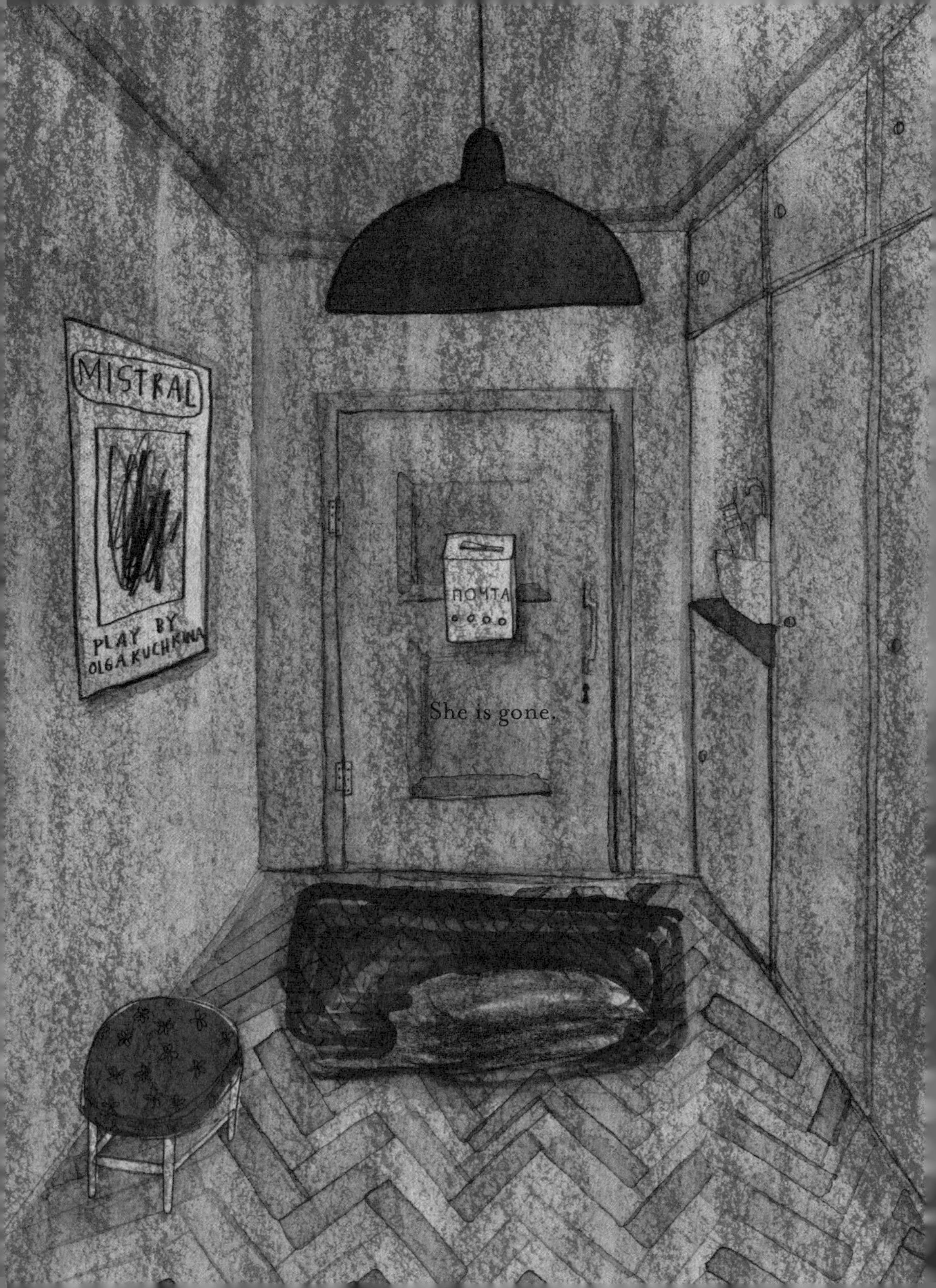
MISTRAL
PLAY BY
OLGA KUCHKINA
ПОЧТА

She is gone.

AUGUST

My grandmother and I get in the car and drive ninety kilometers out of the city to the writers' retreat we go to every year. Usually we go in June, when it's mostly just the writers there, and I wander around aimlessly and pick at the asphalt. But this year we go in August, when other kids will be there. I've never met any of them, but my best friend from school, Masha, usually goes for winter break with her family when they are around, and she's told me ALL ABOUT THEM.

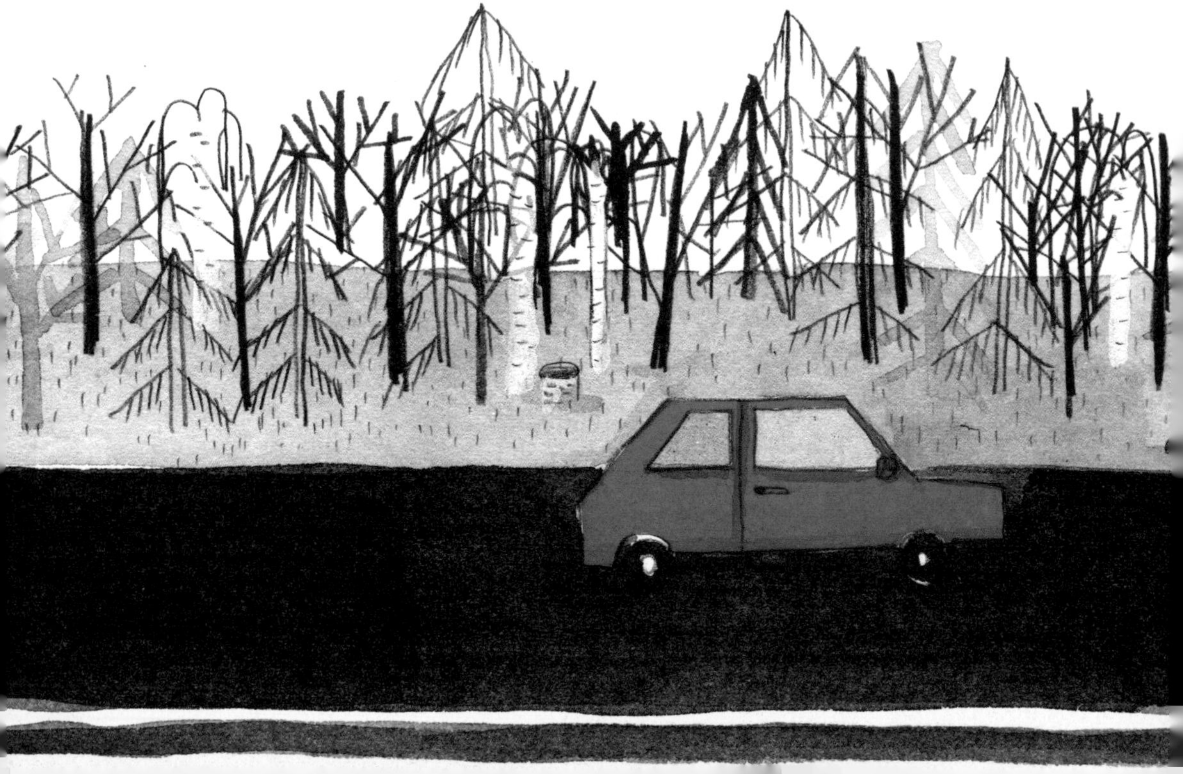

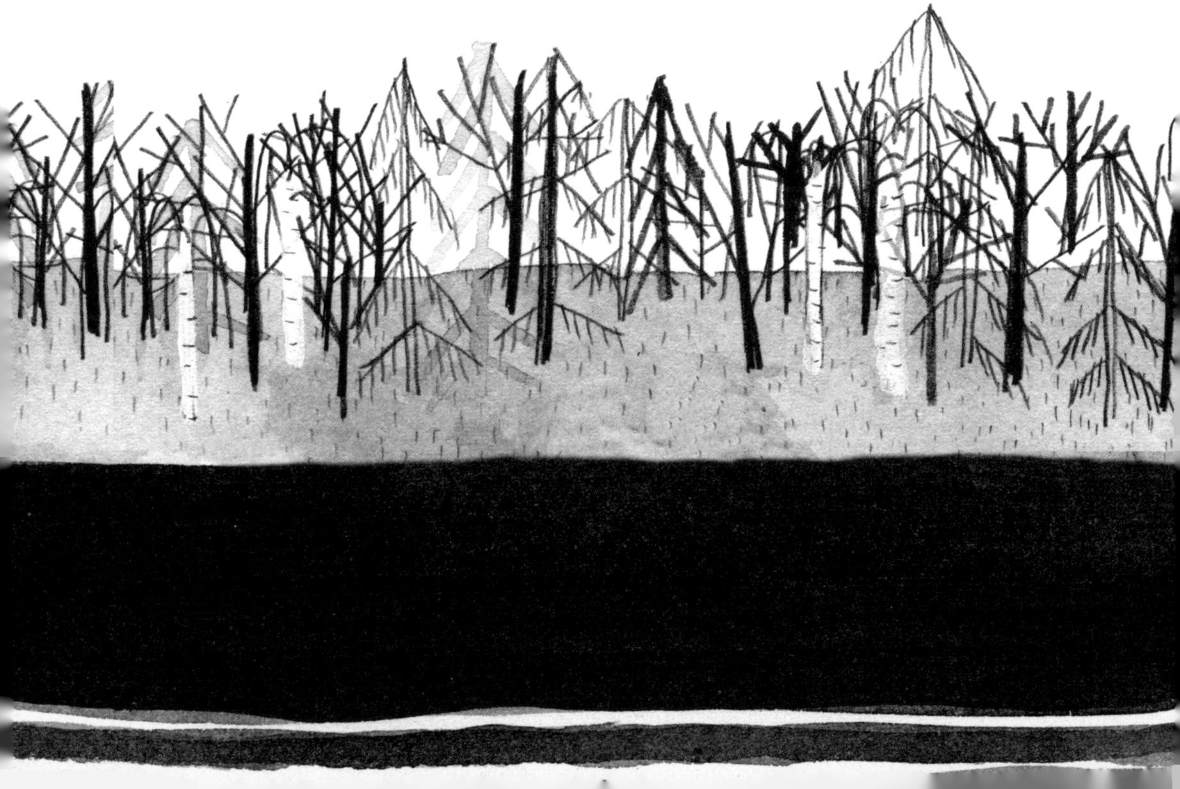

Everyone eats in the same cafeteria and we have assigned seats. My grandmother and I sit with a poetess and her husband. She is a drunk. I like her. She tells me stories.

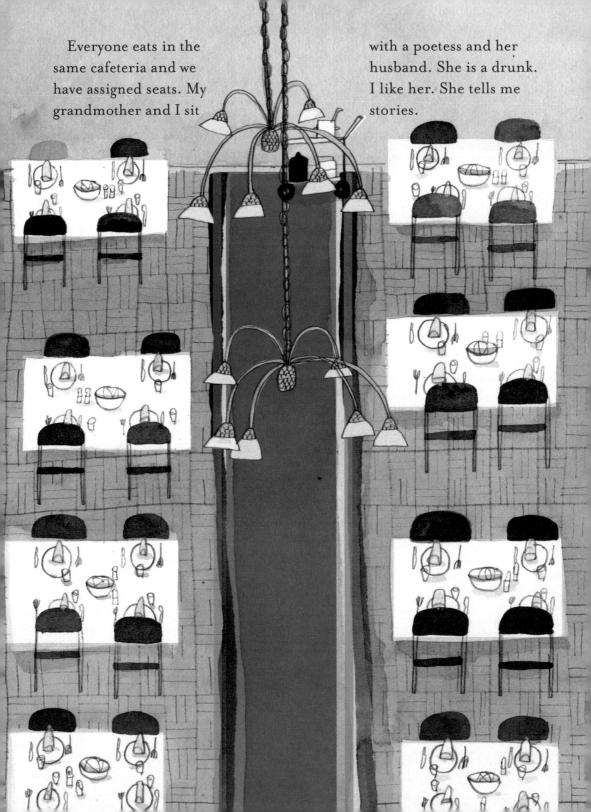

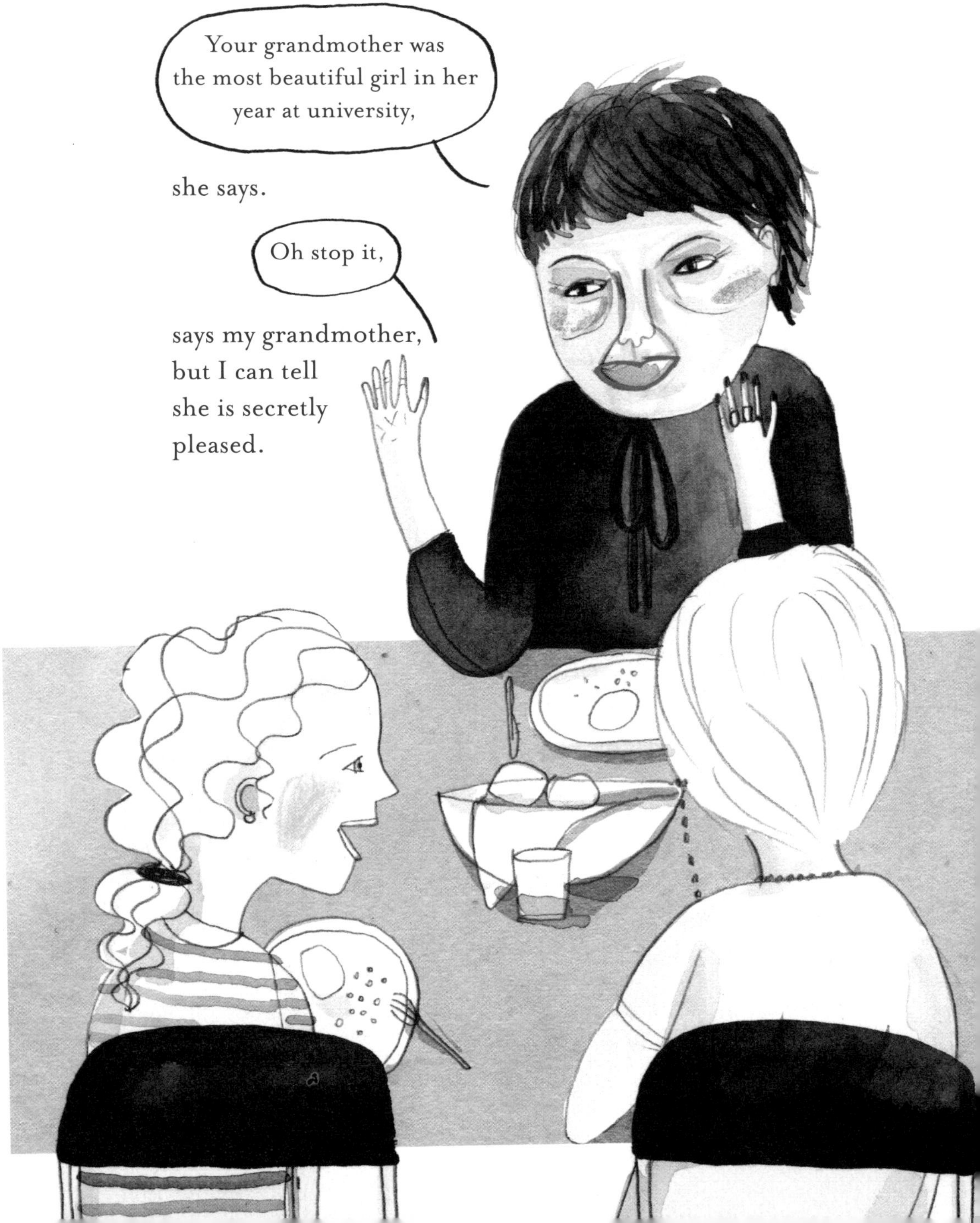
Your grandmother was the most beautiful girl in her year at university,
she says.
Oh stop it,
says my grandmother, but I can tell she is secretly pleased.

I spend my days reading, doodling and lounging about.

Why don't you go play with the other kids?

says my grandmother.

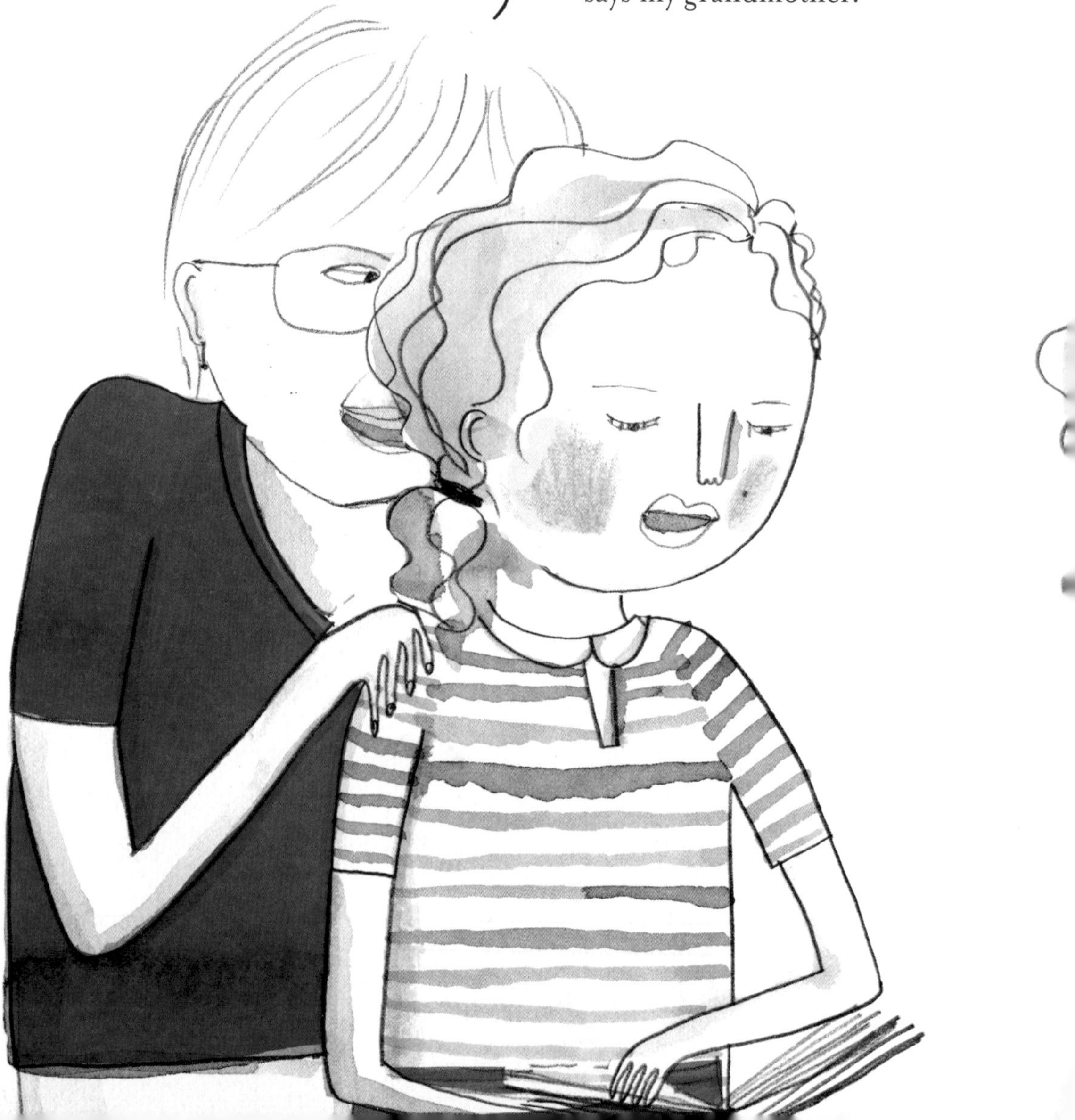

Petya is their leader. His mother is VERY FAMOUS and he himself is an anchor of a children's TV show on Channel 1.

He is FIFTEEN! I am scared of him the most.

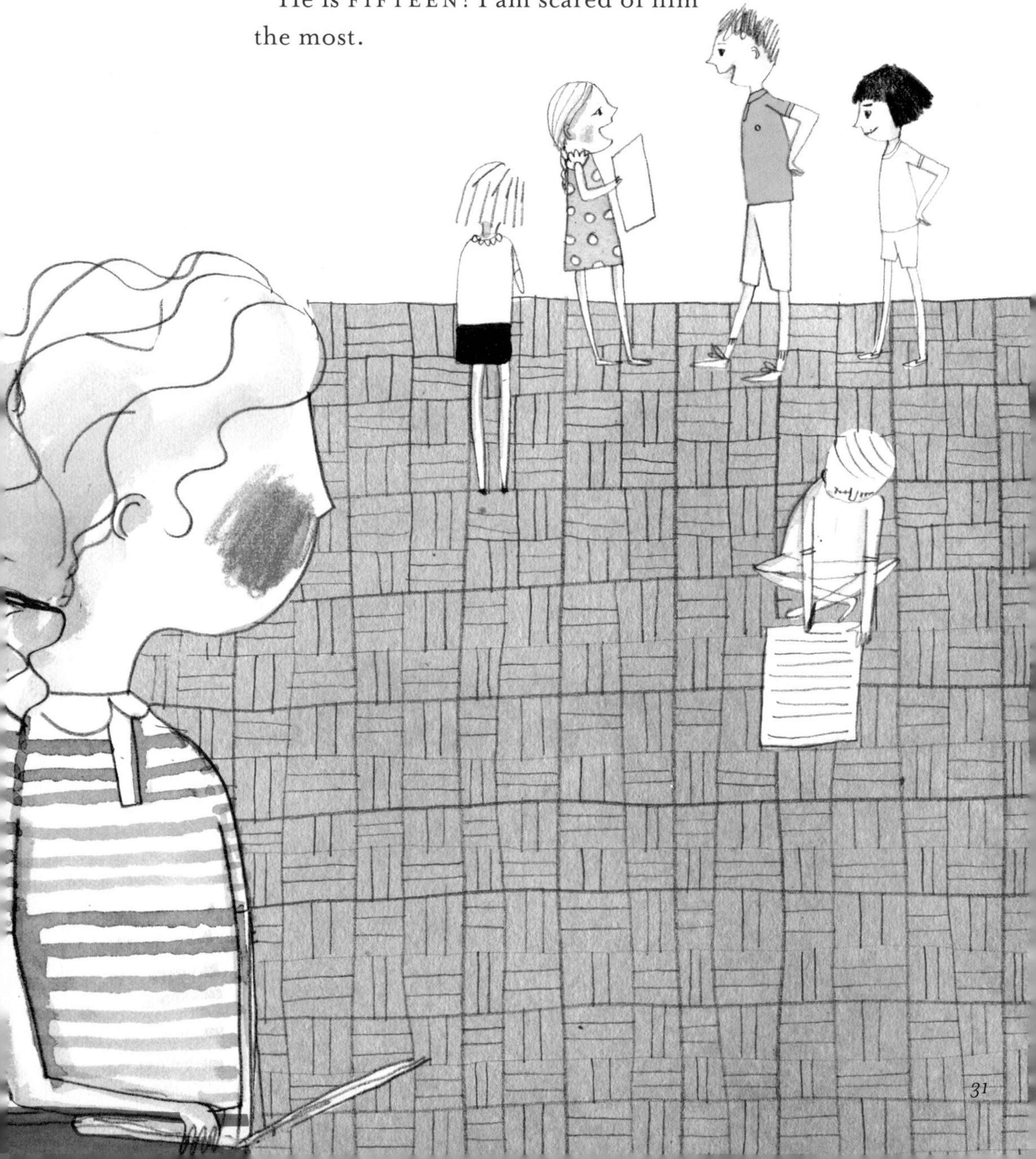

A girl, whose name is Nina, tells me that they are putting on a play, and Petya has sent her to see if I will draw the posters for it.

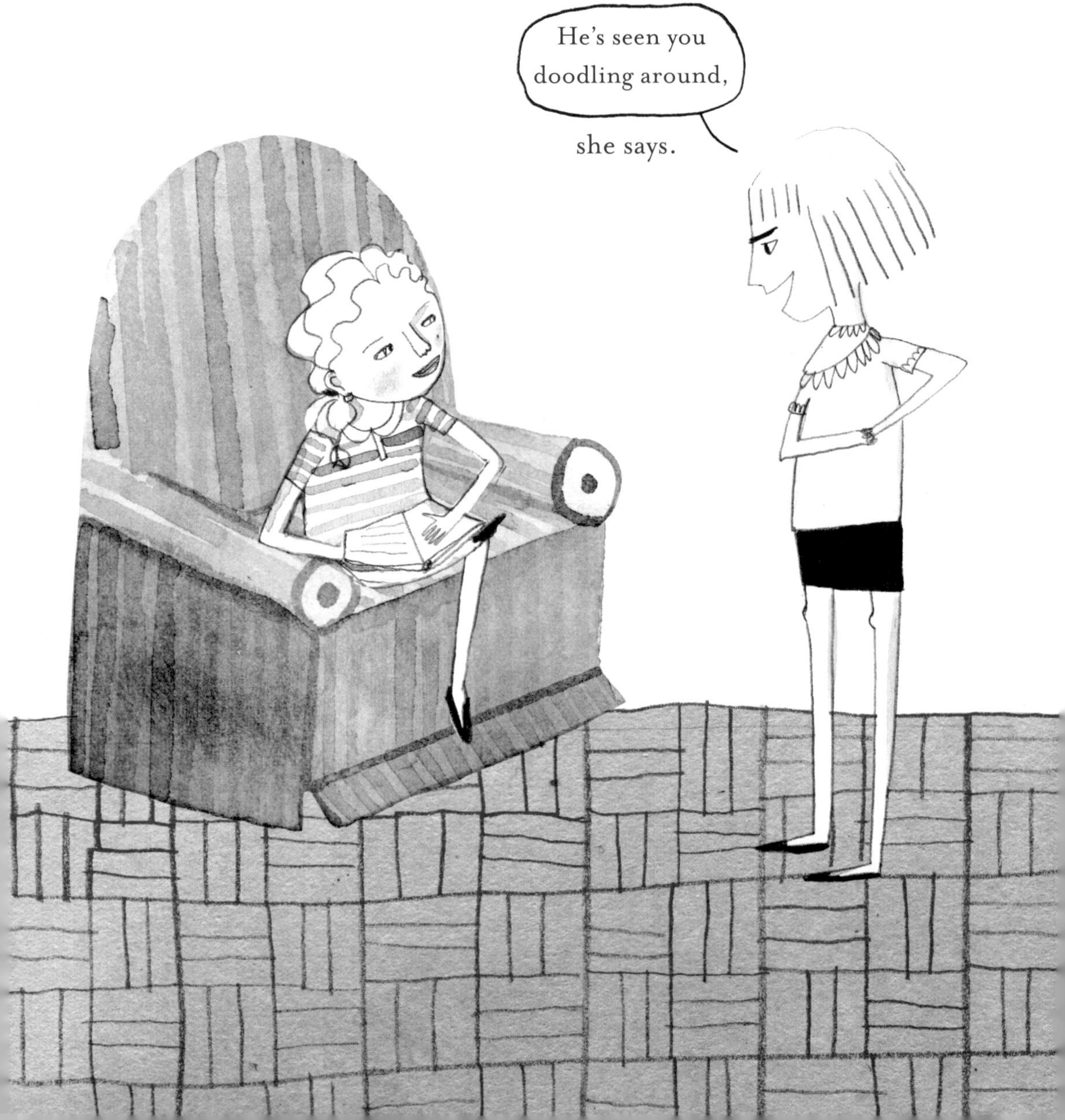
He's seen you doodling around,
she says.

Hiya, I'm Petya,

he says. (As if I don't know who HE is.)

Dasha,

I say.

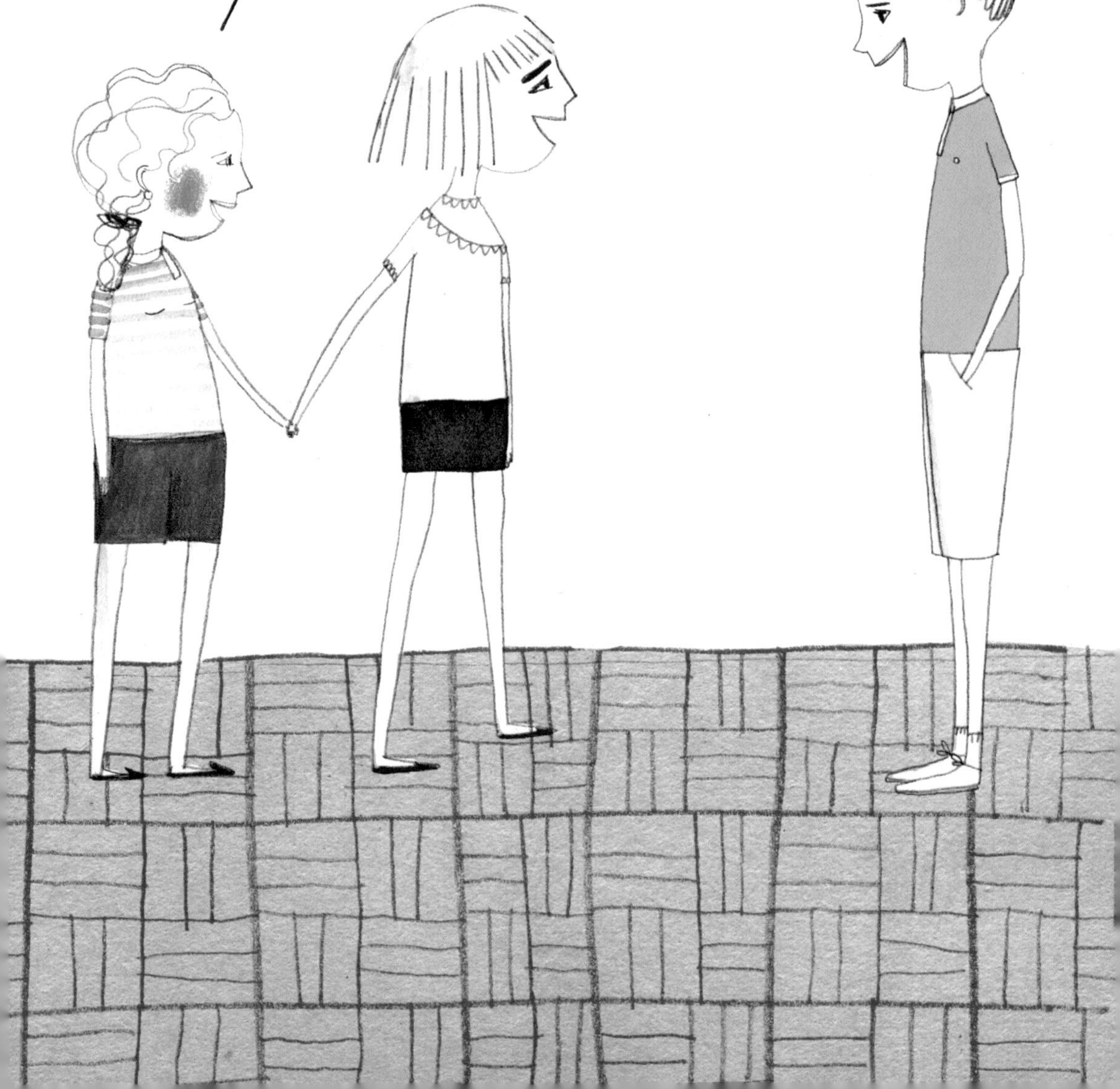

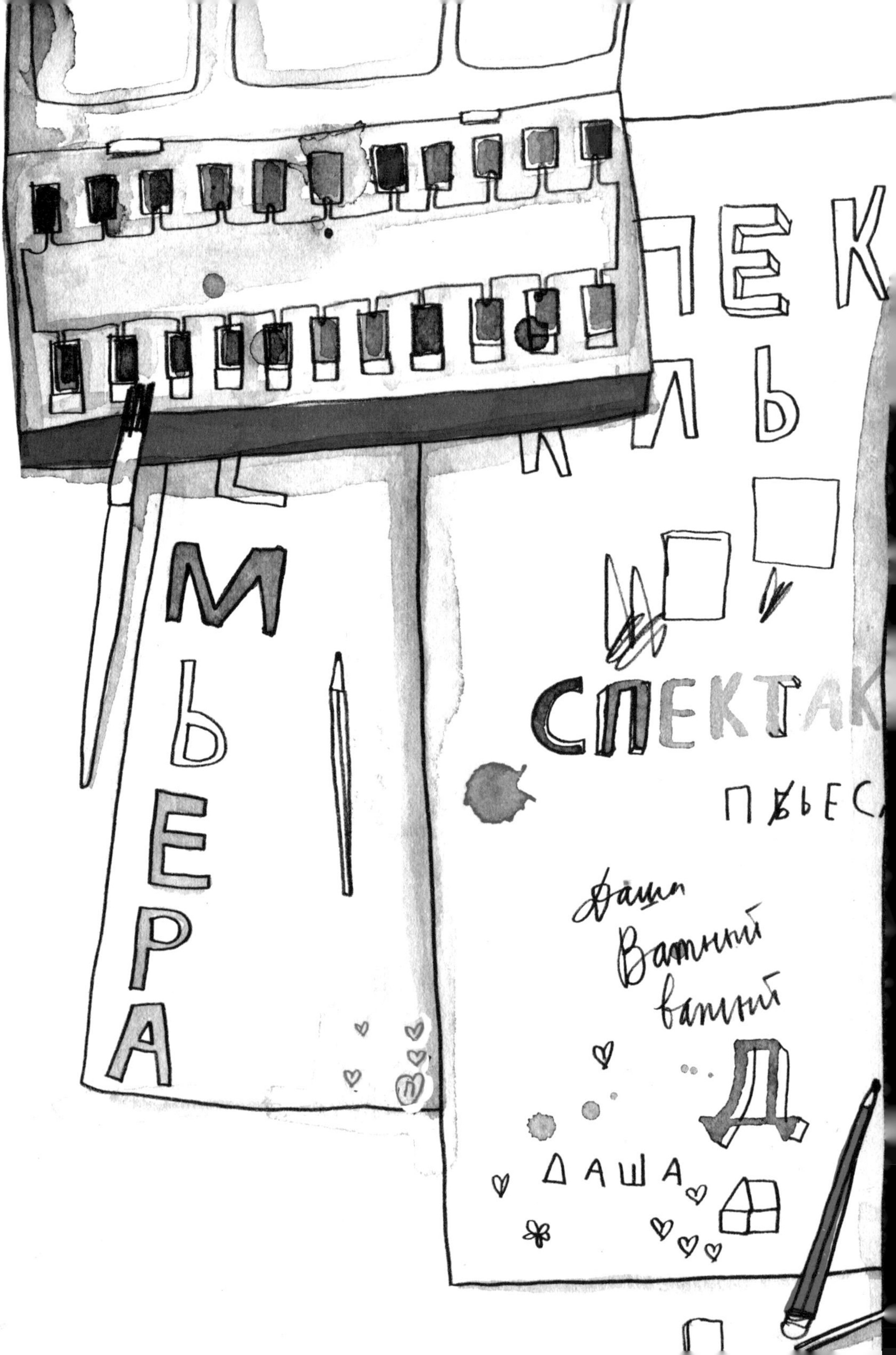

ПЕК
ЛЬ
МЬЕРА
СПЕКТАК
Даша
ДАША

ТА

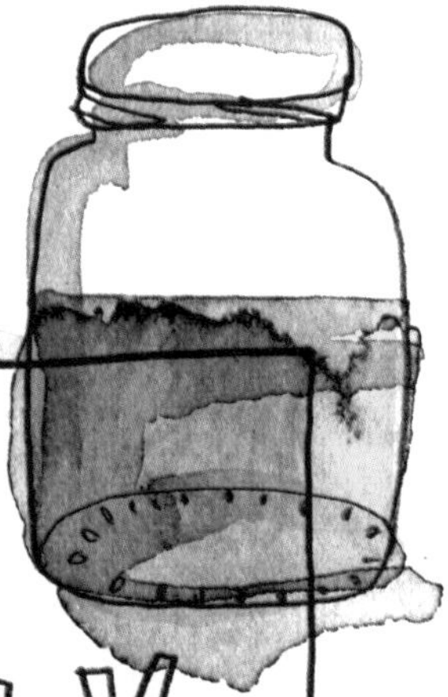

ВО-ПЕРВЫХ

И ВО-ВТОРЫХ

ВАЖНЫЙ СПЕКТАКЛЬ

ПО МОТ

And then one morning we wake up and Gorbachev, the president of Russia, is taken prisoner by some bad people and there are tanks rolling down the streets of Moscow. The TV networks are all shut down except for one that streams *Swan Lake* all day long.

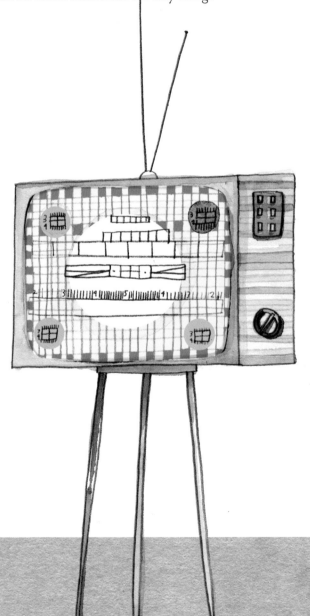

"It's a coup d'état," says my grandmother.

(Coup is pronounced "coo" and every time people say it out loud, which is a lot, I think of small birds nesting.)

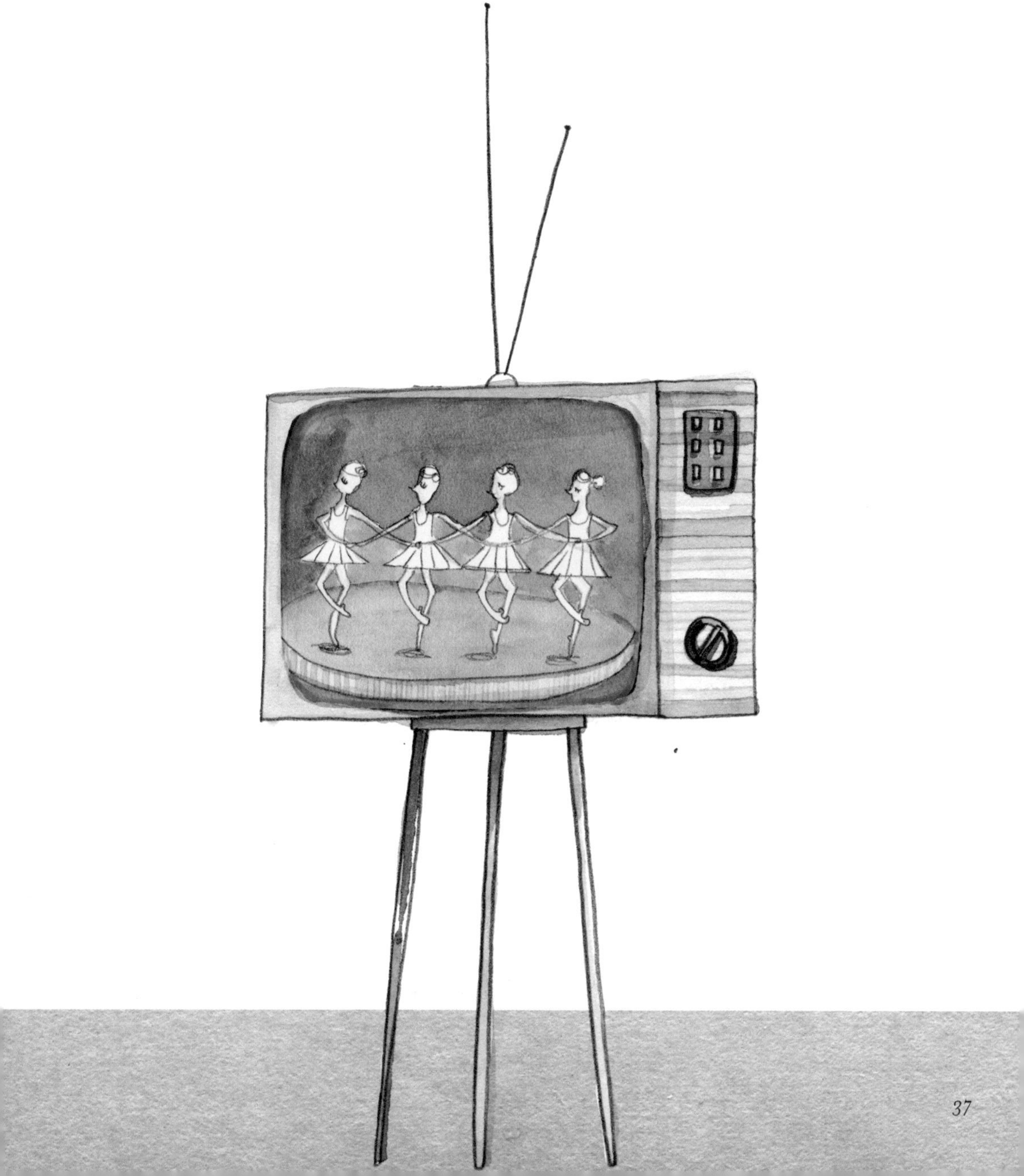

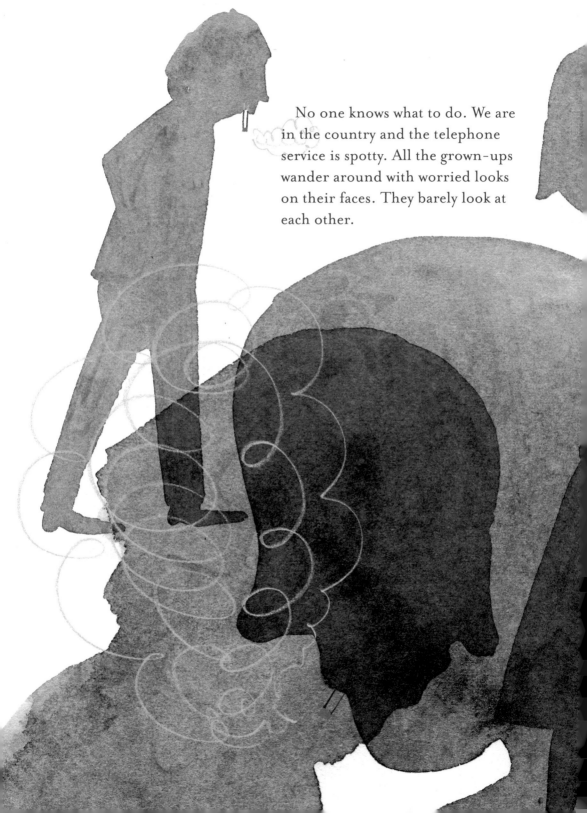

No one knows what to do. We are in the country and the telephone service is spotty. All the grown-ups wander around with worried looks on their faces. They barely look at each other.

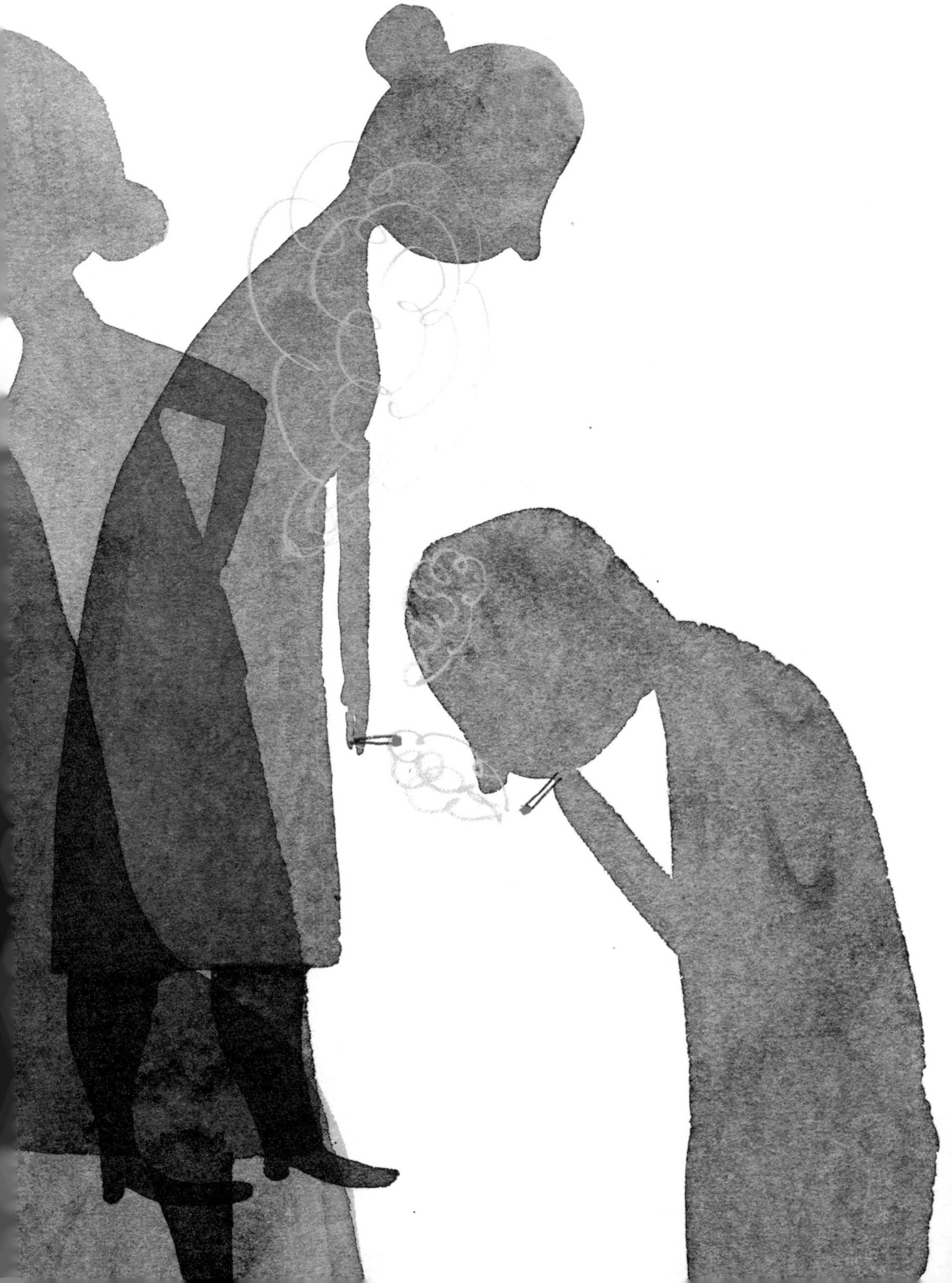

I worry about my mom. Is she watching the news in America? Does she know we are okay?

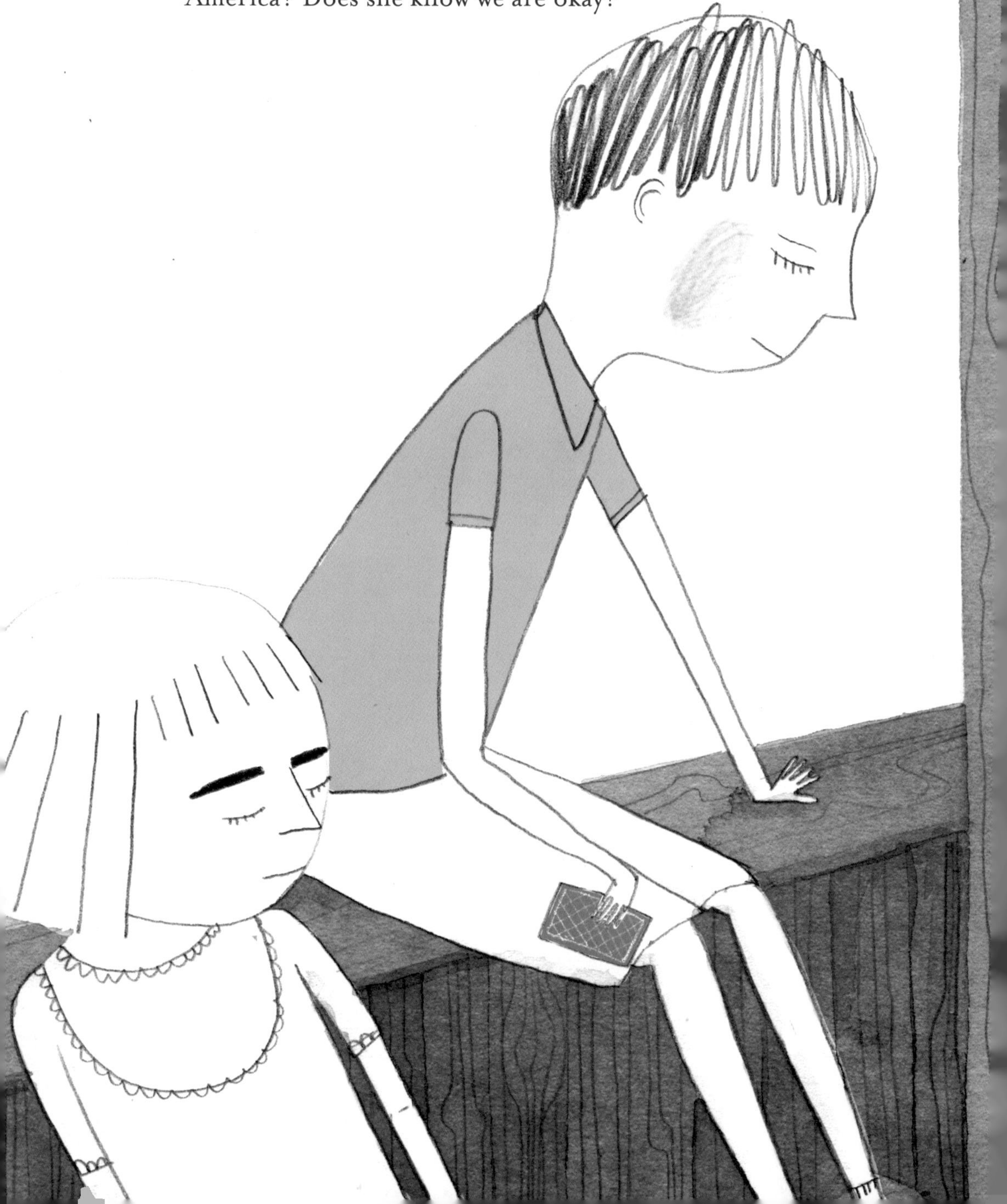

The play is suspended for the moment. Instead everyone plays mafia in the gazebo.

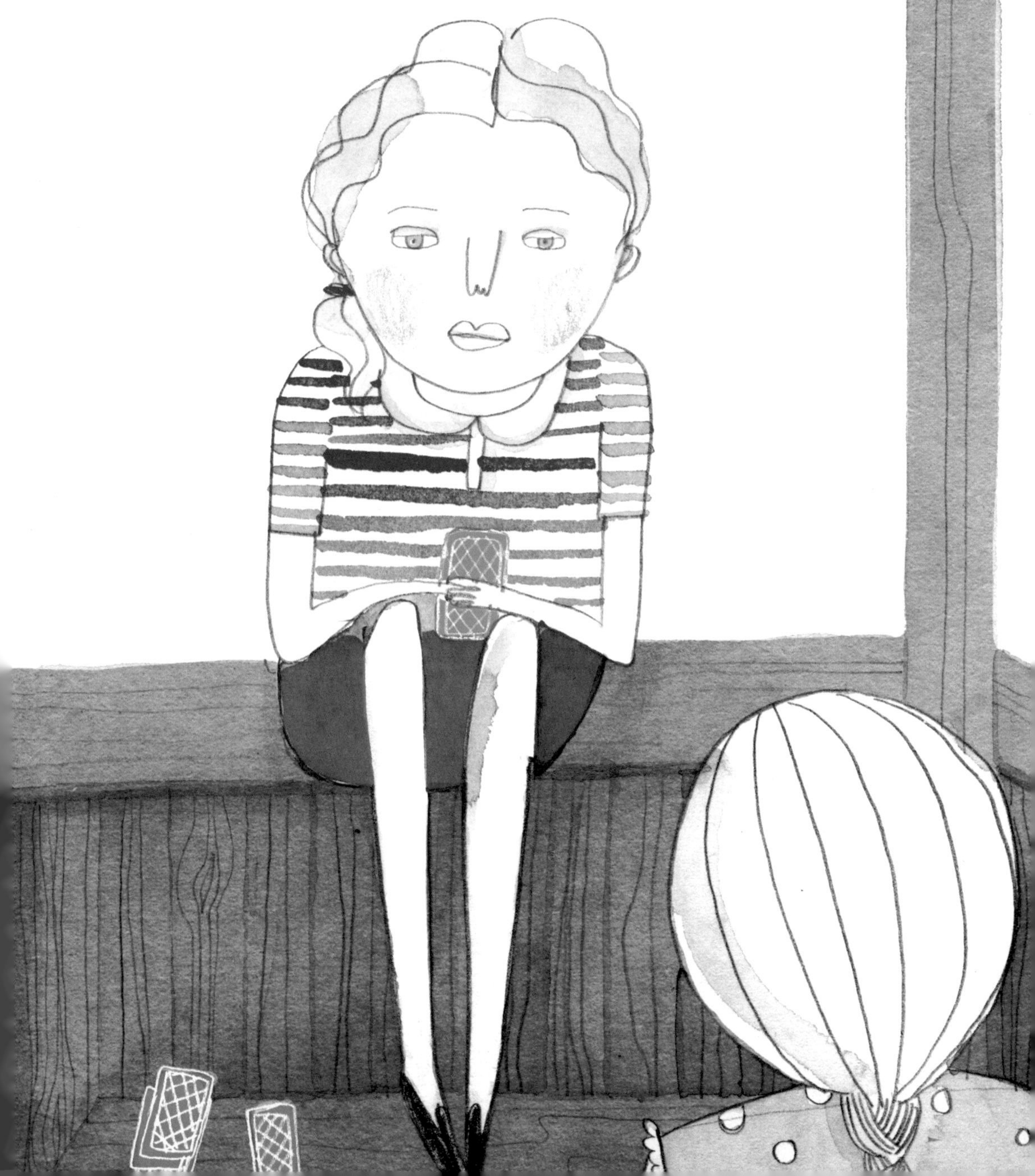

My grandmother cannot reach my
grandfather and decides to drive to the city
to see what's going on and to try to call my
mom in America. After dinner, she leaves
me in our neighbor Bella's care.

"I'll be back in the morning," she says.

Bella asks me if I want to come sleep
in their room, but I say I'll be fine. She
makes sure I brush my teeth, tucks me in
and says to come knock on their door if I
get scared alone. I read for a long time. At
some point I fall asleep.

My grandmother is there (asleep) when I
wake up.

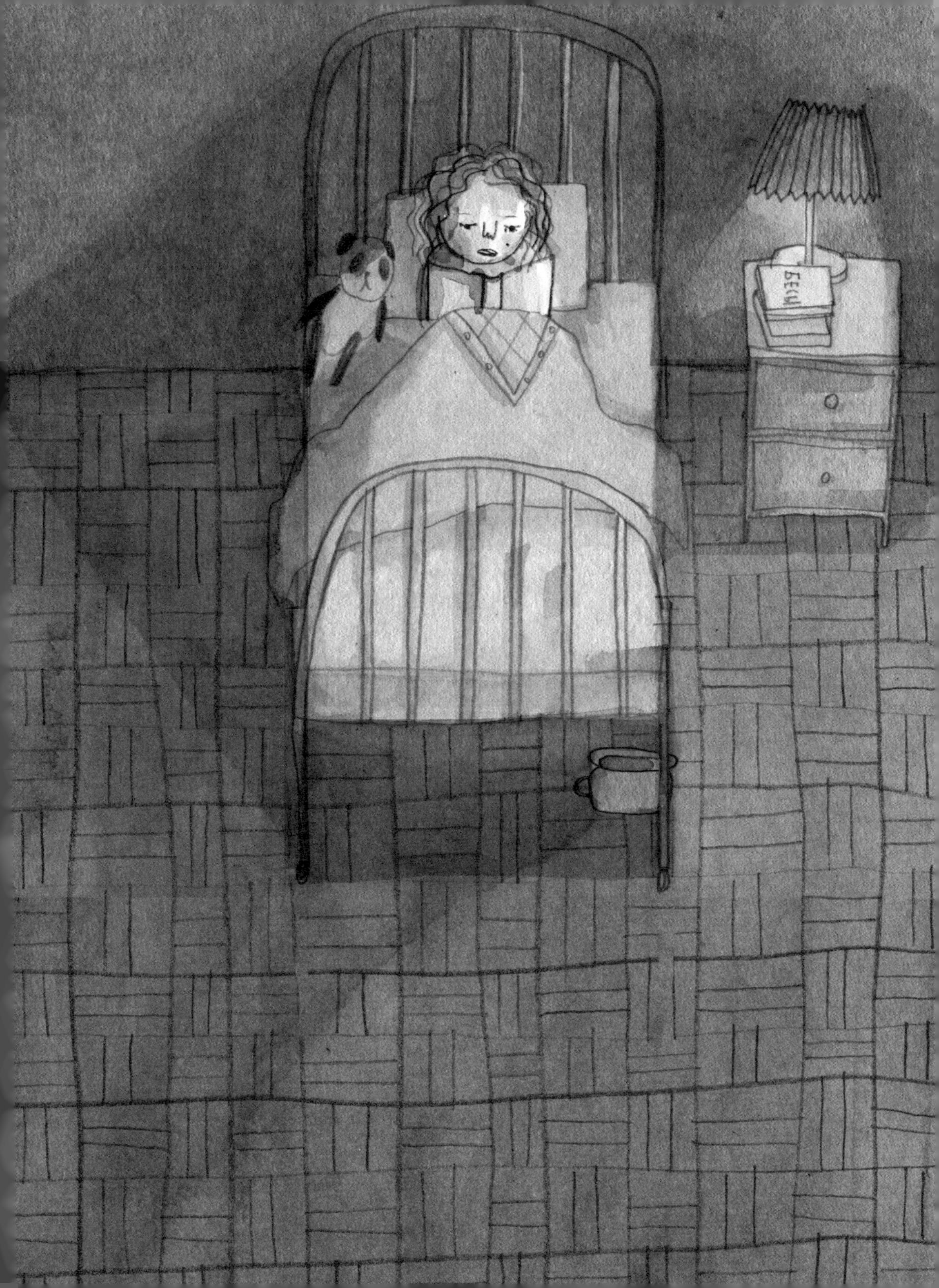
БЕСЫ

Later she tells everyone about what she saw in the city — the tanks and the people protesting the take-over. We went down to the White House with the protesters, she says.

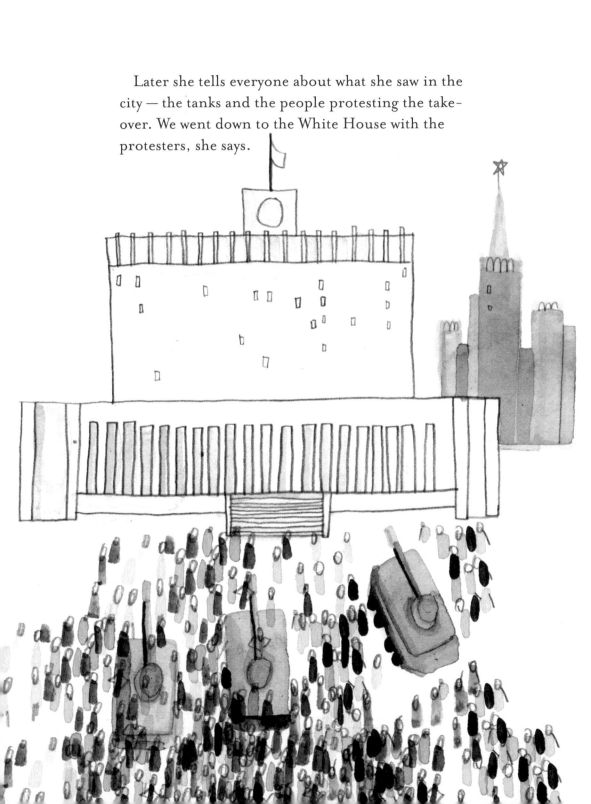

"I was able to get through to your mom and tell her we are okay," she says to me. "I am so happy she is there where it is safe and not here with us."

Then she says, "You know, it's going to be okay. The good guys have to win this one."

And she is right. Good guy Yeltsin, who we learned about at school last year, comes to the rescue and new life begins in earnest.

We put on the play the last week we are at the retreat.

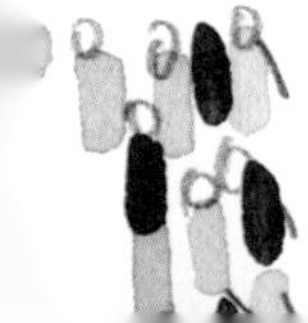

When we get back to the city, I move the rest of my stuff into Mom's room, my mix tapes and books.

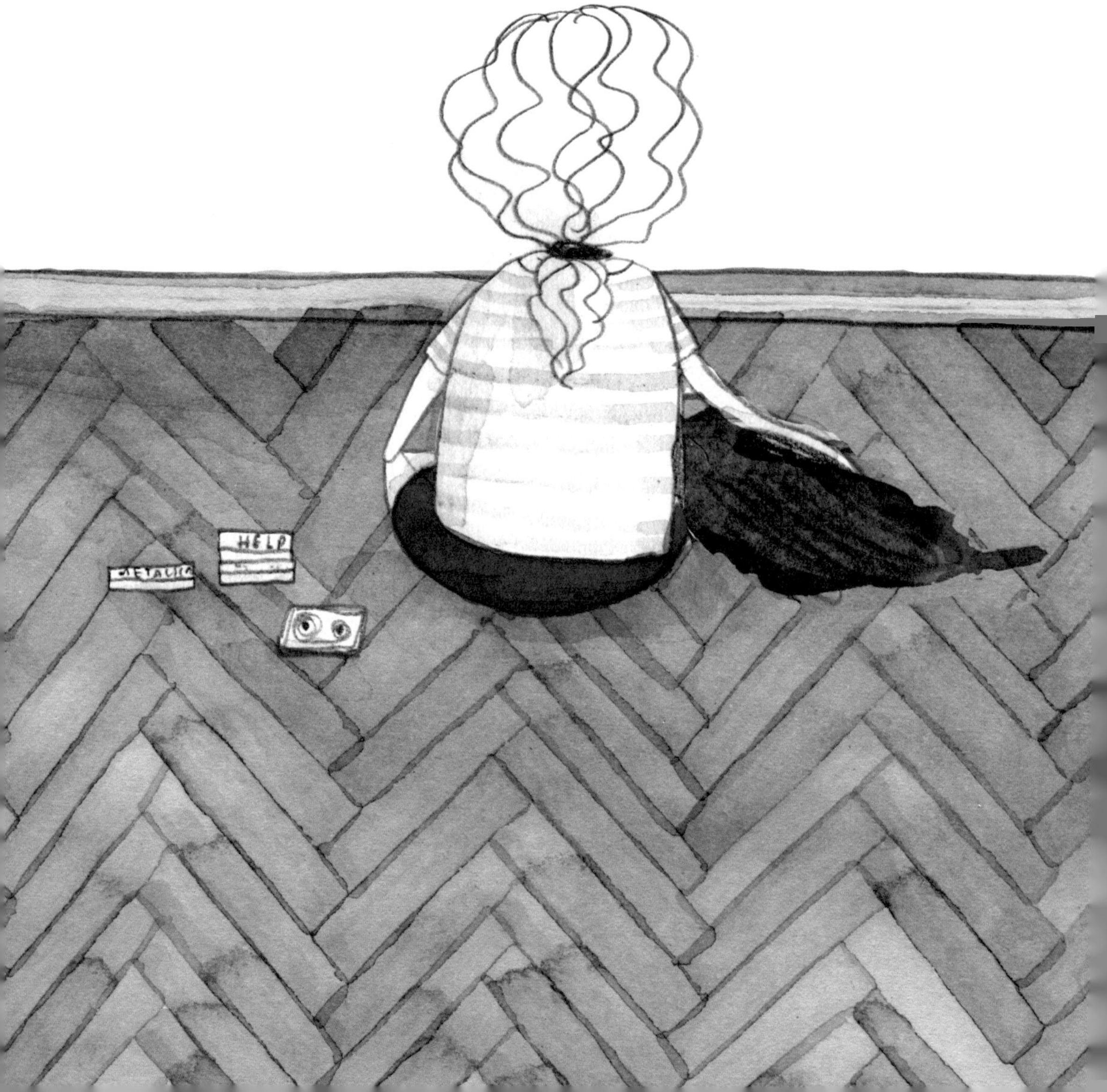
HELP

We settle into a routine. Grandpa wakes
me up and has the tea brewed by the time
I shuffle into the kitchen, but I am on my
own for everything else. I eat toast with jam
(Mom made it last summer with the berries
from our dacha) and then go back to my
room to read. Grandpa walks the dog and
then starts on the day's lunch — some sort
of soup usually. My grandmother wakes
up last. She does not have breakfast, but
instead goes to her typewriter for an hour.
Sometimes I go into her office and read
there.

SEPTEMBER

On September 1 I go back to school. I missed Masha and Natasha SOOO MUCH! They are my best friends. Masha is small and pretty and independent. She has three brothers and a little sister. She went to Paris for the summer to visit her grandmother. Natasha is taller with short black hair and a cool mother who is a journalist. She says things like, "When I get married, I want to marry someone for money, I don't want to marry for love. I want to marry an old man for money and take a young lover." Masha and I are horrified by this, but Natasha is the only one of us who has ever had a boyfriend.

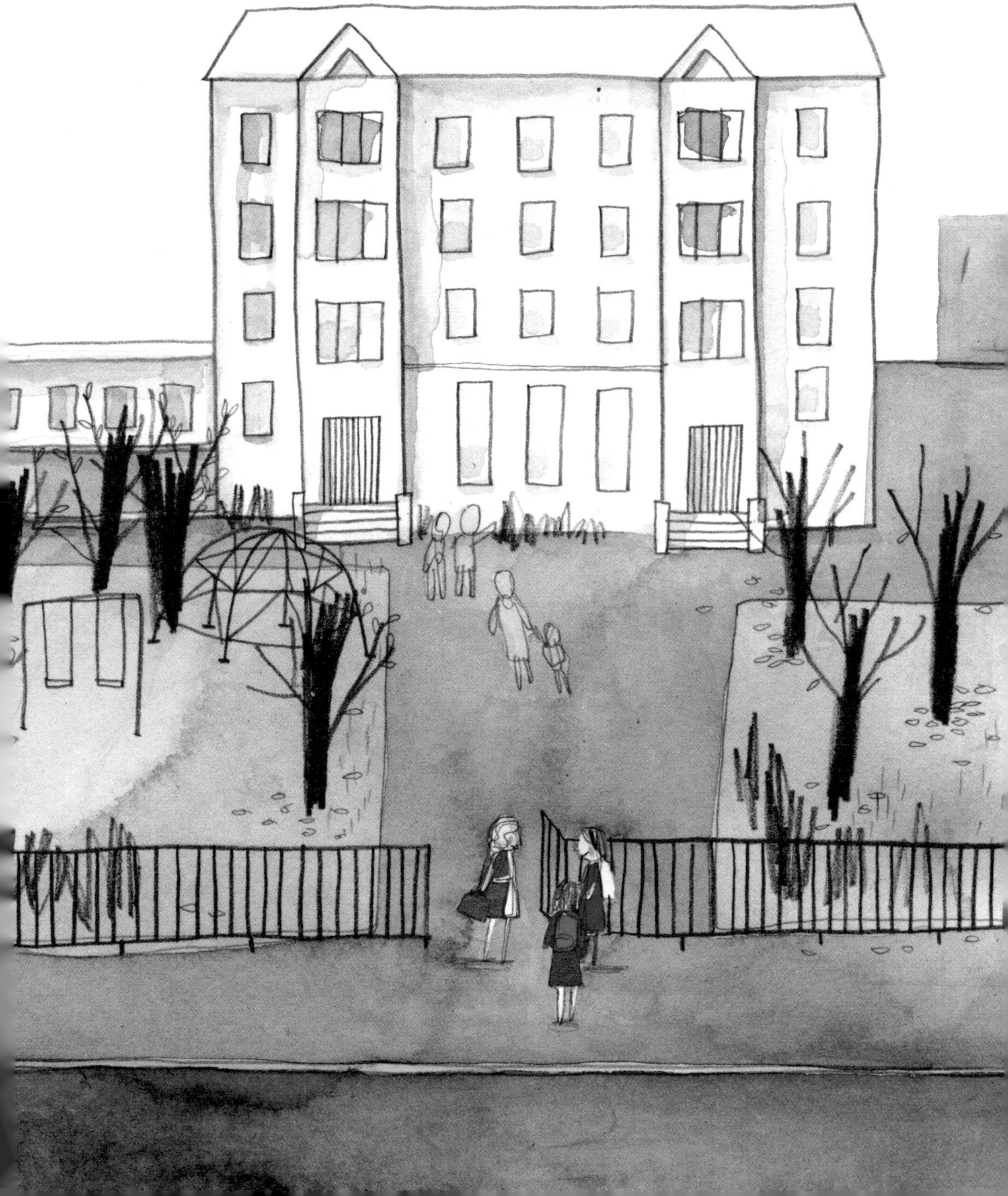

Most days we hang out after school. Masha wants to know all about the writers' retreat kids.

Did Smetanka get any taller? Is Nina still so weird? Did you swim a lot? I wish we went in the summer, so we could swim. Did you play cops and robbers?

I met Petya,

I say.

Oh hiiiim. He is in my brother's class.

Masha rolls her eyes.

Oh, meee too! Isn't Louise Poindexter the best?

I say.

I am happy for the change in subject. Masha makes me nervous, and I am sorry I even brought Petya up.

She is fine.

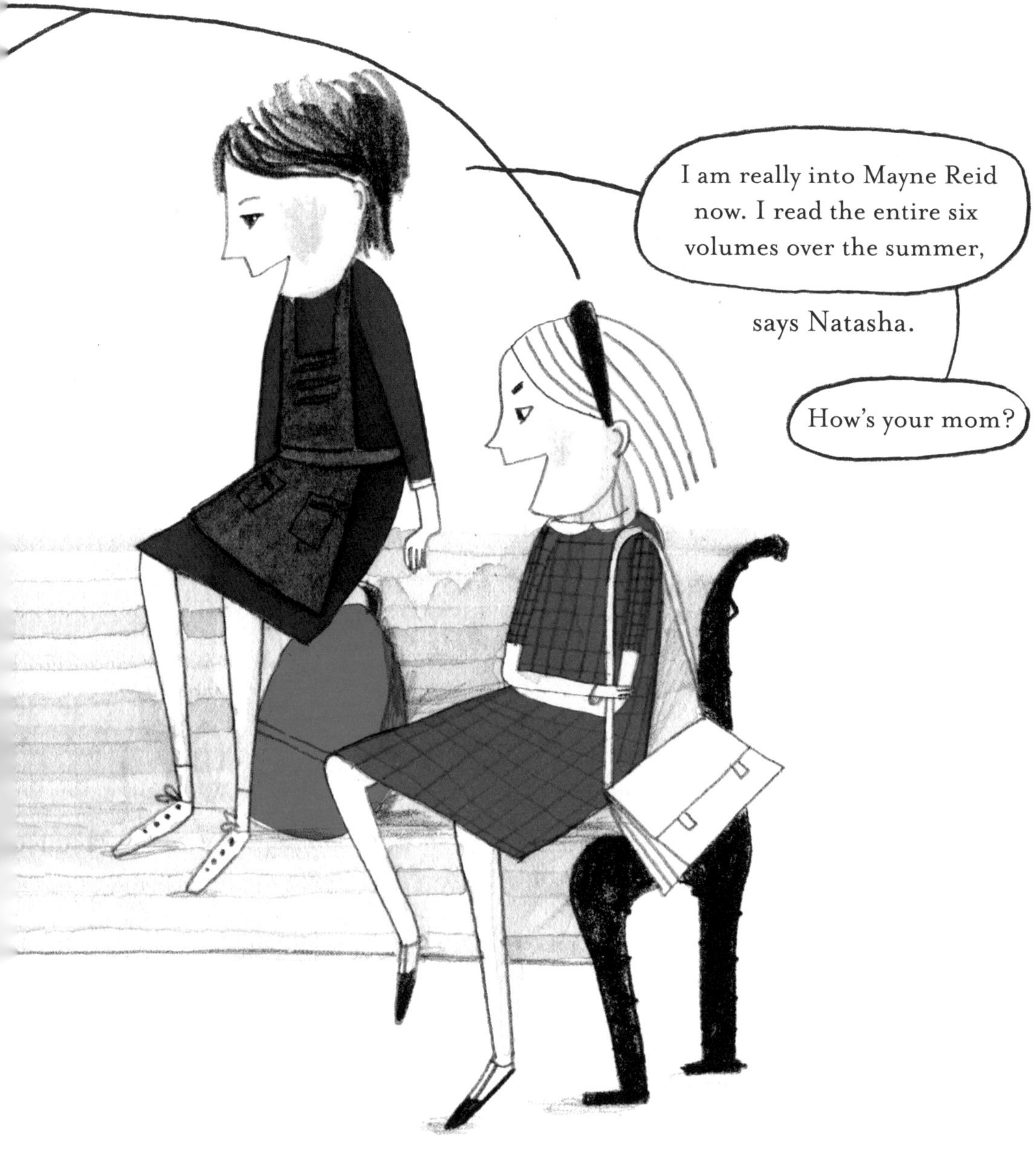
I am really into Mayne Reid now. I read the entire six volumes over the summer,
says Natasha.
How's your mom?

$$E = \frac{mv^2}{2}, \text{Дж} \quad \left(\text{Дж} = \frac{\text{кг } м^2}{c^2} \right)$$

Потенциальная энергия

$$E = mgh, \text{Дж}$$

$$Q = cm \, (t_2 - t_1)$$

c — теплоёмкость, $\frac{\text{Дж}}{\text{кг} \cdot °c}$

$$C = \frac{a}{m(t_2 - t_1)} = \frac{Q}{m \, \Delta t}$$

$$p = \frac{F}{S} = \frac{F}{ab}, \text{ т.к } S = ab$$

$F = 600 \text{ H}$
$a = 20 \text{ см} = 0,2 \text{ м}$
$p = 0,5 \text{ мм} = 0,005 \text{ м}$

———————————————
найти p

$$p = \frac{600 \text{ H}}{0,2 \text{ м} \cdot 0,005 \text{ м}} =$$

$$p = 600 \text{ к Па}$$

$$60000 \text{ Па} = 600 \text{ к Па}$$

$N = 83$

$м = 5r = 5000 \text{ кл}$
$h = s = 20 \text{ м}$
$N = 30 \text{ к Вт} = 30000 \text{ Вт}$
$g = 10 \text{ H / кг}$

———————————————
$t - ?$

$N = \frac{A}{t}$

$A = F_c \cdot S$

$F_c = mg$

$A = mgs$

$t = \frac{A}{N}$

$t = \frac{m \cdot g \cdot s}{N}$

$t = \frac{5000 \text{ кл} \cdot}{300}$

$$= \frac{100000 \text{ H} \cdot}{30000 \text{ В}}$$

We have a new class I am excited about
— physics! Even though the teacher seems
a little scary, I pay attention and get a 5 on
our first test (Russian grades go from 1 to
5, 5 being the best).

On Tuesdays, Wednesdays, Fridays and
Saturdays, I go to the art school after my
regular classes. It's on the other side of
town. I go with my little cousin, Varya, who
is nine months younger than me. We study
drawing, composition, painting, sculpture
and art history. On Saturdays, I take a cos-
tume history class.

$$\frac{Ic_2 \cdot 20_u}{r}$$

$$= 33{,}3c$$

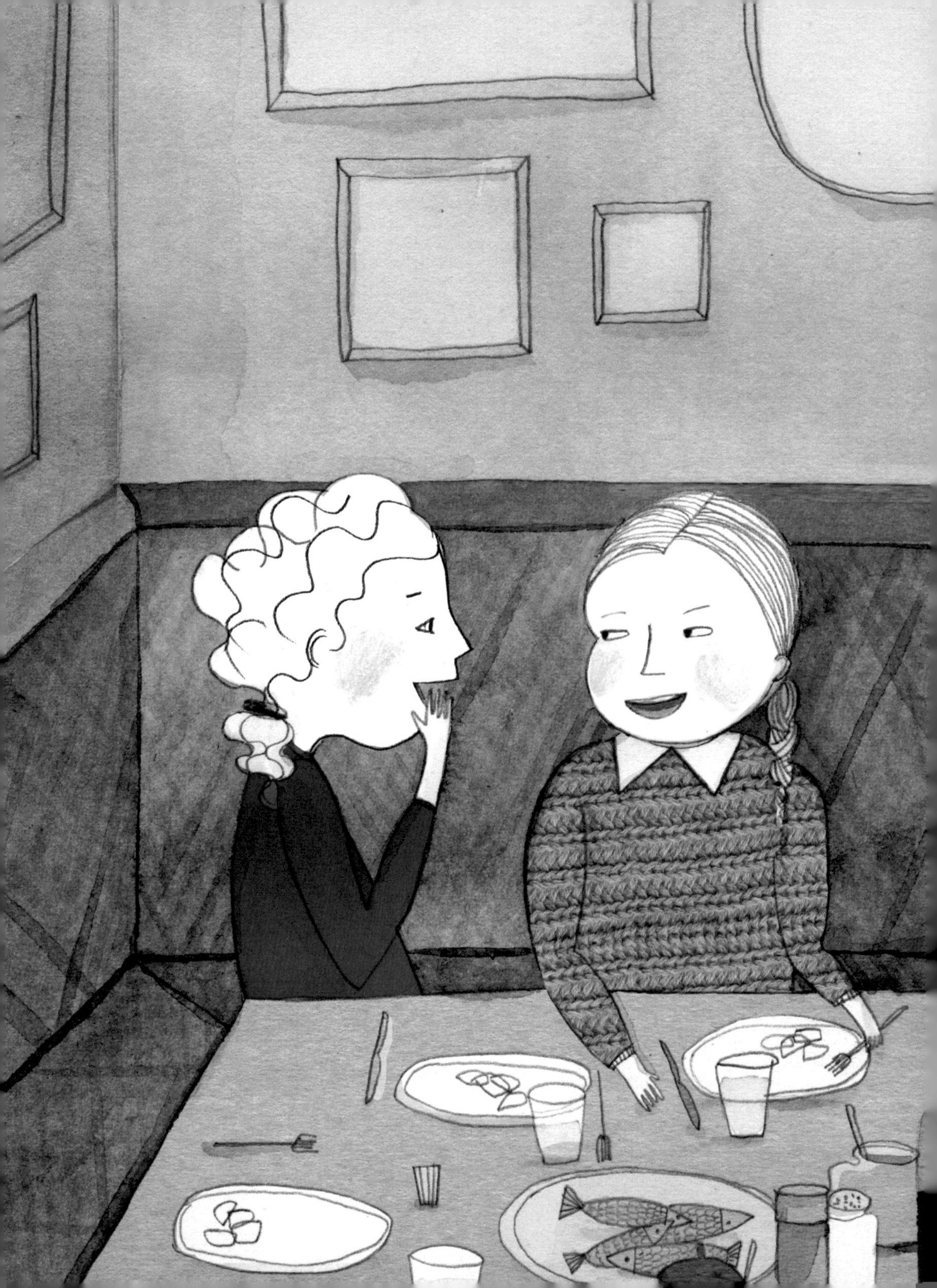

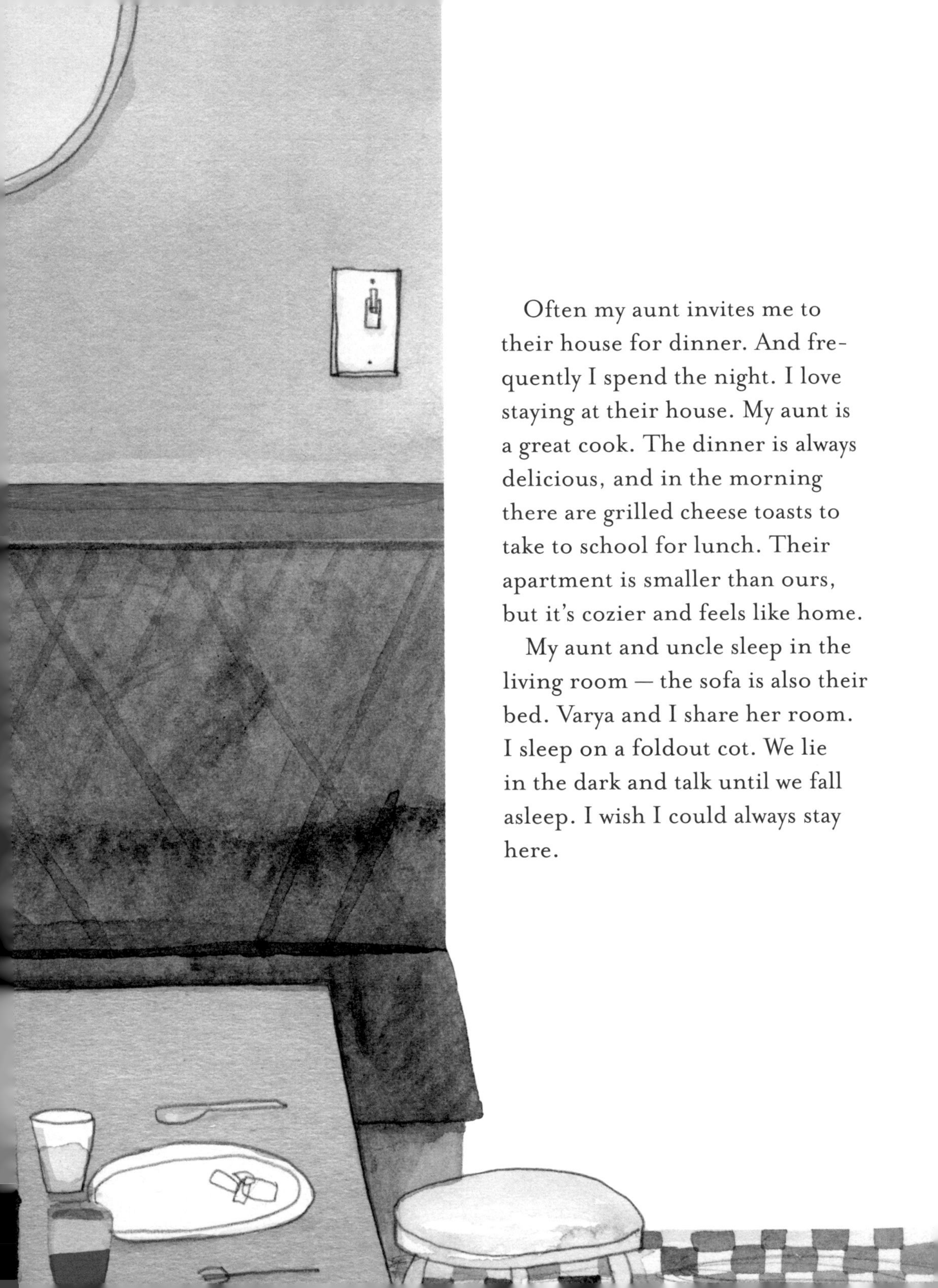

Often my aunt invites me to their house for dinner. And frequently I spend the night. I love staying at their house. My aunt is a great cook. The dinner is always delicious, and in the morning there are grilled cheese toasts to take to school for lunch. Their apartment is smaller than ours, but it's cozier and feels like home.

My aunt and uncle sleep in the living room — the sofa is also their bed. Varya and I share her room. I sleep on a foldout cot. We lie in the dark and talk until we fall asleep. I wish I could always stay here.

OCTOBER

My mom left me this tape. It's a letter she recorded for me. I listen to it most nights as I fall asleep.

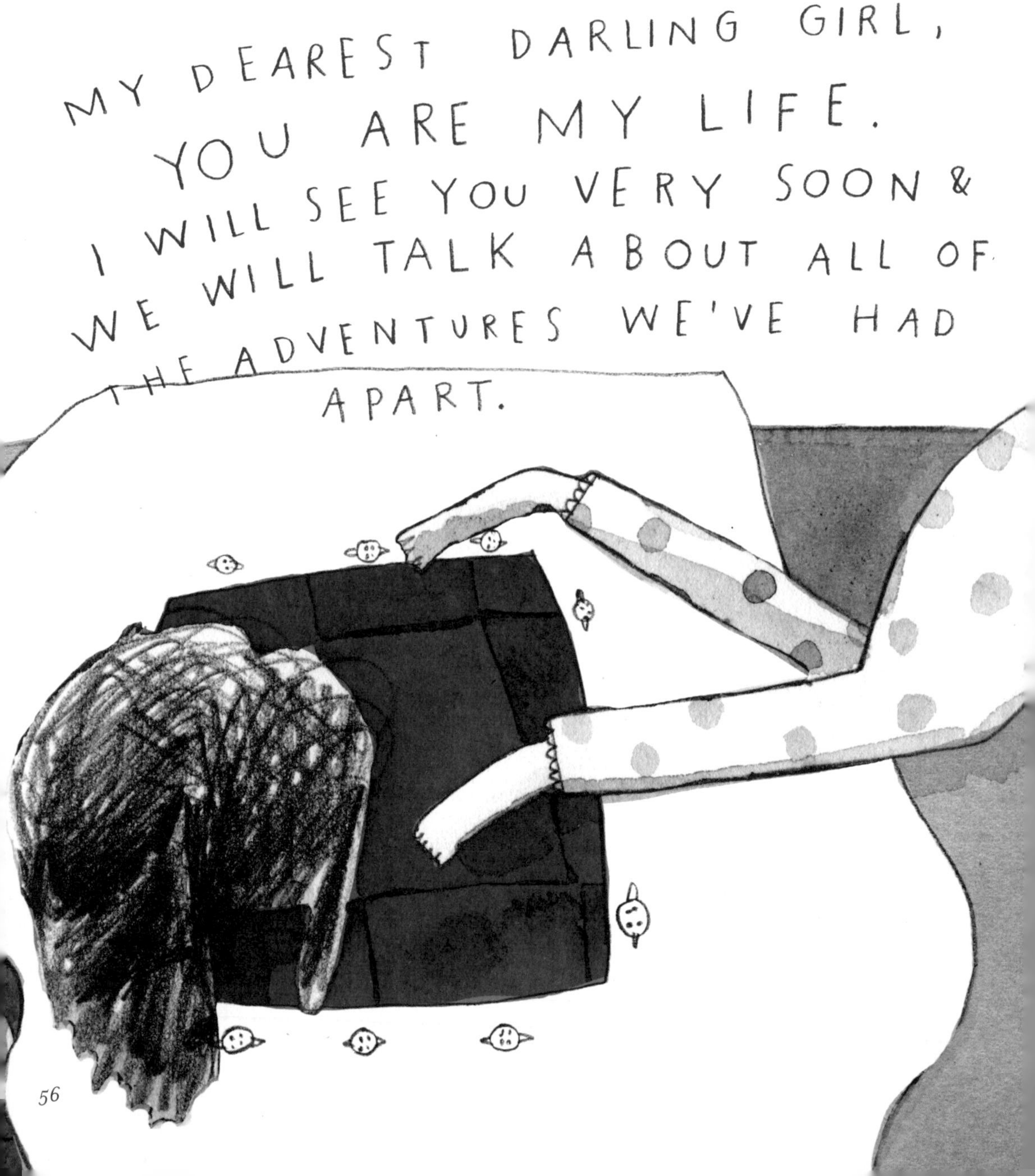
MY DEAREST DARLING GIRL,
YOU ARE MY LIFE.
I WILL SEE YOU VERY SOON &
WE WILL TALK ABOUT ALL OF
THE ADVENTURES WE'VE HAD
APART.

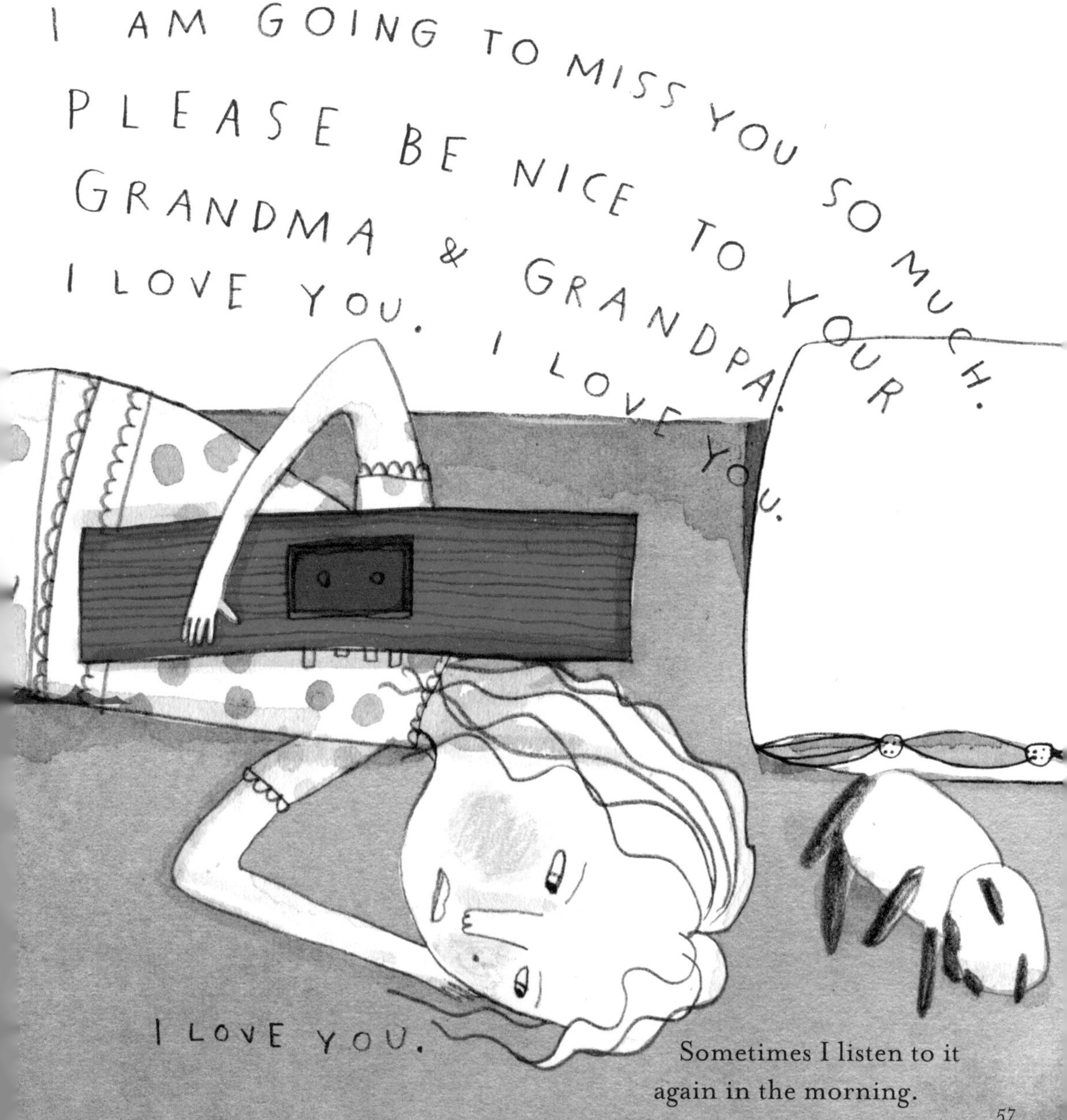
I AM GOING TO MISS YOU SO MUCH.
PLEASE BE NICE TO YOUR
GRANDMA & GRANDPA.
I LOVE YOU. I LOVE YOU.
I LOVE YOU.

Sometimes I listen to it again in the morning.

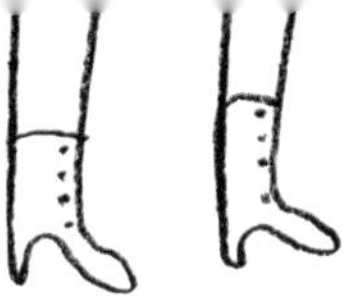

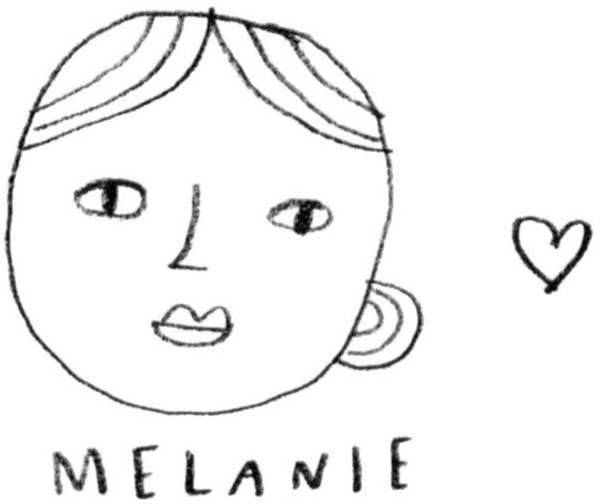
MELANIE

I read a lot. I've decided to learn more about America so I can better imagine where my mom is. I'm reading *Gone with the Wind*. Scarlett is obviously mesmerizing, but I want to be just like Melanie — she is so good and pure.

Masha and Natasha and I play that we are ladies from the 1860s. We write each other letters with nib pens and seal them with wax. I wish I could have a real feather pen. We make up new aristocratic names for ourselves. Both Masha and I want to be named Louisa, so we compromise by picking different last names for ourselves.

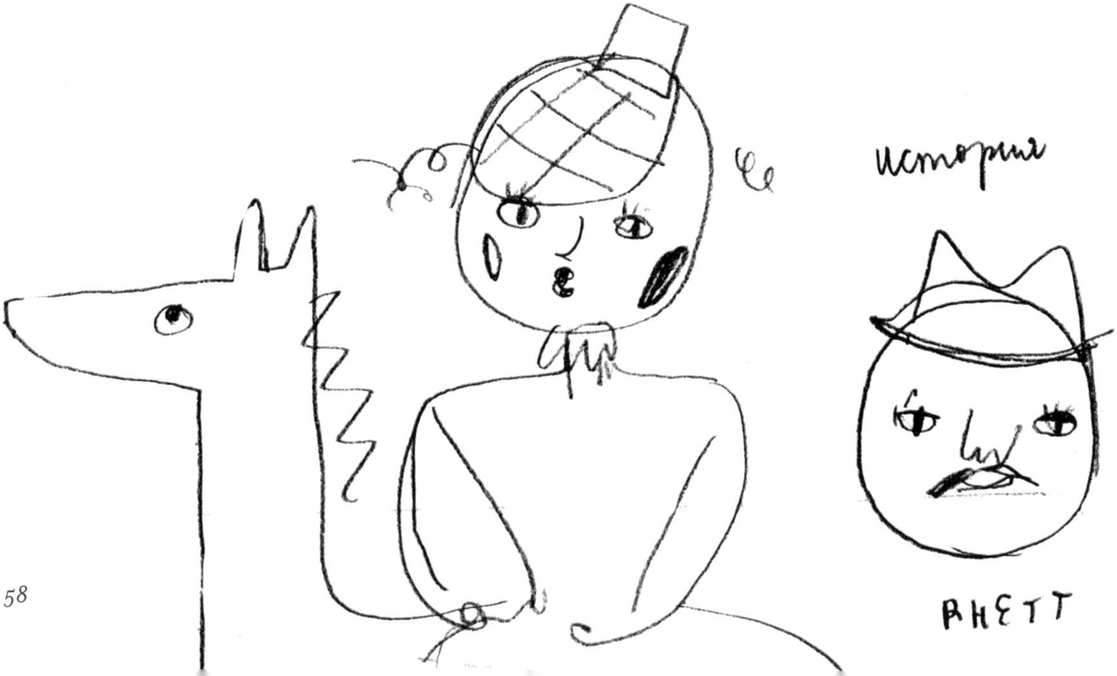
история
RHETT

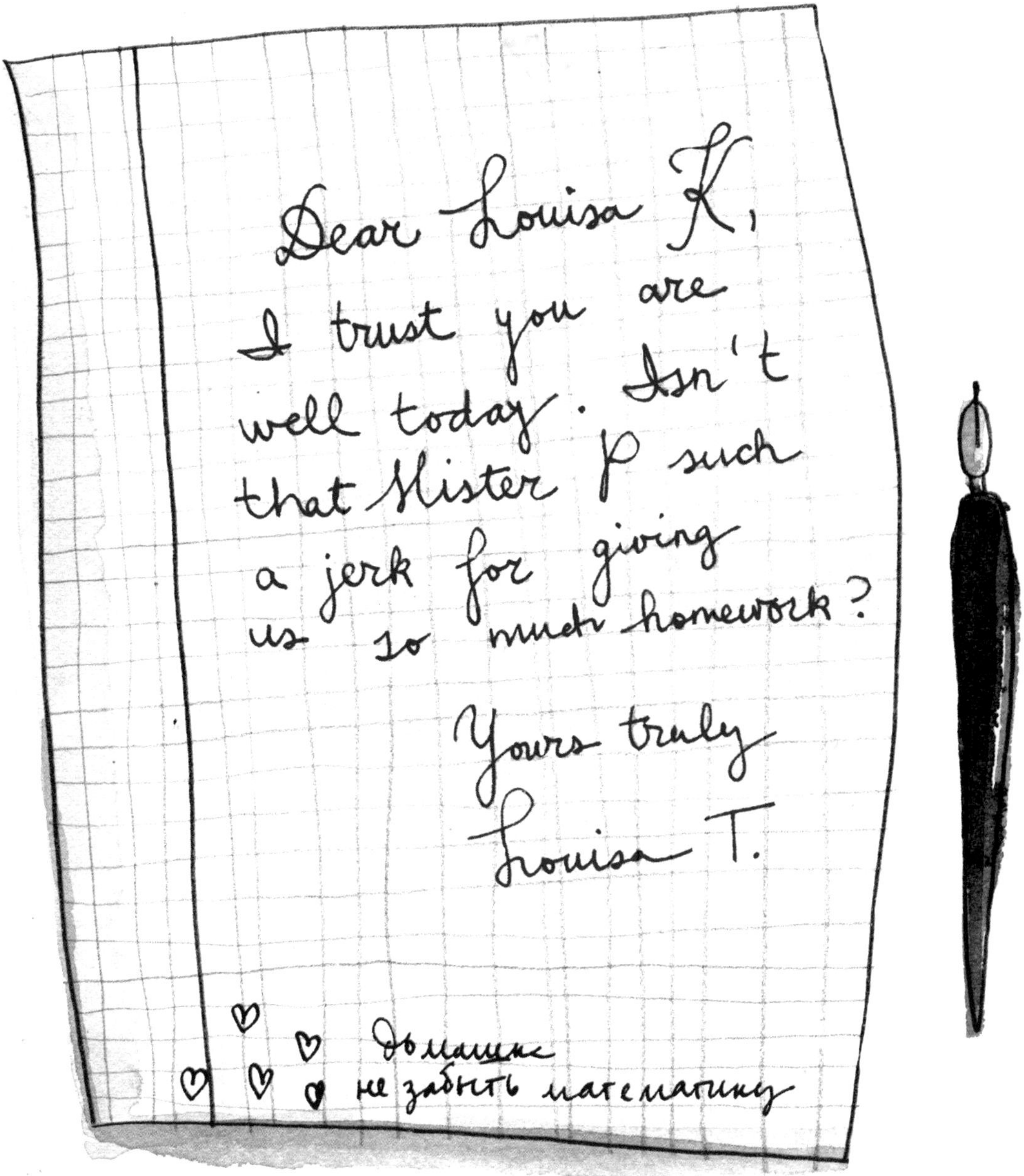
Dear Louisa K,
I trust you are
well today. Isn't
that Mister P such
a jerk for giving
us so much homework?
Yours truly
Louisa T.
не забыть математику

NOVEMBER

On Monday, Natasha says that she is not going to history. It's stupid, she says. Masha says that she won't go either. I am torn. I don't want to skip. We stand around on the sidewalk until the first bell rings and it's clear that I am going to be late. I remember that we have a quiz and run as fast as I can!

HMMM

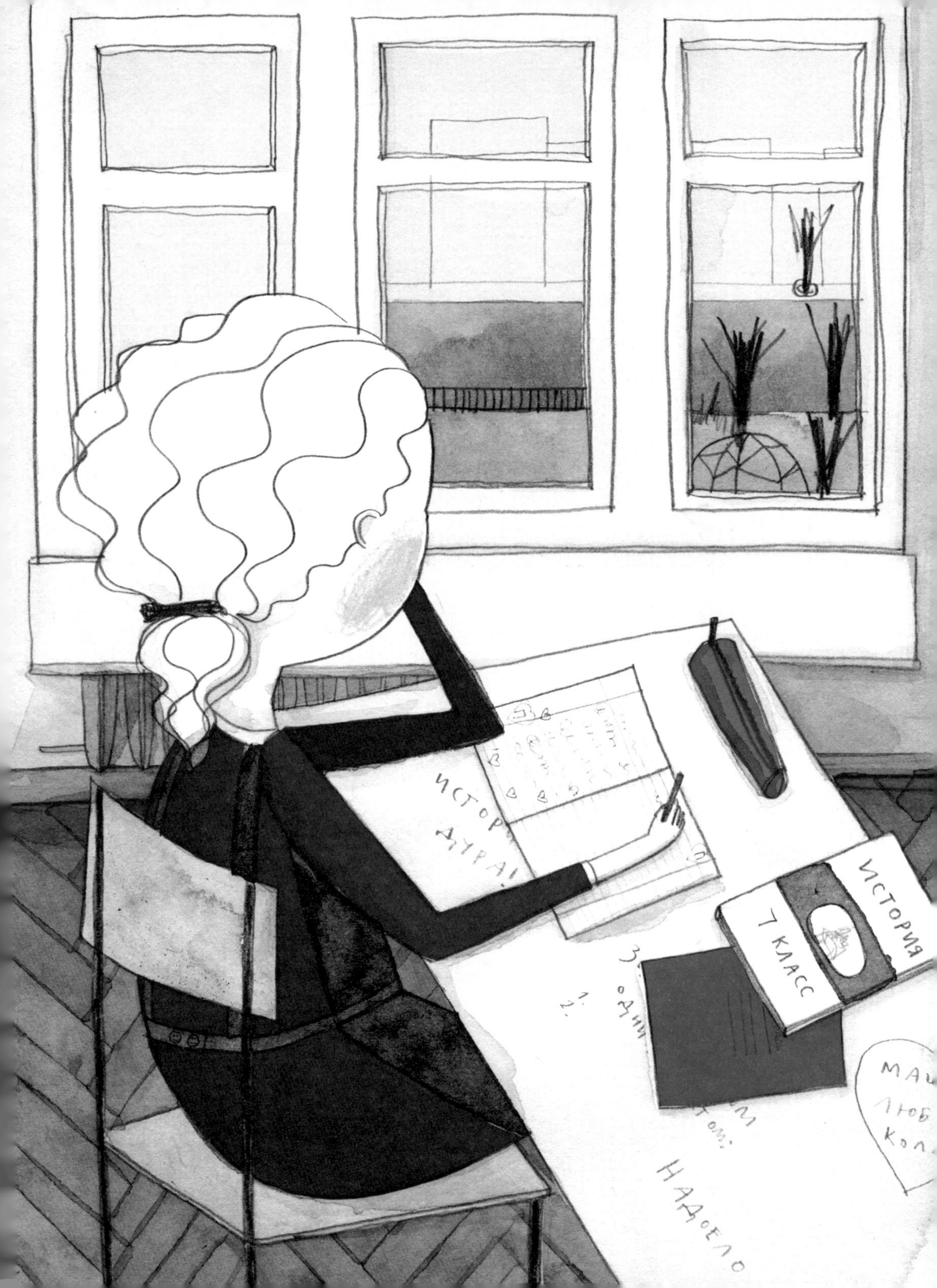
ДУРА!
ИСТОРИЯ
7 КЛАСС
НАДОЕЛО

I call Petya when I get home. (I got his number from my grandmother's book back in August — she is friends with his mom.) I don't know what to say to him, so I just hold the receiver to my ear for a minute and listen to him say, "Hello? Hello?"

I wonder what it would be like to have him be my BOY-FRIEND — and tell him about the girls and my day, the quiz and everything.

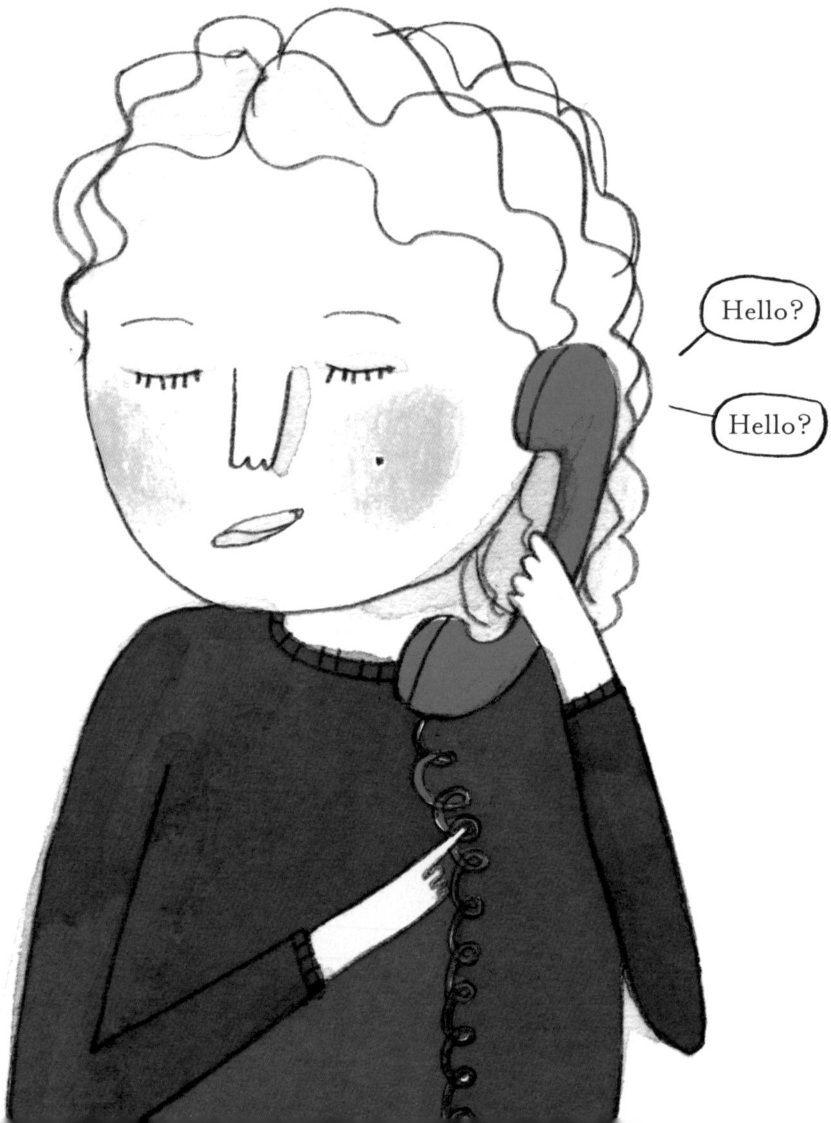
Hello?
Hello?

Then my grandfather picks up his extension and says,

DASHA! GET OFF THE PHONE!

I AM WAITING FOR A CALL.

I could just die.

DECEMBER

It's completely dark now in the morning, and it's hard to get up for school.

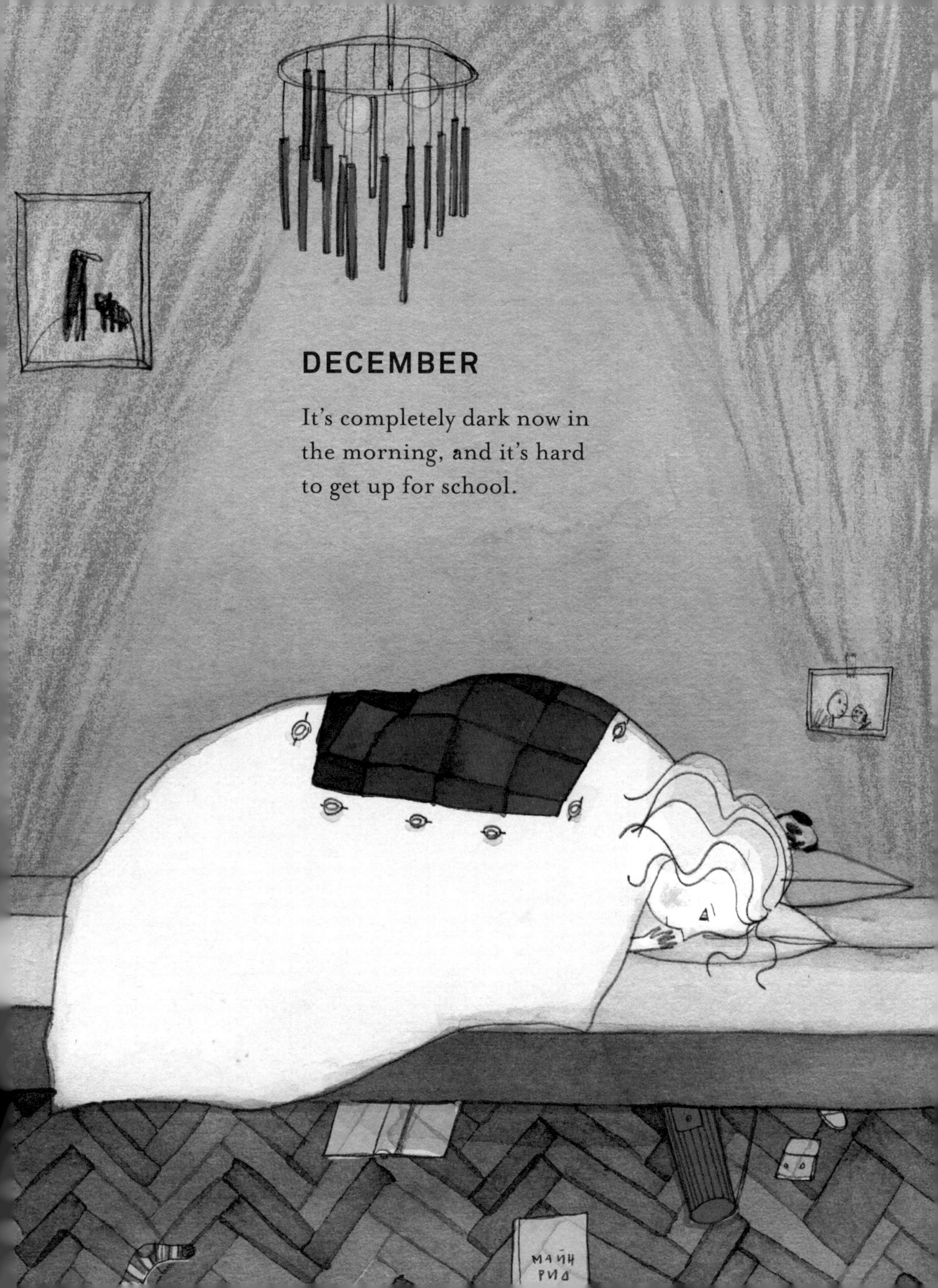
МАЙН
РИД

A lot of days M and N are not there for first period. I know they are just sleeping in and not hanging out somewhere together, but still it makes me sad, being at school by myself.

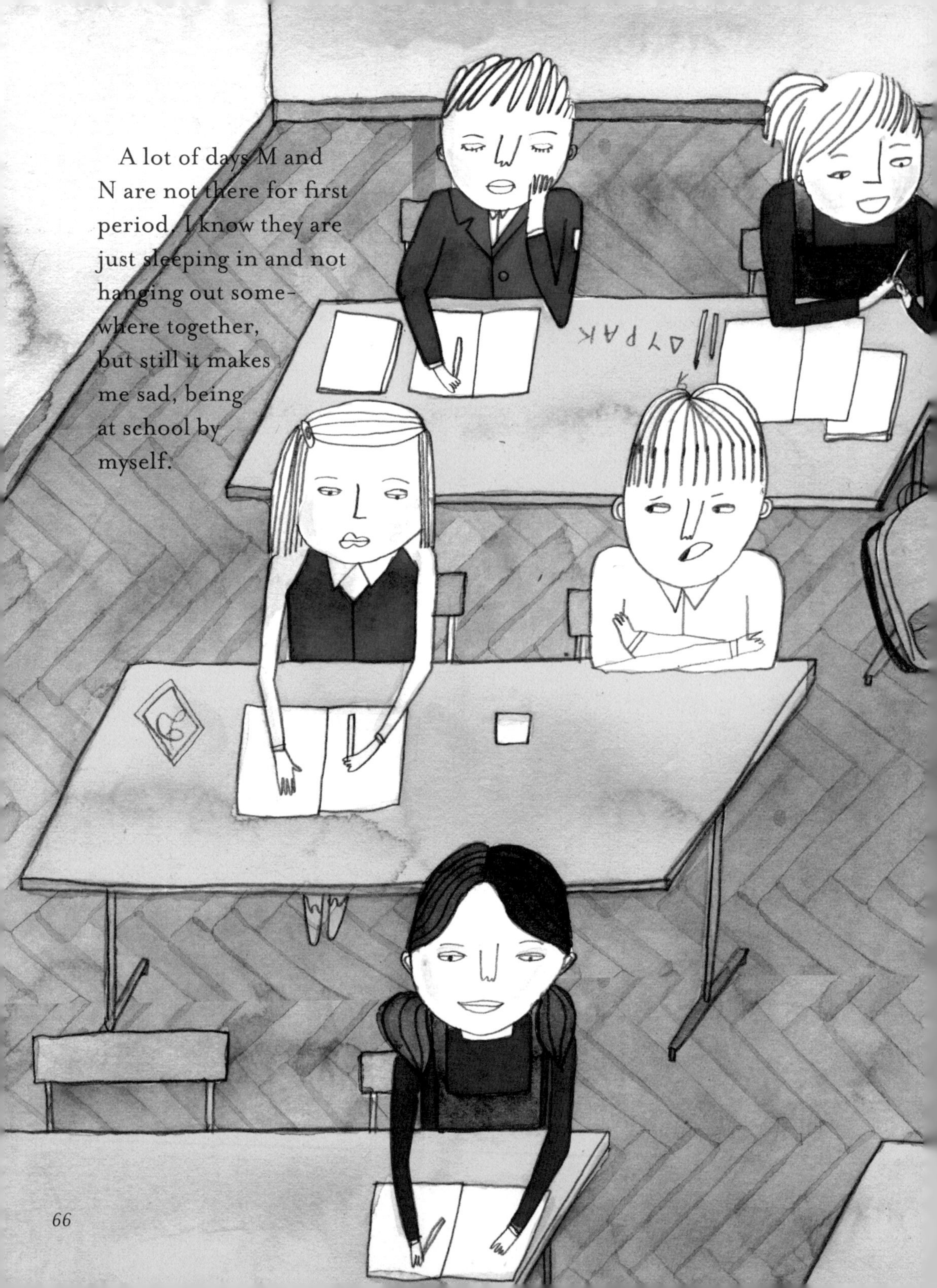
ДУРАК

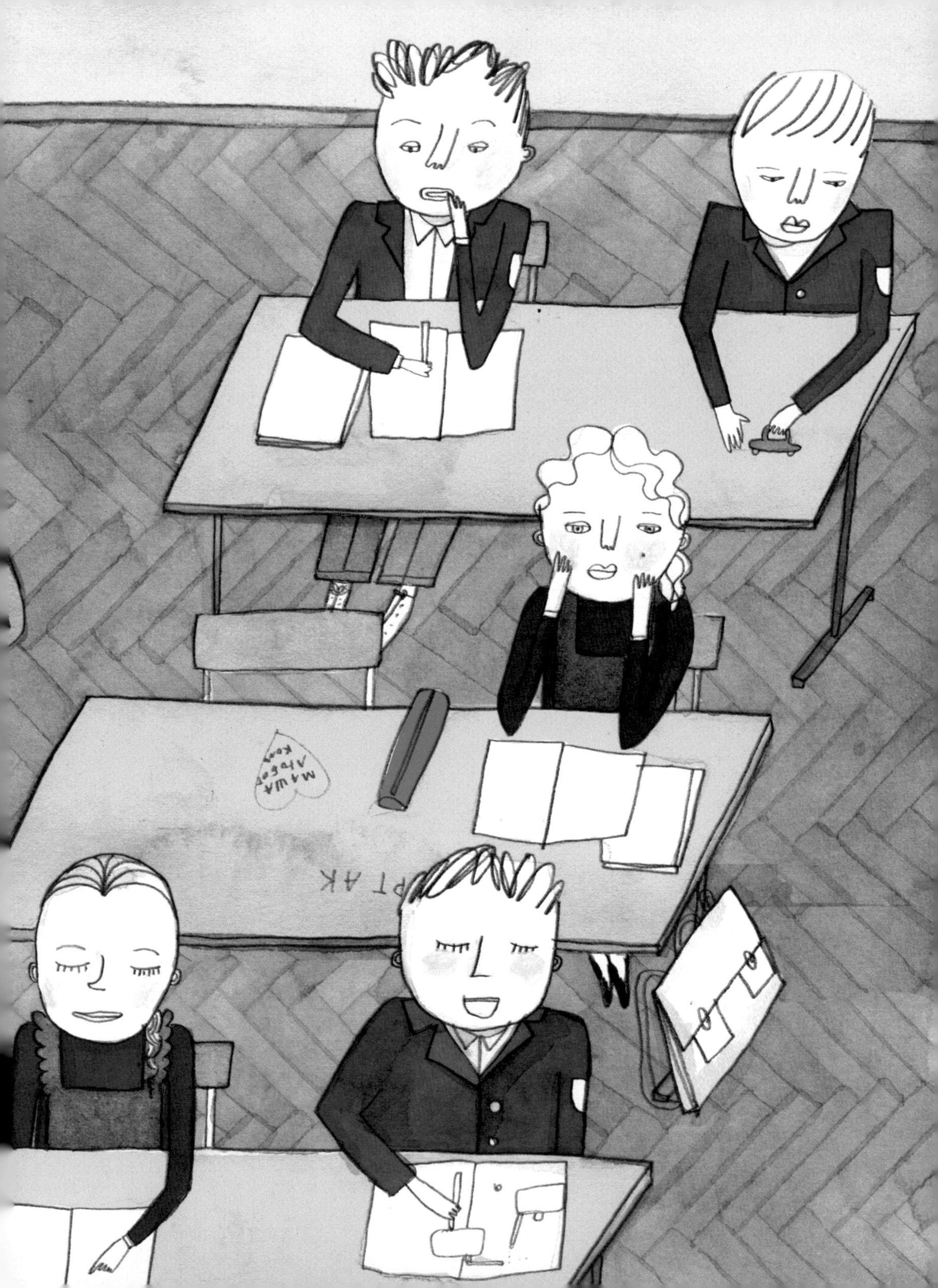

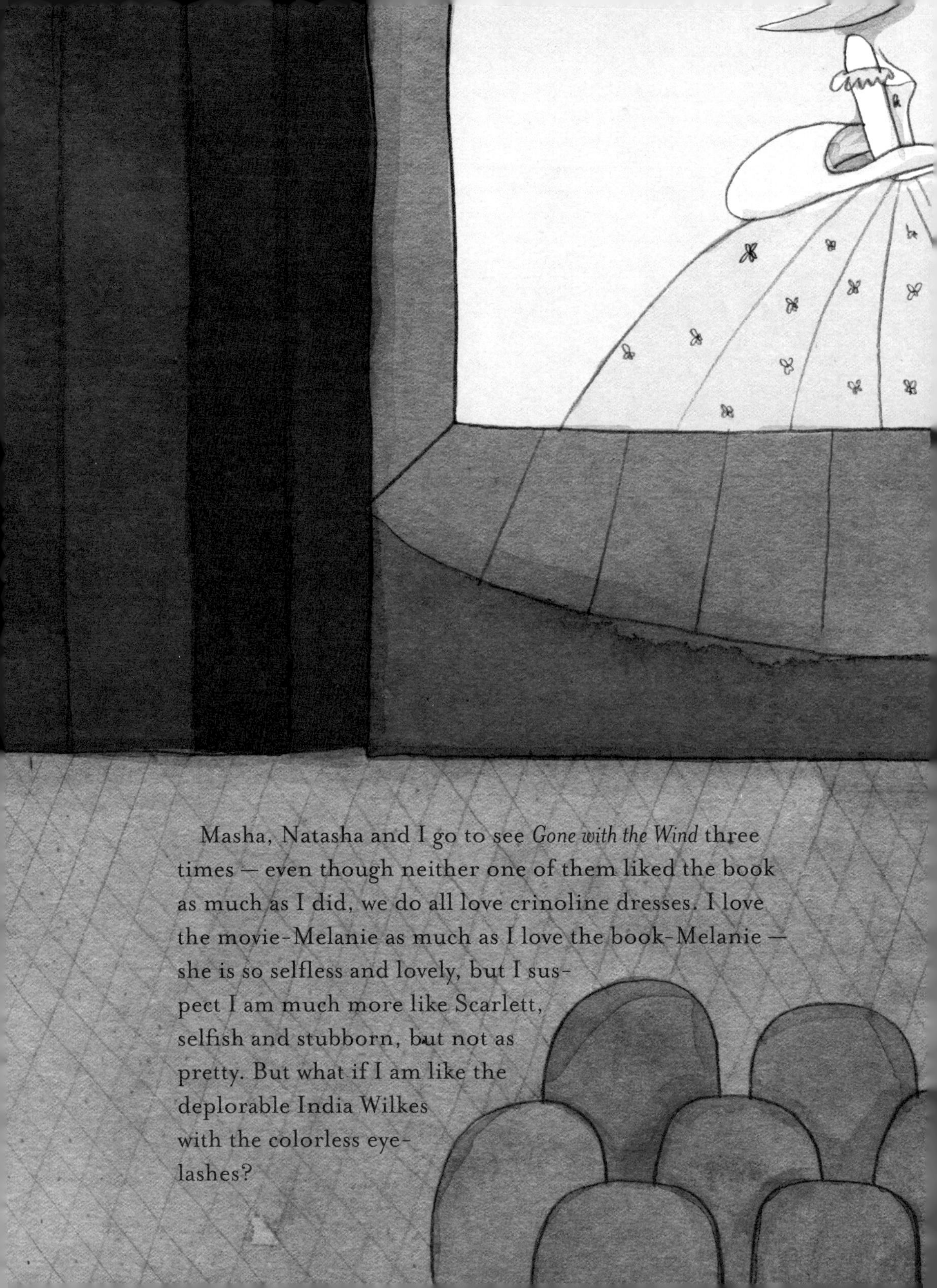

Masha, Natasha and I go to see *Gone with the Wind* three times — even though neither one of them liked the book as much as I did, we do all love crinoline dresses. I love the movie-Melanie as much as I love the book-Melanie — she is so selfless and lovely, but I suspect I am much more like Scarlett, selfish and stubborn, but not as pretty. But what if I am like the deplorable India Wilkes with the colorless eyelashes?

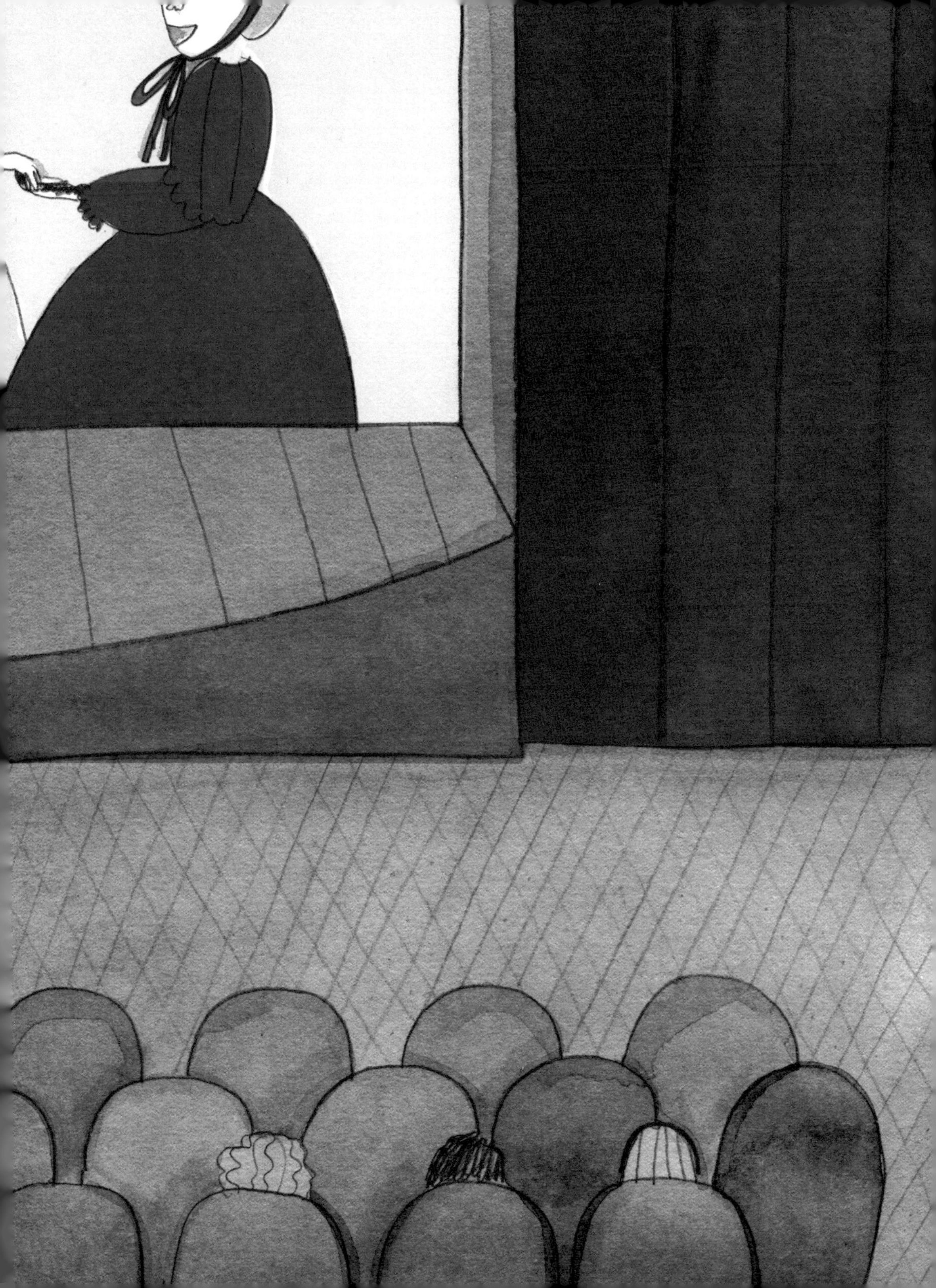

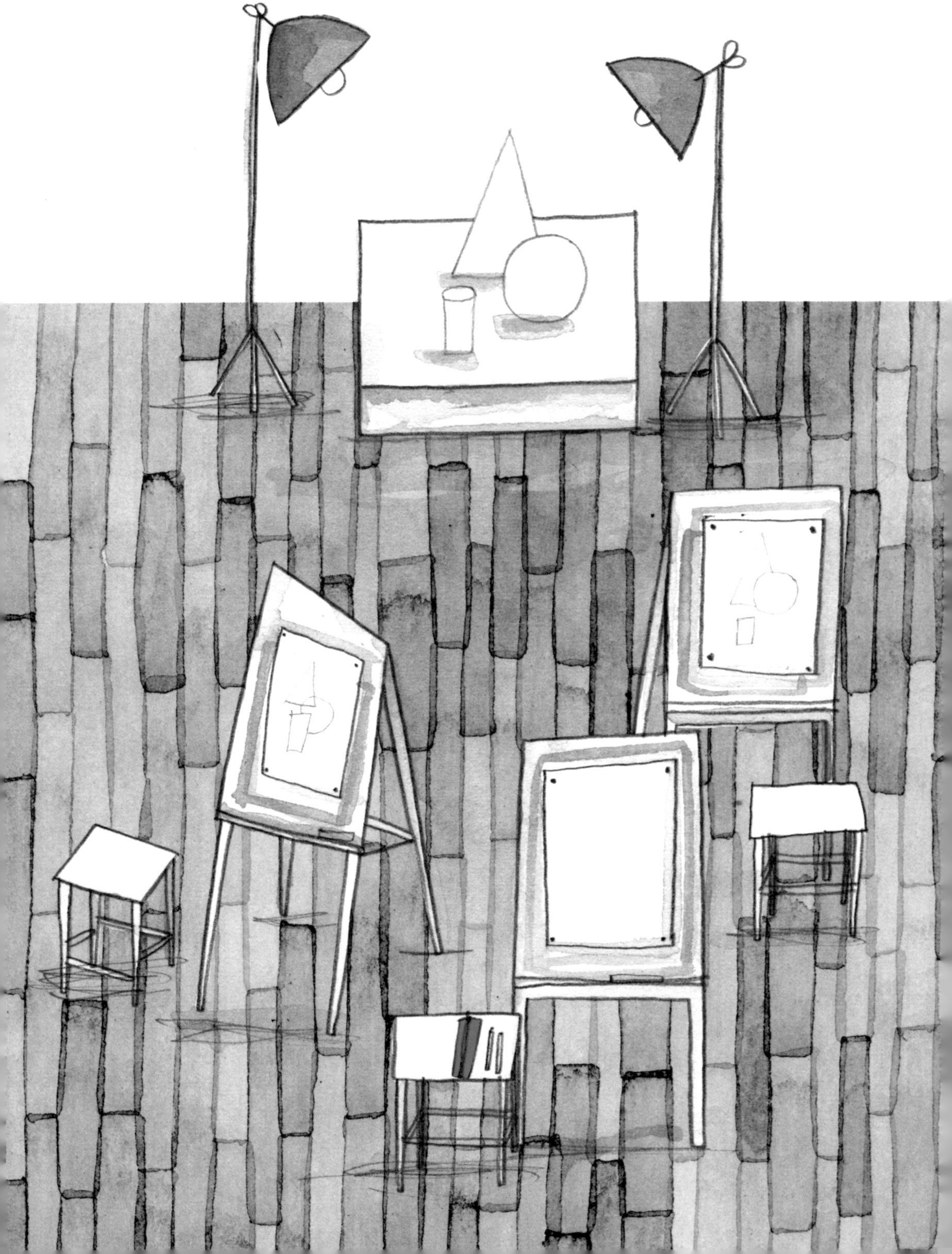

At art school we are working on composition — where you place objects on your page. It's all still lifes all day long. There is this boy, Maxim, who is always sitting so close. I get to class early just to make sure I can get away from him, but he always ends up sitting right next to me. Ugh. His drawings are really good too! I hate him.

Right before winter break, I can hold it in no longer and I tell Varya about Petya.

I love him!

I say.

Varya never likes anyone, but she is very loyal, and she knows to ask the important questions.

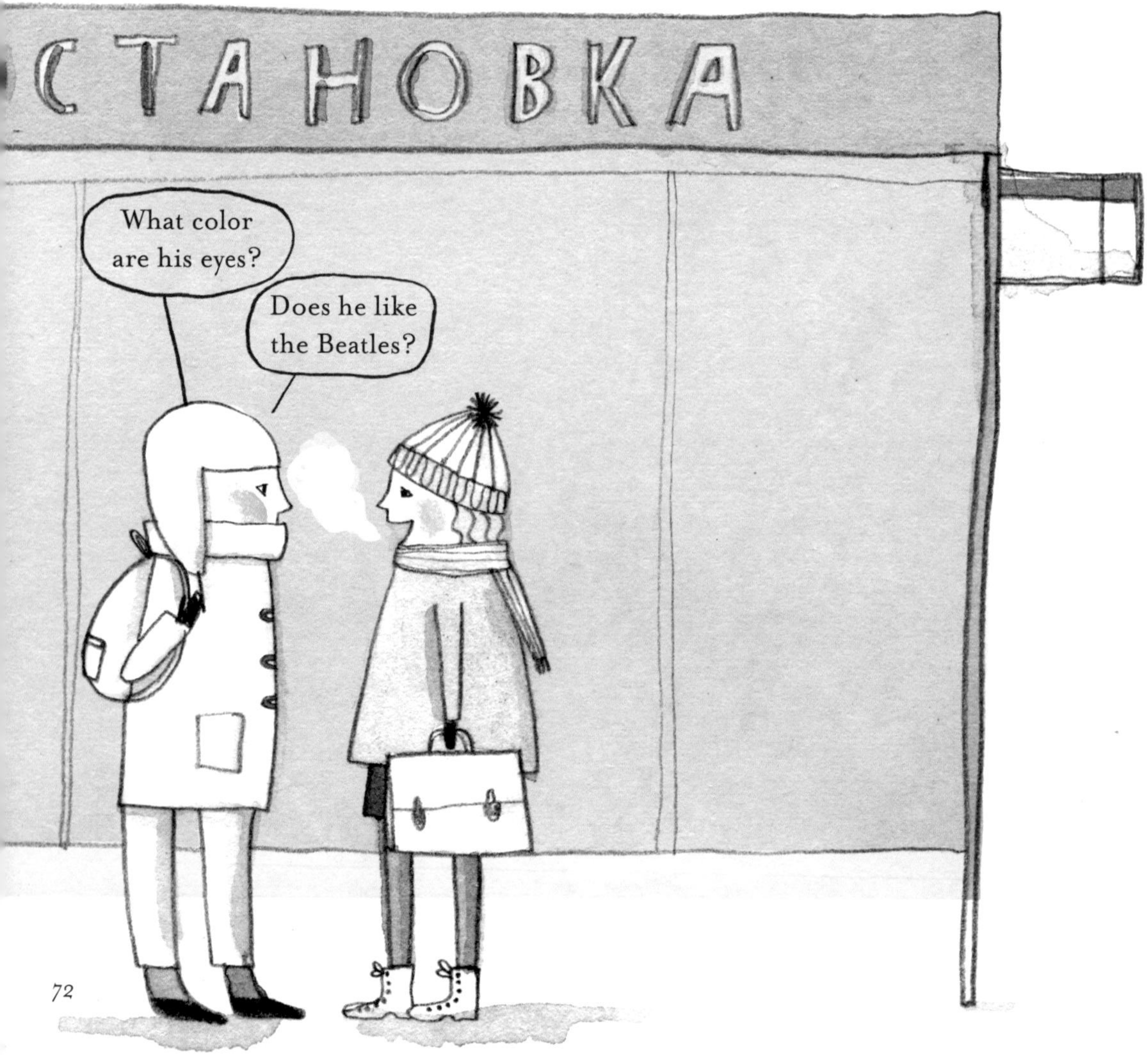
СТАНОВКА
What color are his eyes?
Does he like the Beatles?

WINTER BREAK

We go to Germany to see my grandmother's friends Vadim and Anita. I don't really want to go. I'd rather be going to the writers' retreat. Masha and her whole family are going — and P...

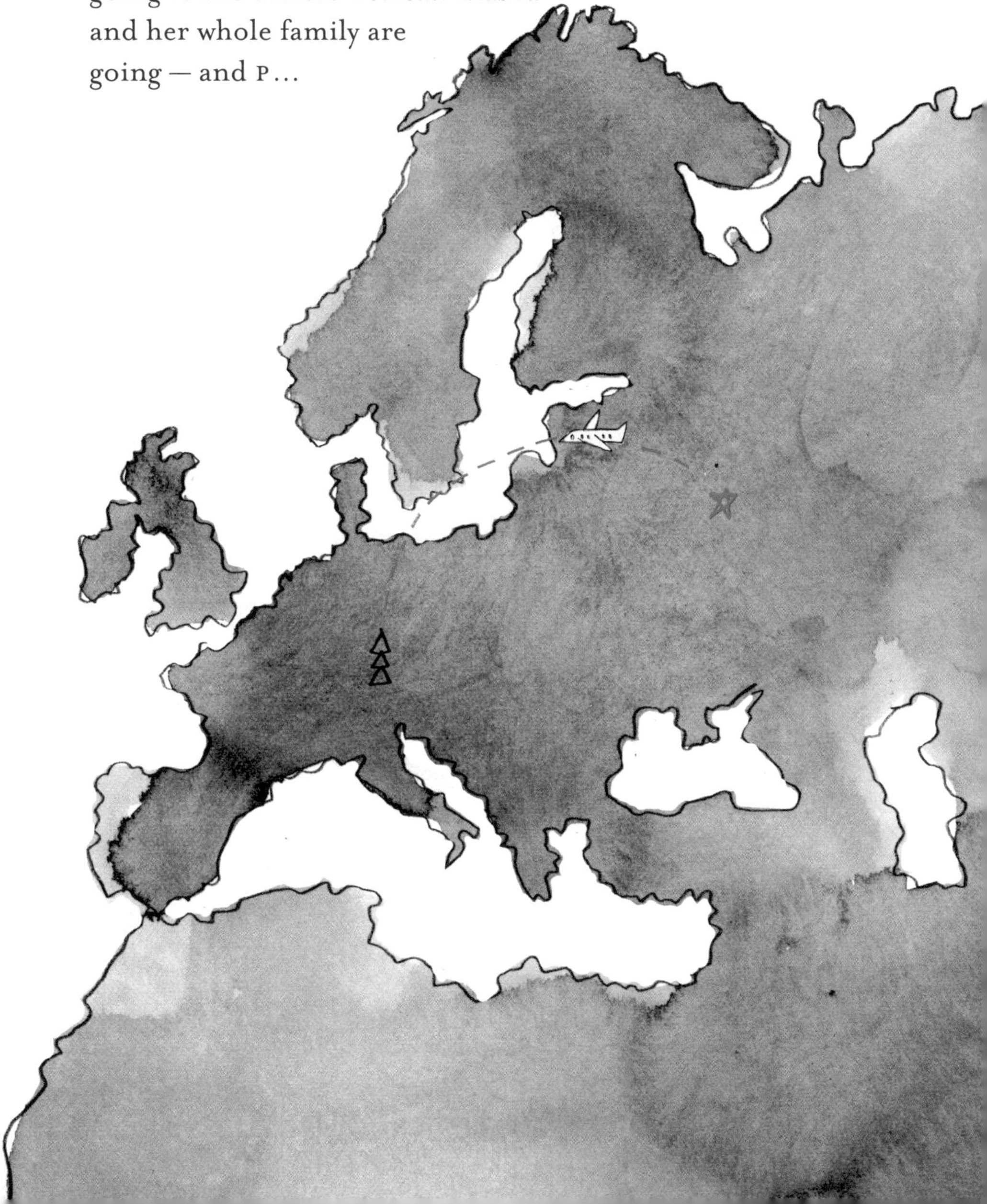

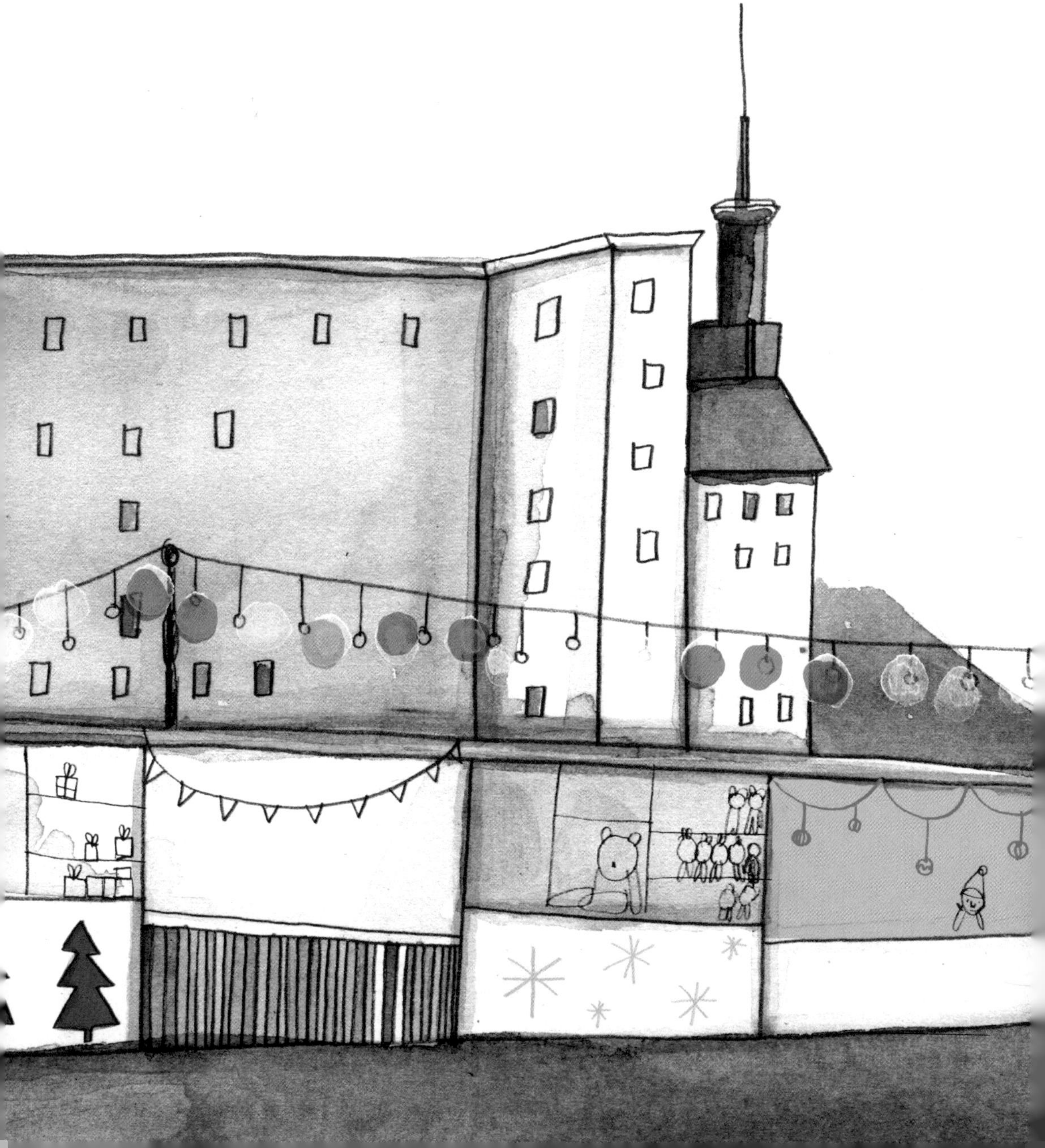

Everything is pretty for Christmas in Munich. Vadim is a journalist at Radio Liberty, a real intellectual. He takes us to see his office straight from the airport. He and my grandmother talk about politics nonstop. When we get to the house, my grandfather cooks for everyone. I fall in love with Anita, who has kind eyes and reminds me of Olivia de Havilland.

"Have you seen *Gone with the Wind*?" I ask her to make conversation.

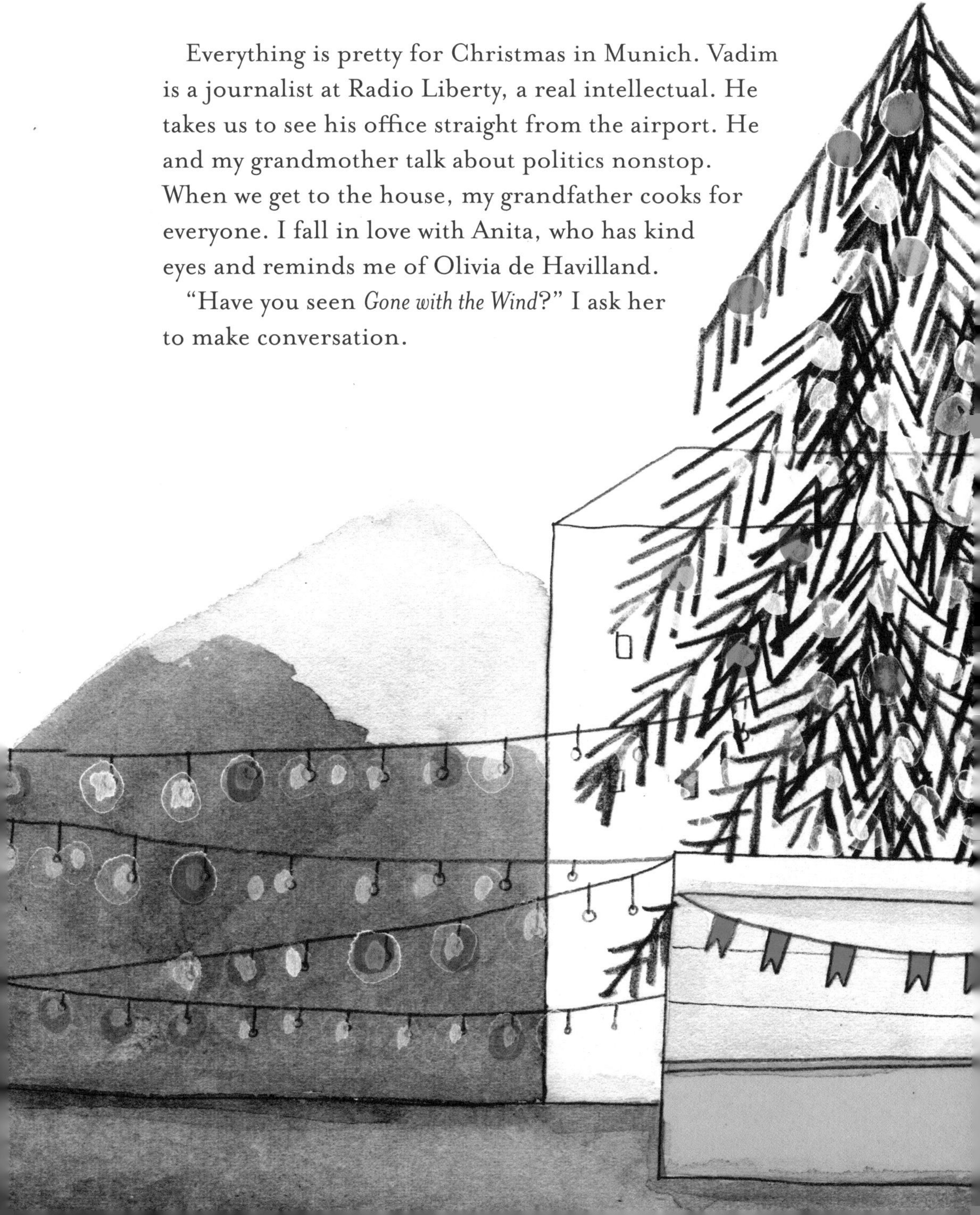

The only thing is, my grandmother has forgotten that I am allergic to cats, and Anita and Vadim have a cat.

All the grown-ups say, "Well, maybe it will be okay. Let's see how this first night goes."

I wake up in the middle of the night and I cannot breathe. I decide I will just wait it out on the balcony without waking anyone up, but it's December and it's cold.

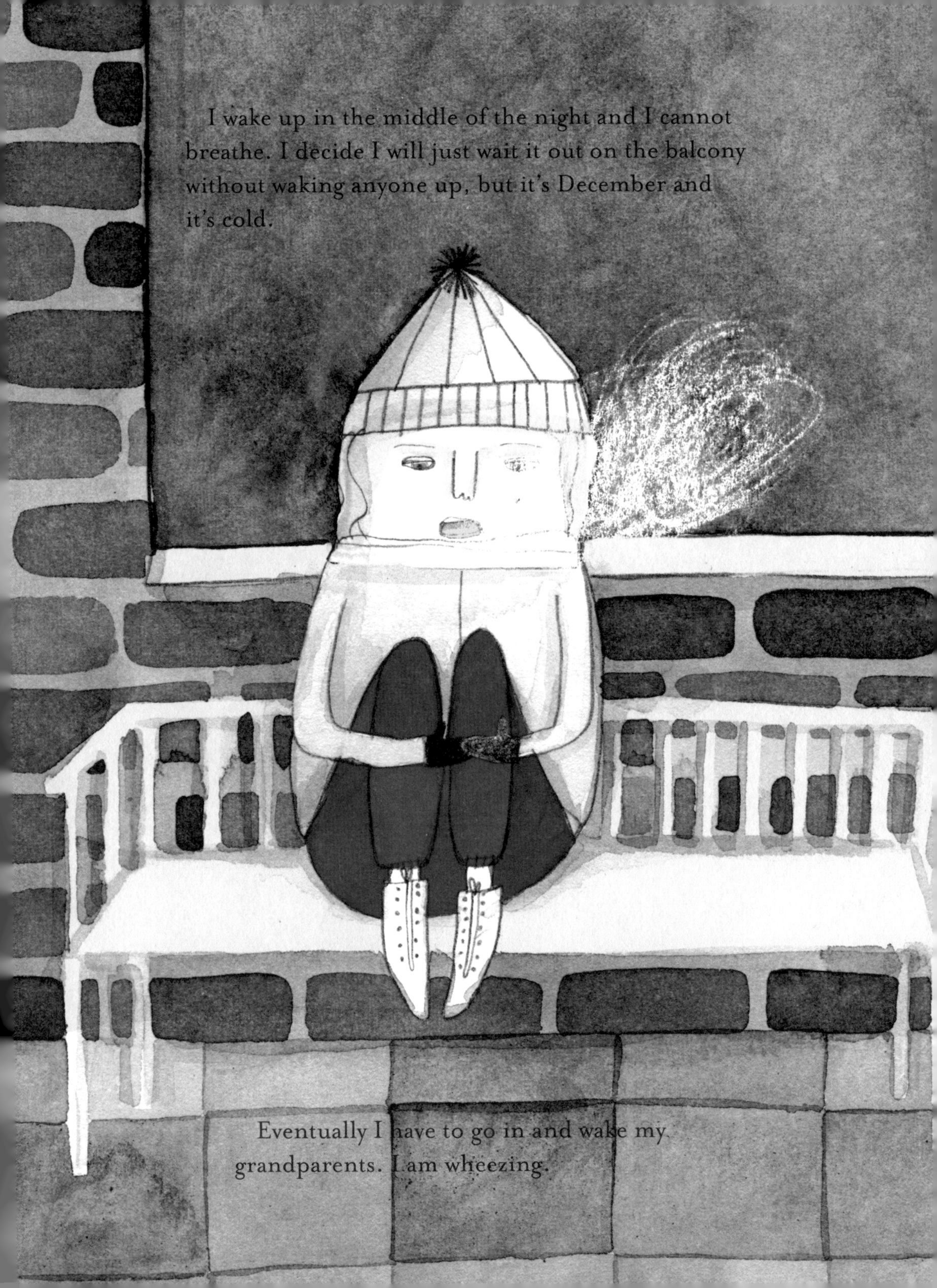

Eventually I have to go in and wake my grandparents. I am wheezing.

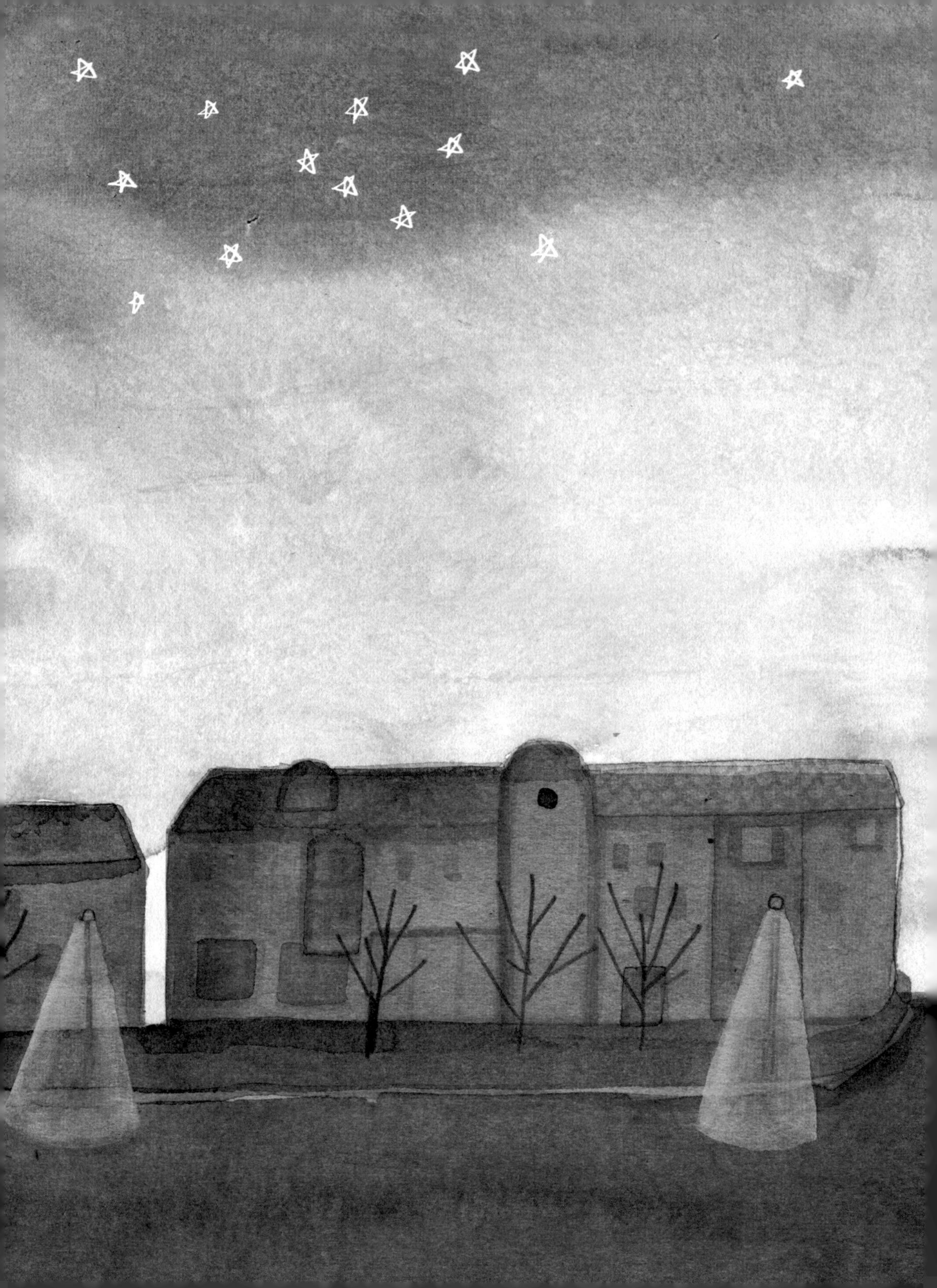

Vadim drives us to the emergency room. He talks on the way about how it's going to be expensive and how they might not even see us because we don't have insurance.

I am barely breathing in the back seat.

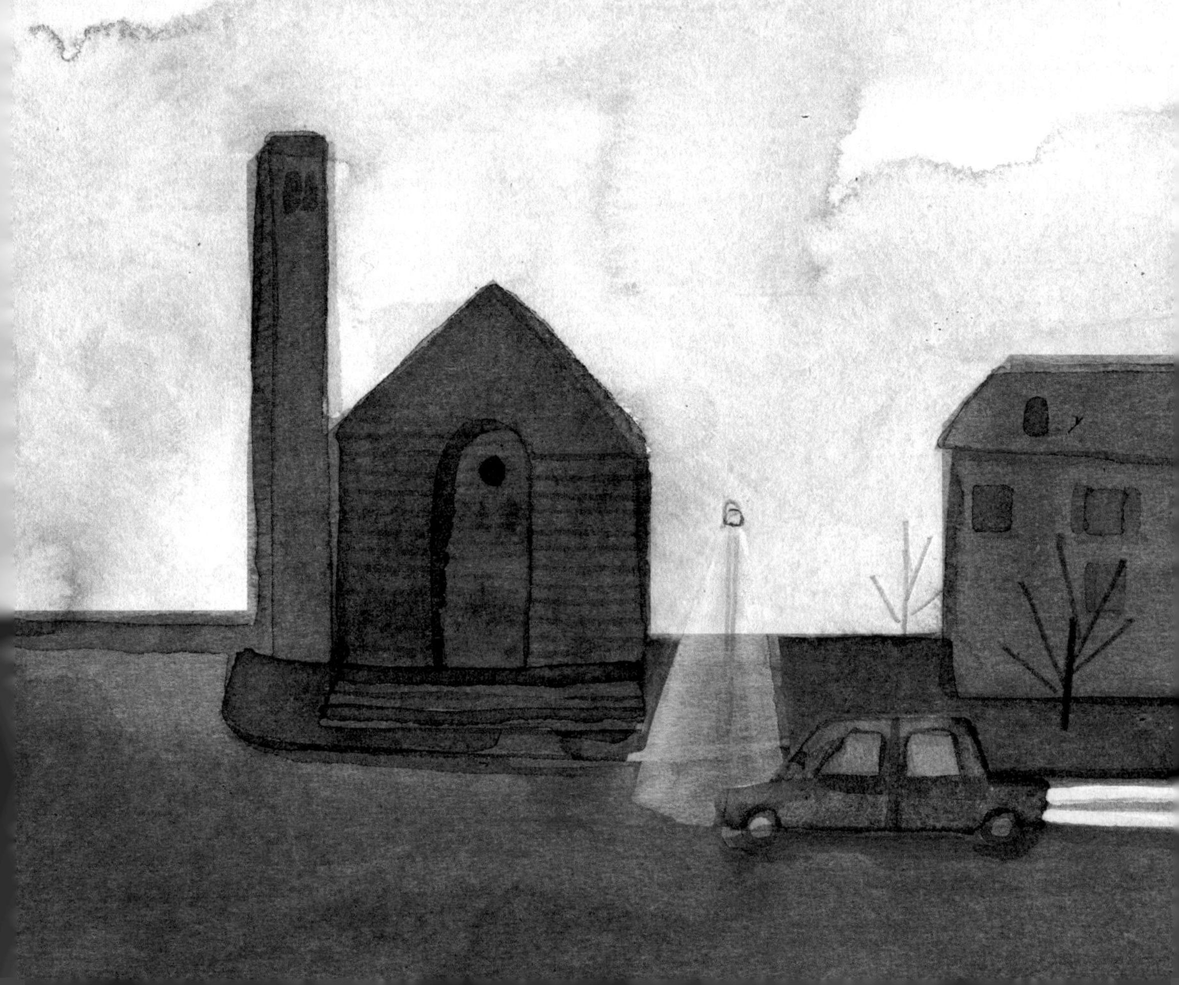

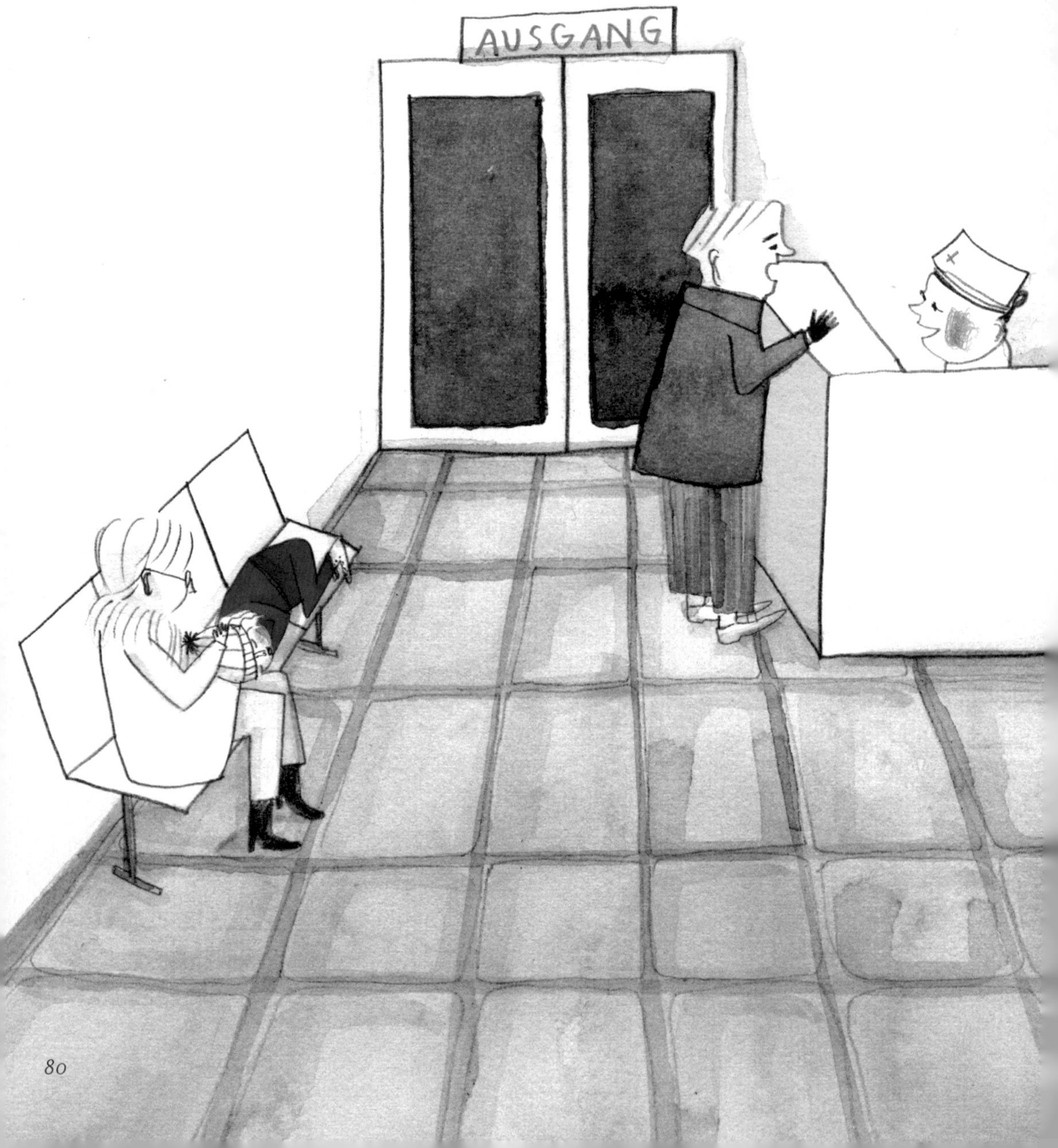
AUSGANG

The emergency room is very white and there is no one there. We are ushered into a room to wait. My grandmother calls my mother from a pay phone to tell her what is happening. A young, sleepy doctor comes in. I think he is kind of cute. I sit quietly while he readies the needle for my shot — he is going to have to give me adrenaline. I watch as he ties the rubber tube above my elbow and inserts the needle. He draws out a little blood, and I see it mix with the liquid inside the syringe.

The doctor says we don't owe him any money.

I can breathe again. We go to a hotel.

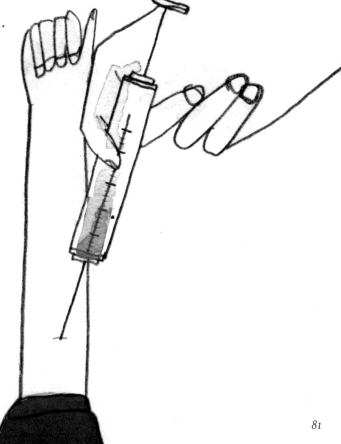

We celebrate Christmas in the hotel. It's cold and damp here, but this is my first proper Western Christmas on December 25. Vadim and Anita bring us a tree and homemade traditional German treats.

And there is a surprise!

My mom has sent us presents! I get candy and Sharpies and a kaleidoscope and a big huge book of music and lyrics for all the Beatles songs ever written.

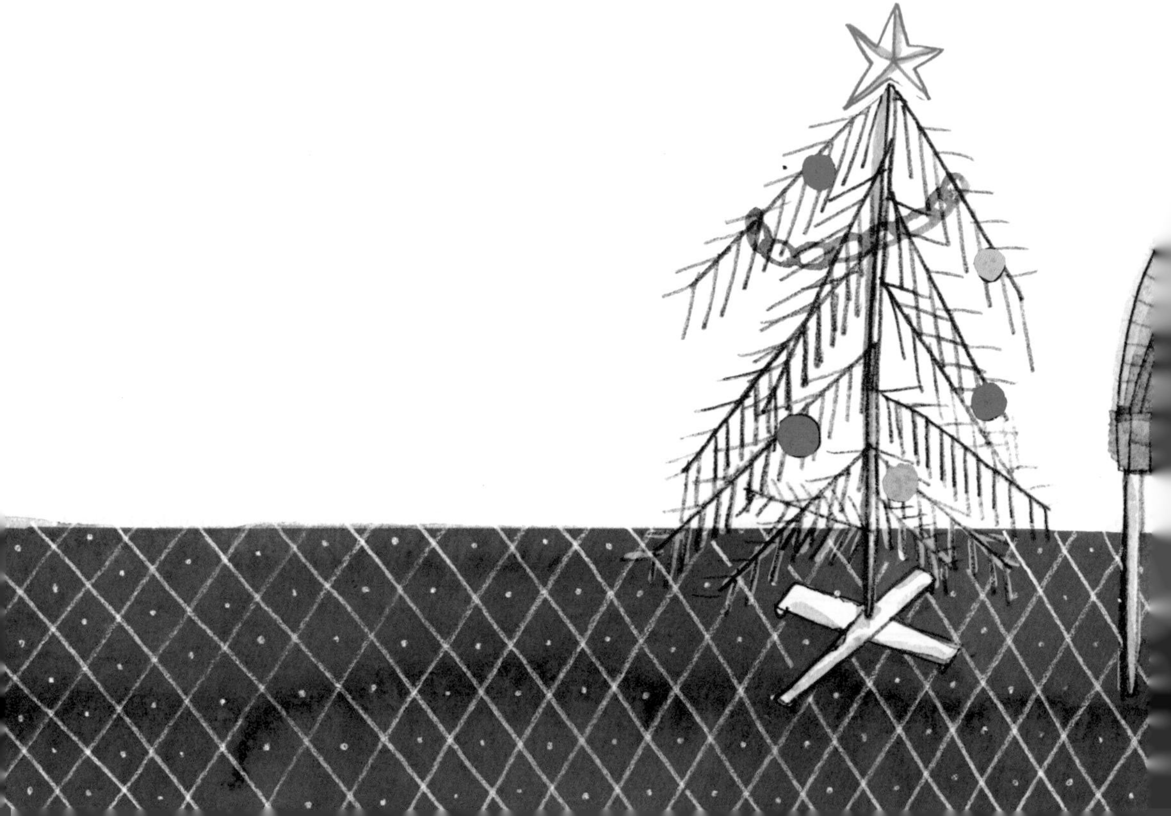

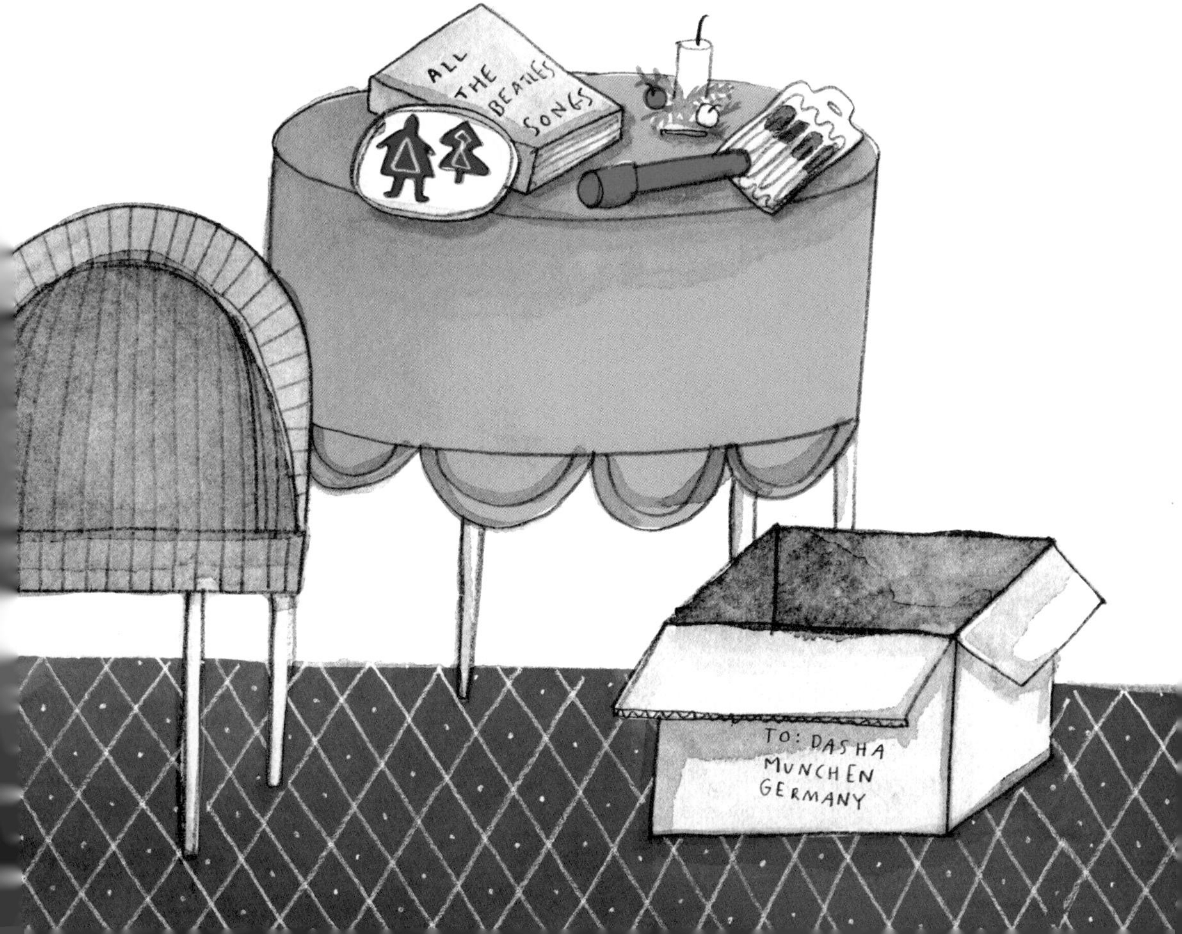
ALL THE BEATLES SONGS
TO: DASHA
MUNCHEN
GERMANY

JANUARY

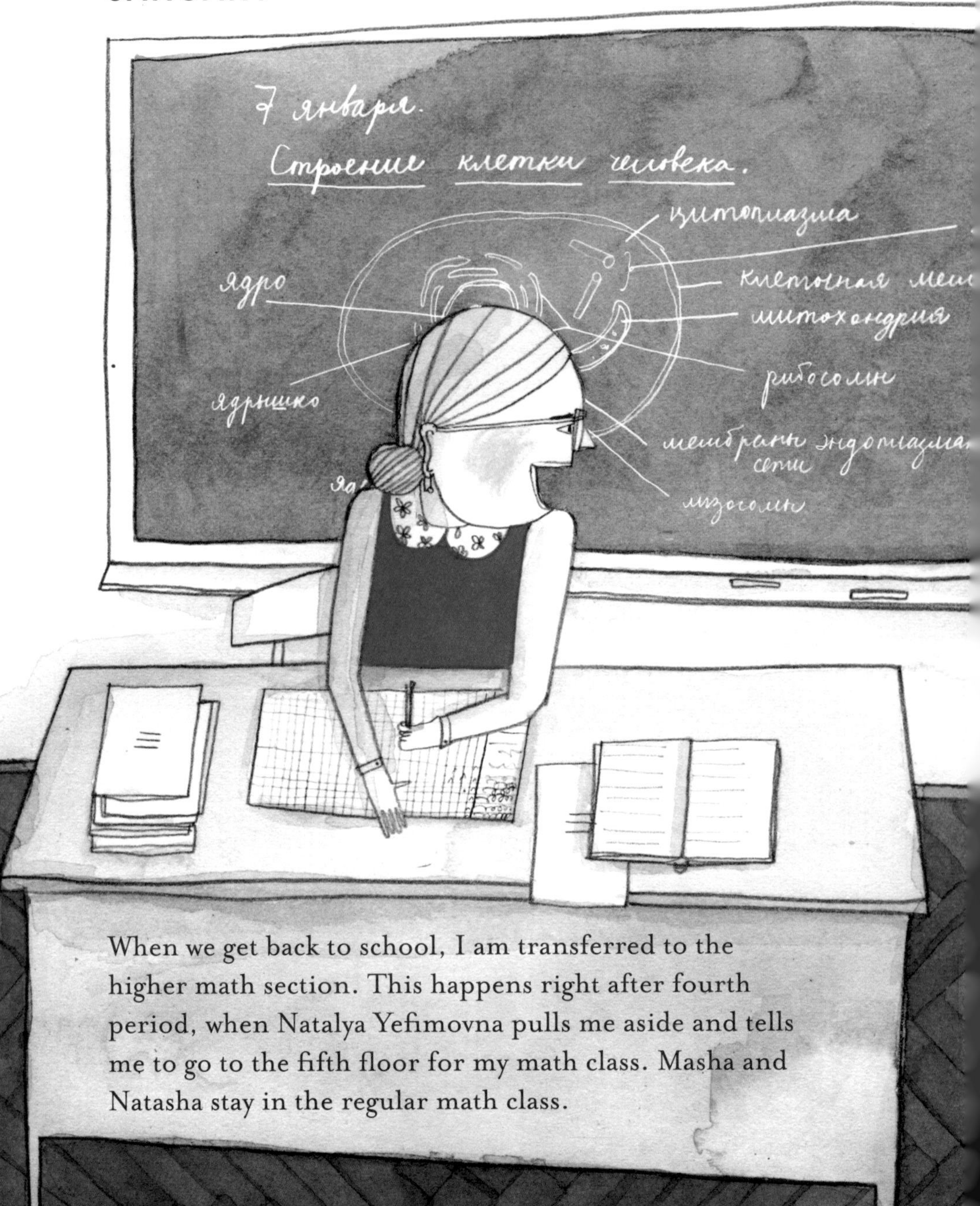
7 января.
Строение клетки человека.
цитоплазма
ядро
митохондрия
рибосомы
ядрышко
лизосомы

When we get back to school, I am transferred to the higher math section. This happens right after fourth period, when Natalya Yefimovna pulls me aside and tells me to go to the fifth floor for my math class. Masha and Natasha stay in the regular math class.

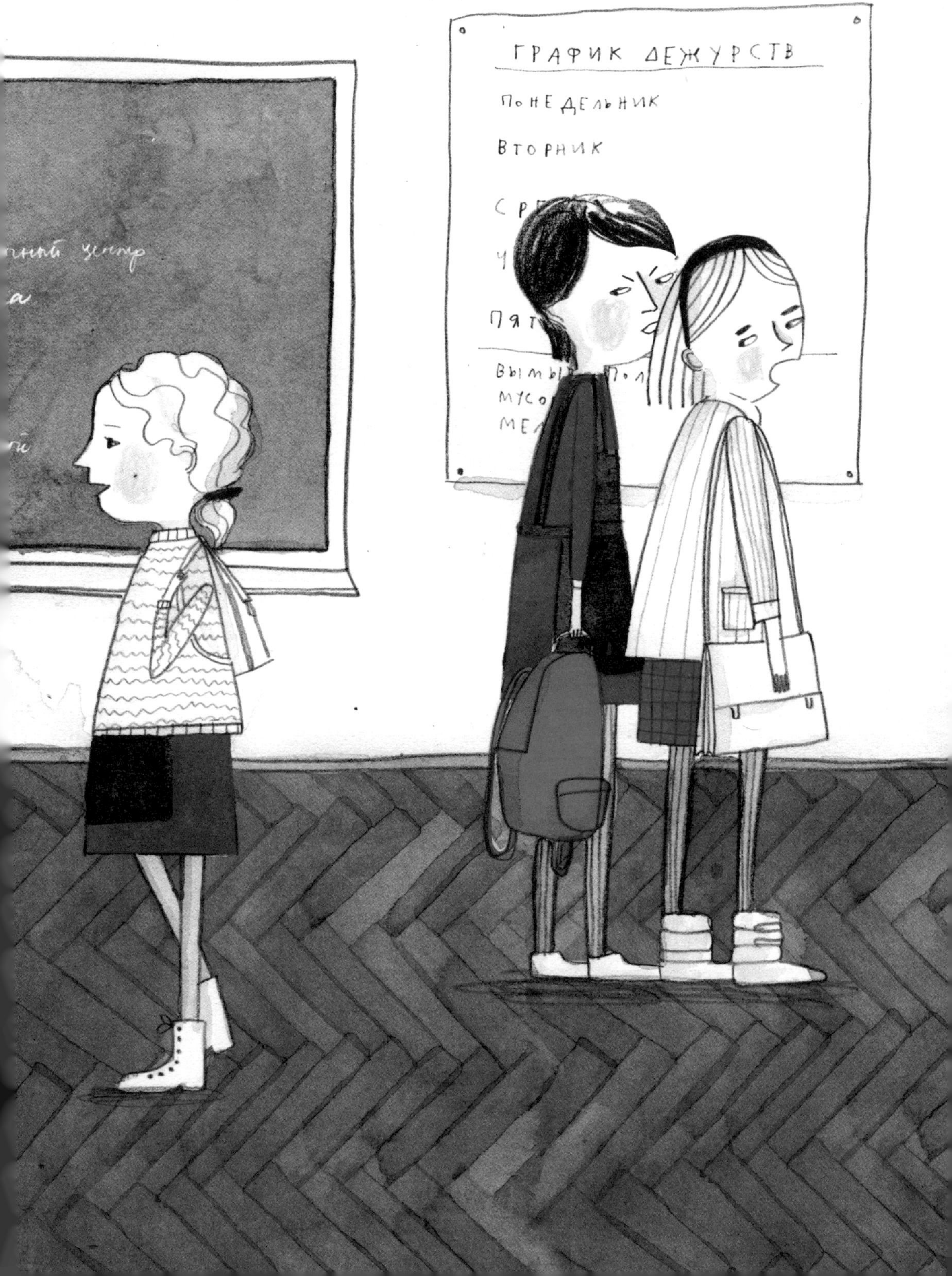
ГРАФИК ДЕЖУРСТВ
ПОНЕДЕЛЬНИК
ВТОРНИК

We only have five periods on Mondays, but when I come back to the cloakroom M and N are nowhere to be found.

I walk home alone. It's cold, and when I get home no one is there. There's just a note telling me to eat soup, walk the dog and not stay up too late — Grandma and Grandpa are out for the night at the Pen Club. I wish I was at Natasha's house eating toast. I call her, but no one picks up.

I read until my eyes won't stay open anymore.

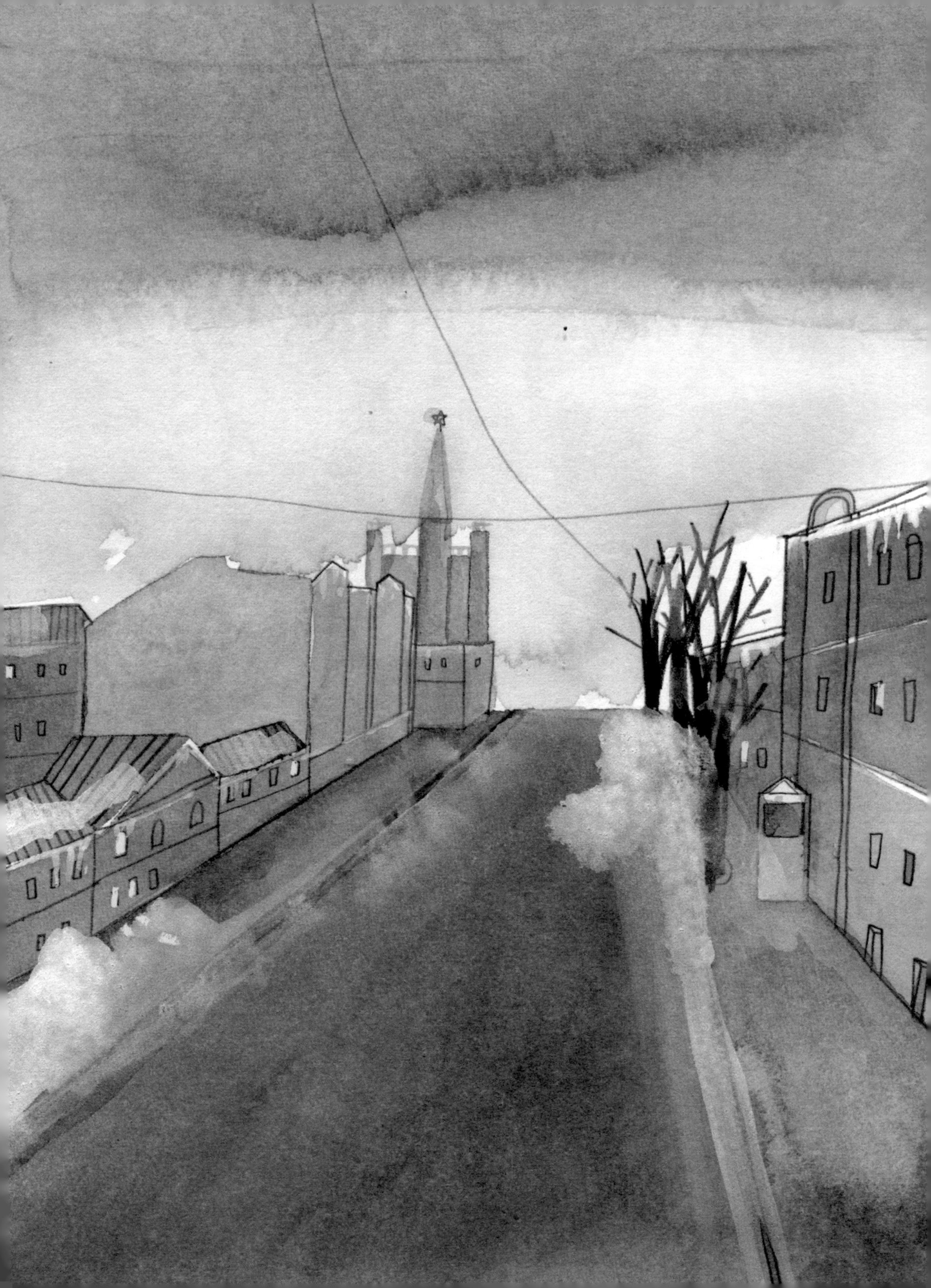

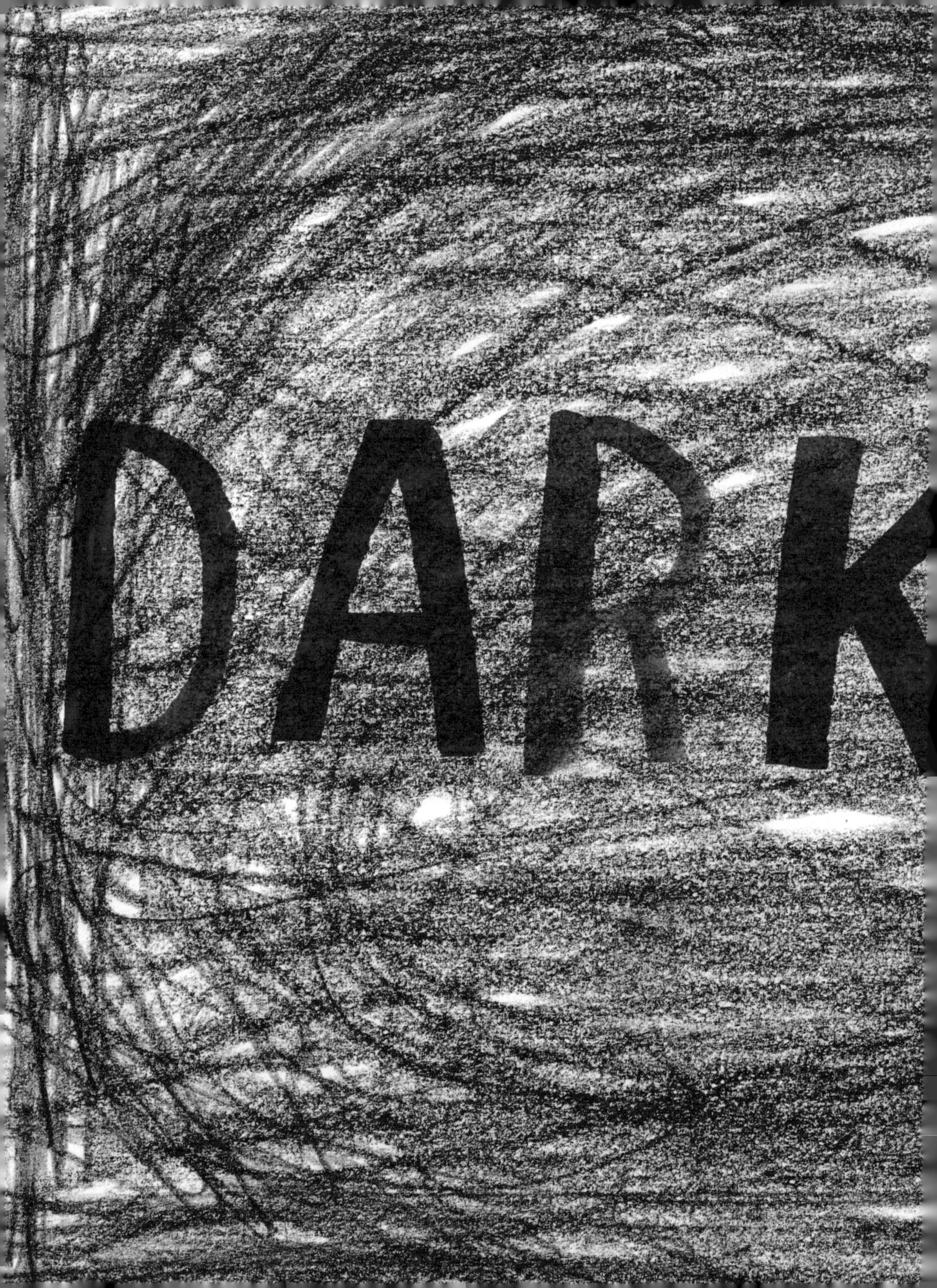
DARK

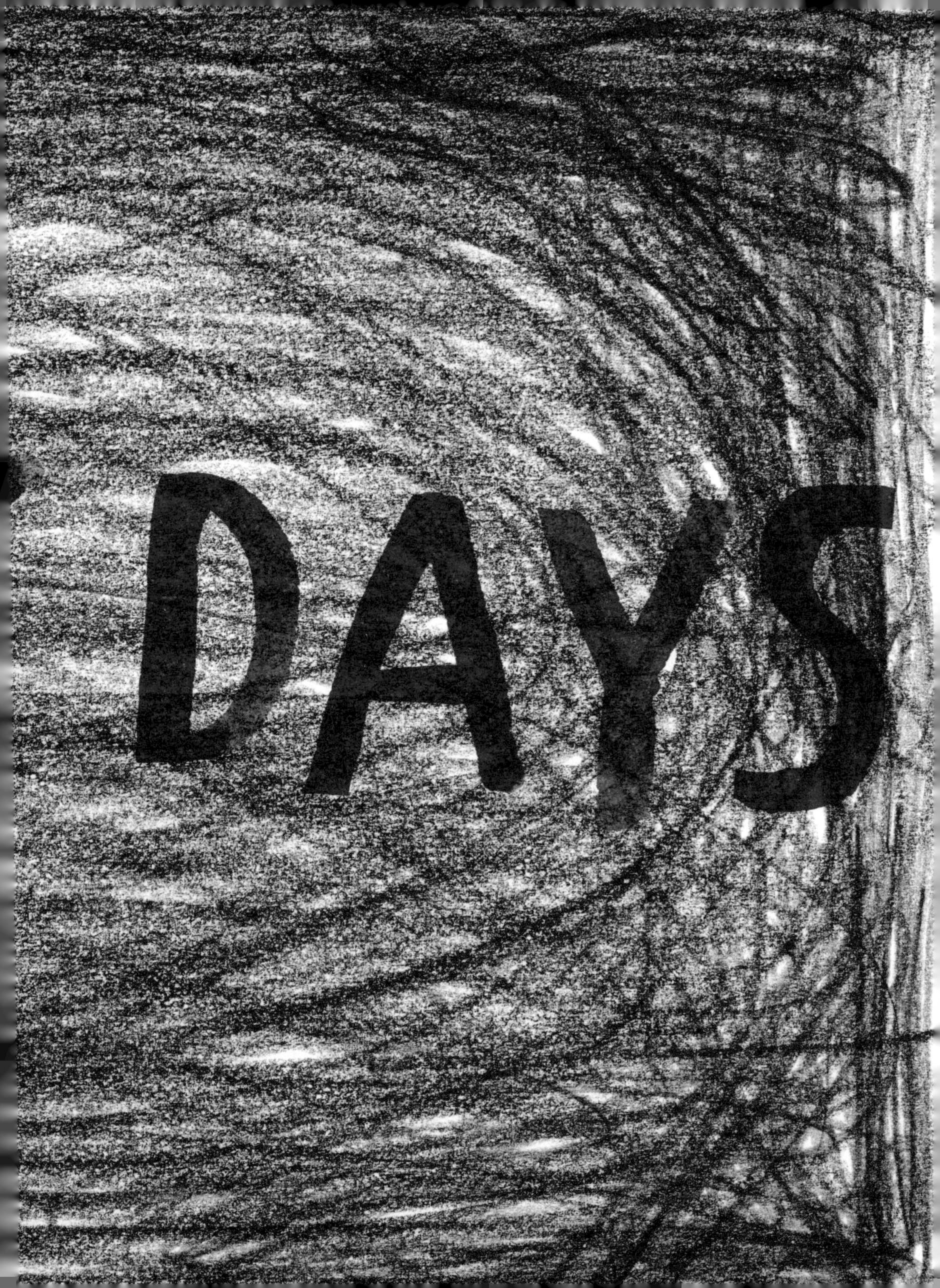
DAYS

Masha and Natasha don't talk to me for two days, but on Friday they wait for me by the front gate of the school and say hello as I approach.

We never talk about what happened.

FEBRUARY

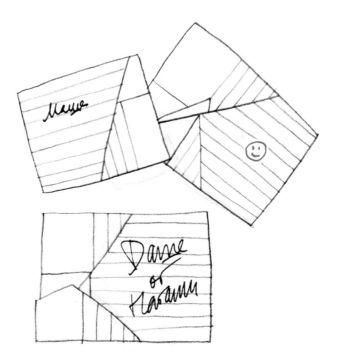

We are passing notes and hanging out after school.
Masha's brother comes by and tells us that Petya invited
us to see the absurdist poets play at their school.

It's on February 14 and that feels like a special sign.

I am a little nervous about going. I haven't really told Masha and Natasha how I feel about P. I'm scared they'll think it's stupid. He hangs out at Masha's house with her brother a lot, and Masha always rolls her eyes when she tells me about this. (I always try to pretend that I am not interested in every single, teeny detail.) Masha has really high standards.

I wear my favorite dress the day of the play, but I have to put on these really hideous leggings because it's -7°C outside. We take the trolley and the whole time I worry about my leggings, even though both Masha and Natasha tell me they are fine.

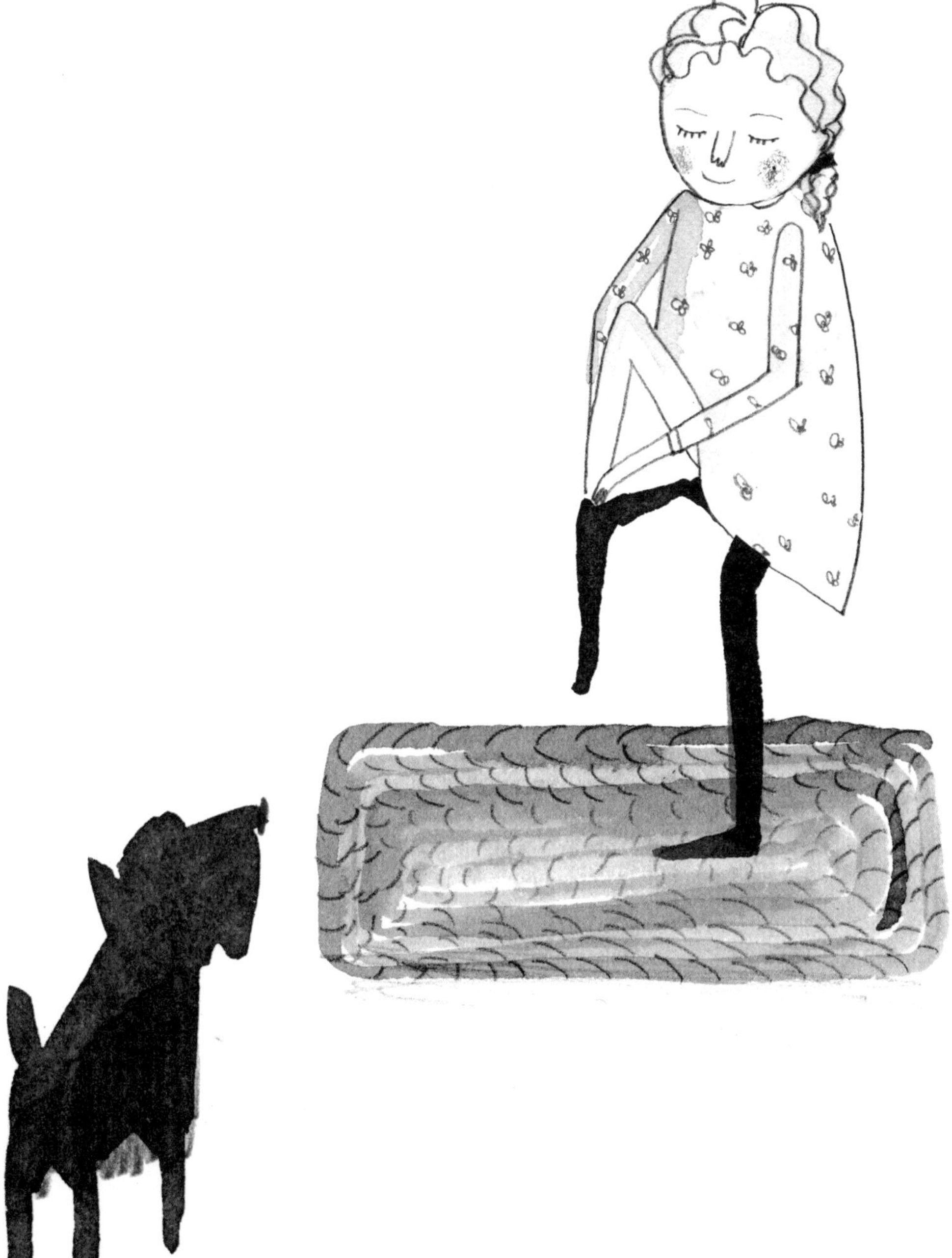

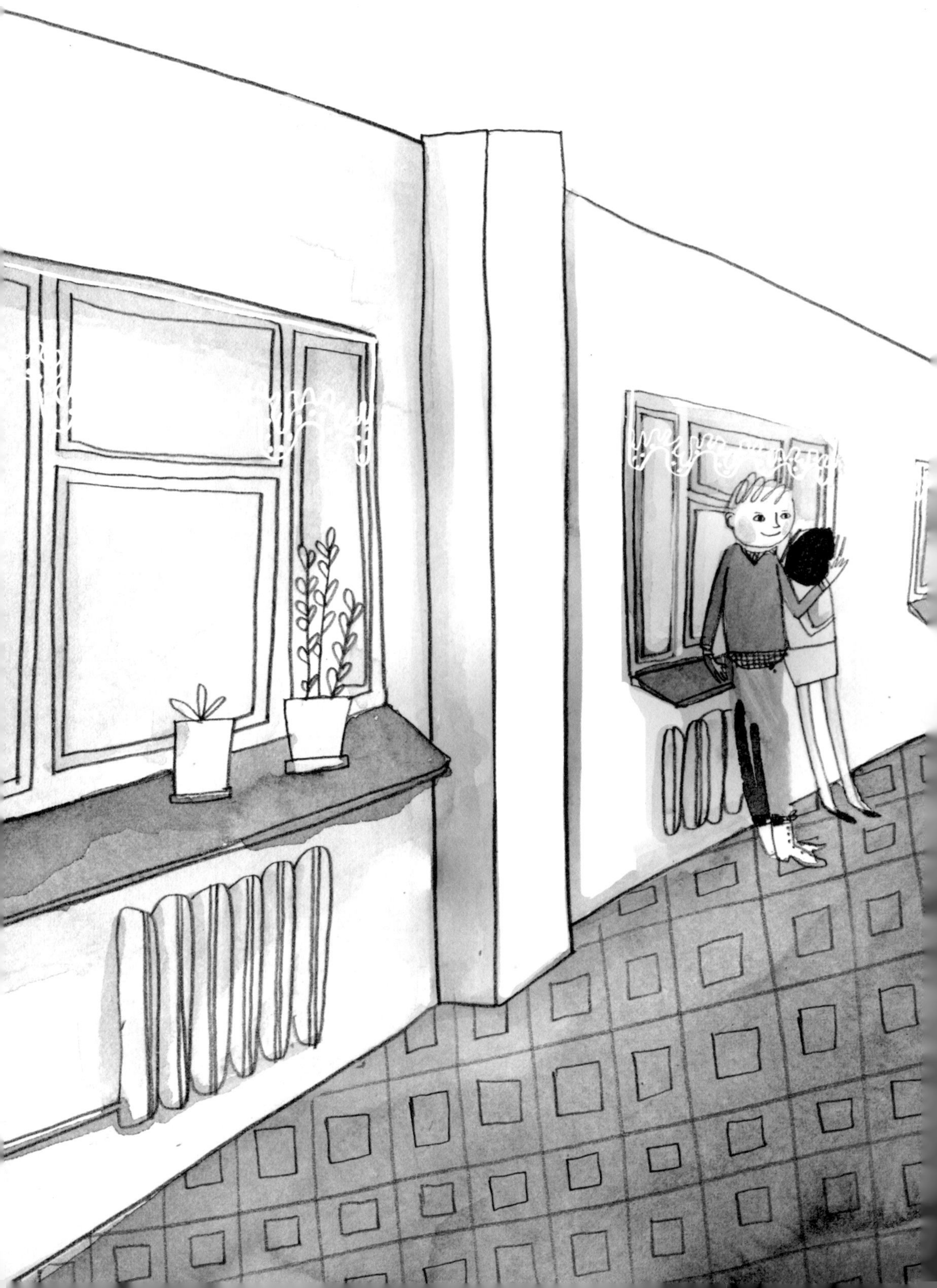

When we get to Petya's school (School 67), it's awesome! It's big and light and there are kids sitting around in the hallway studying and having deep conversations. I love it here.

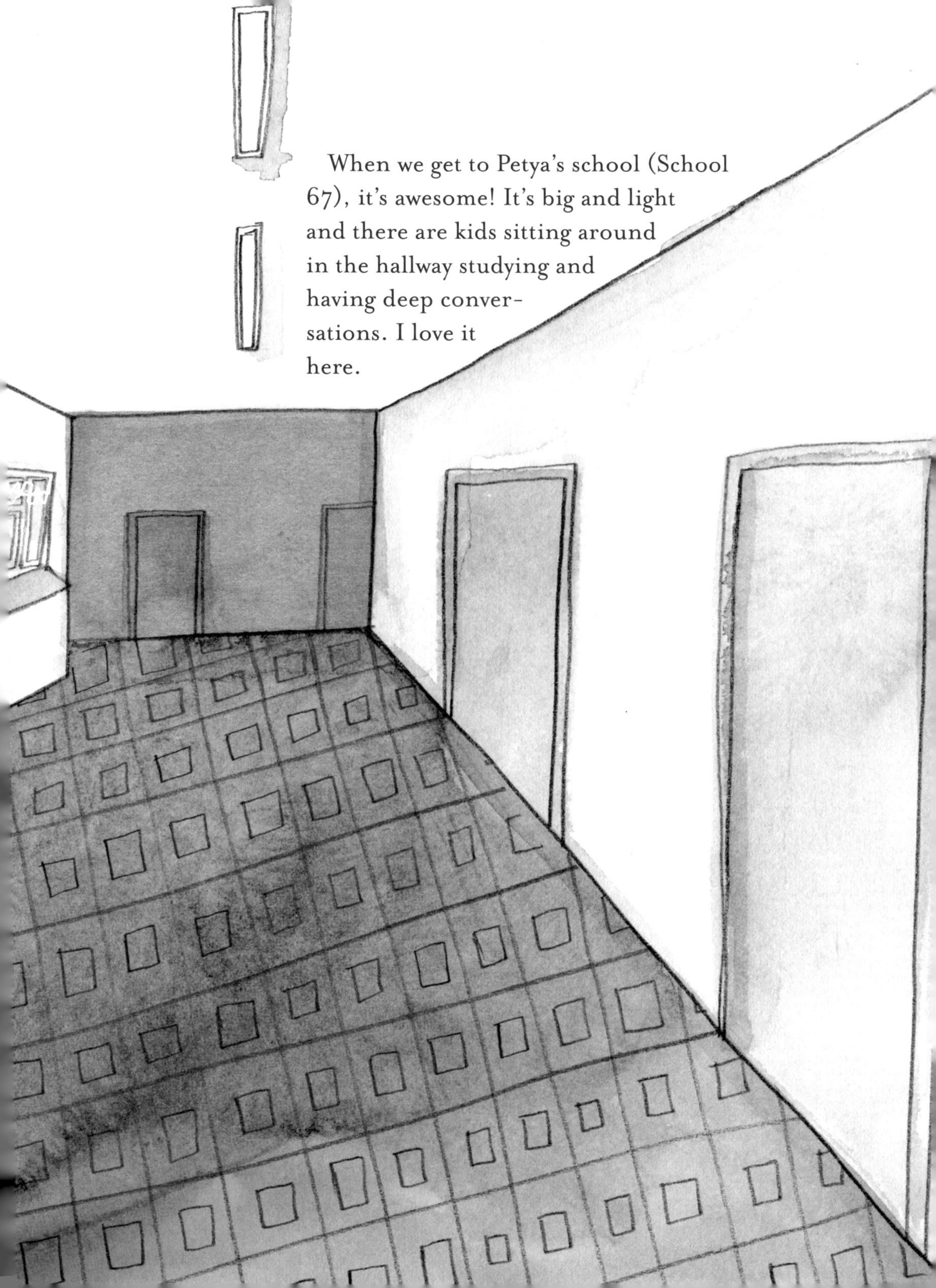

Petya gives me a huge hug when he sees me.

"Did you notice we used your posters again?" he asks.

I beam.

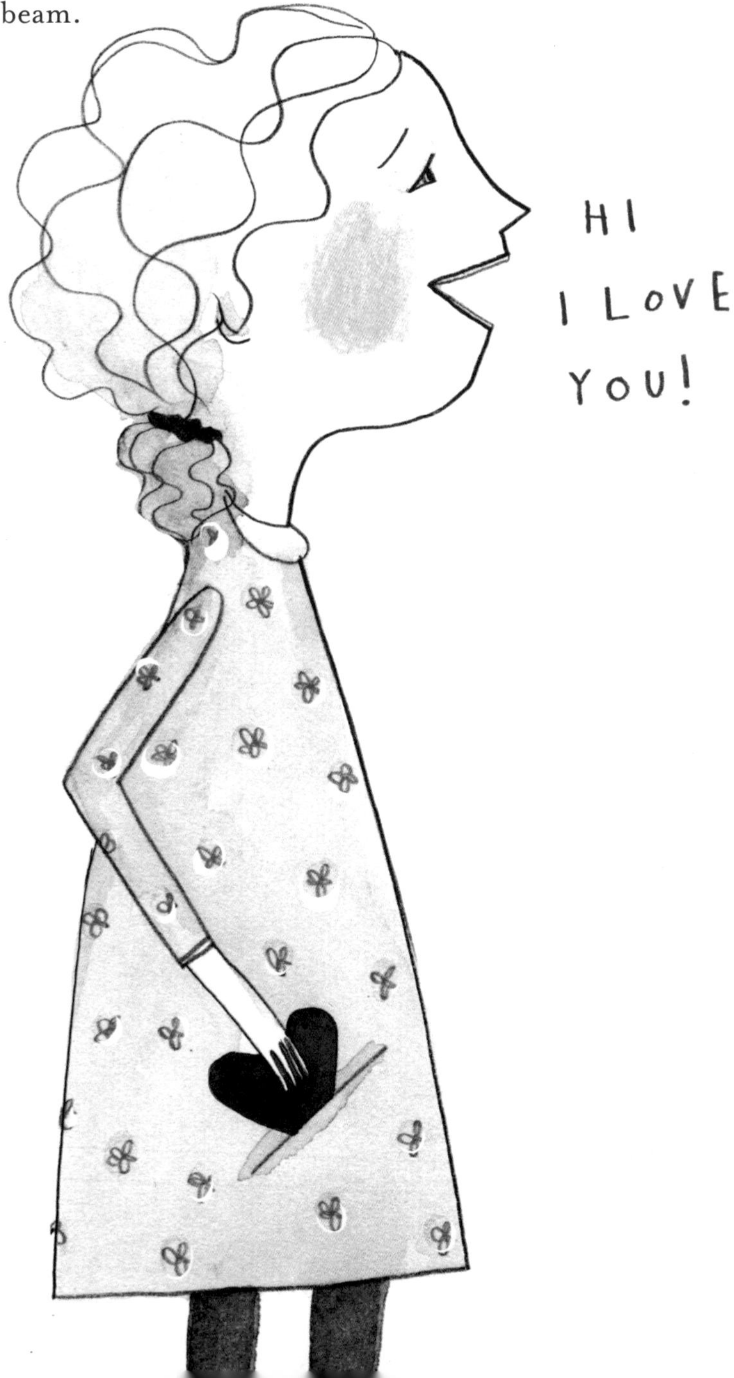
HI
I LOVE
YOU!

"Did you meet Katya?" he says.

He has his arm around this girl. She has short black hair and HUGE eyes and wears black nail polish — and she is SMOKING! IN THE SCHOOL HALLWAY!

The rest of the day is hazy. The play is
fine. All of the writers' retreat kids are
there, but I can barely say hello. Luckily,
Masha knows all of them, so I don't have to
make introductions or anything.

On the ride back to our neighborhood,
M and N talk about the play and the school
and Masha's brother's friends (Natasha has
a crush on one of them!), but I just stare
out of the window and think about Petya
and Katya. She was soooo cool. I am never
going to be cool like that.

MARCH

I don't care about anything anymore.
It's cold and dark out. I am not cool.
Petya will never like me. School is
boring. Everything sucks.

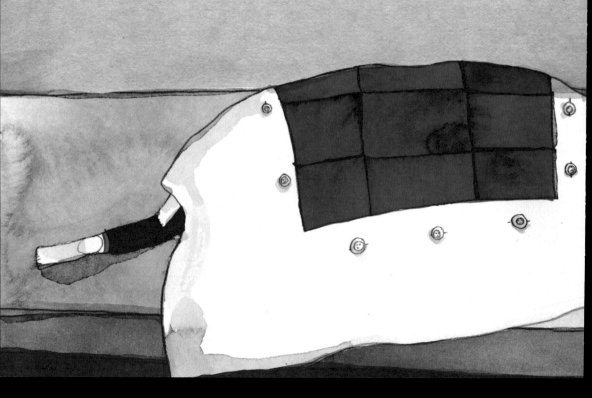

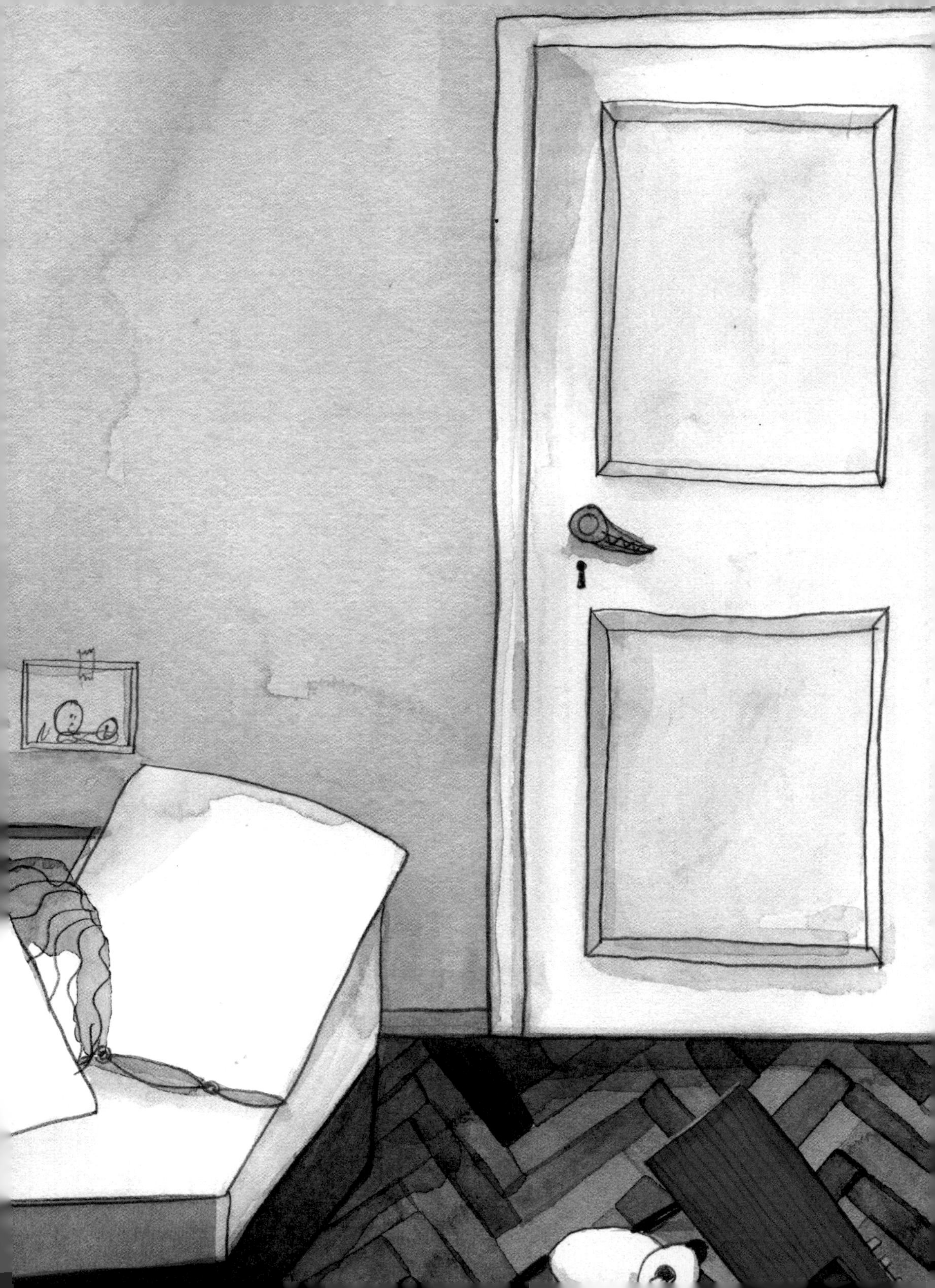

Dad comes to visit from LA.

He brings me a jean jacket that he says is all the rage. I'm not convinced. It's very short with very long sleeves.

My dad is very cool.

We drive around and go to dinner. He asks me about my friends and Varya and what I like to do. He asks me if I still play tennis. He likes the idea of me playing tennis. But I haven't played in a year, and that makes me sad. I worry that he will like me less because I don't play tennis anymore.

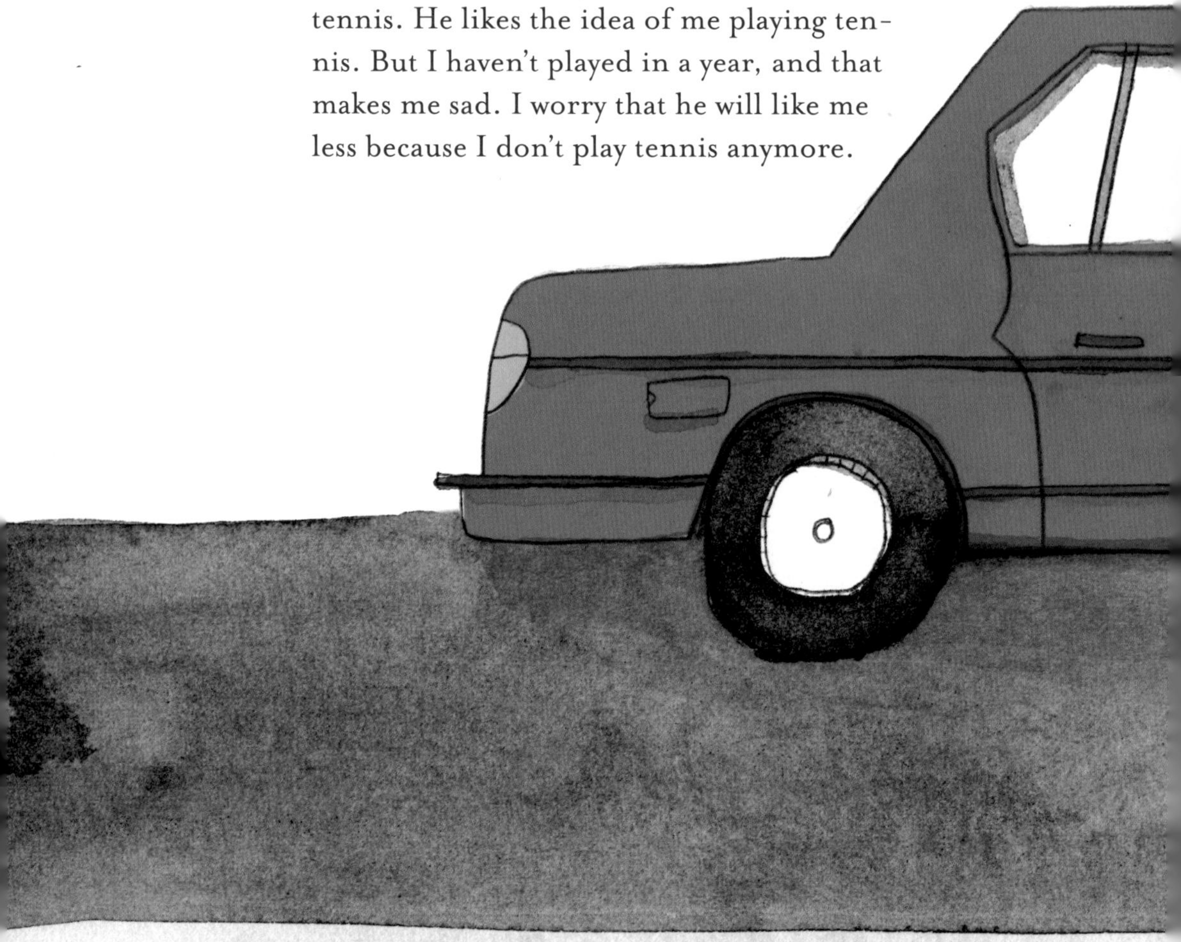

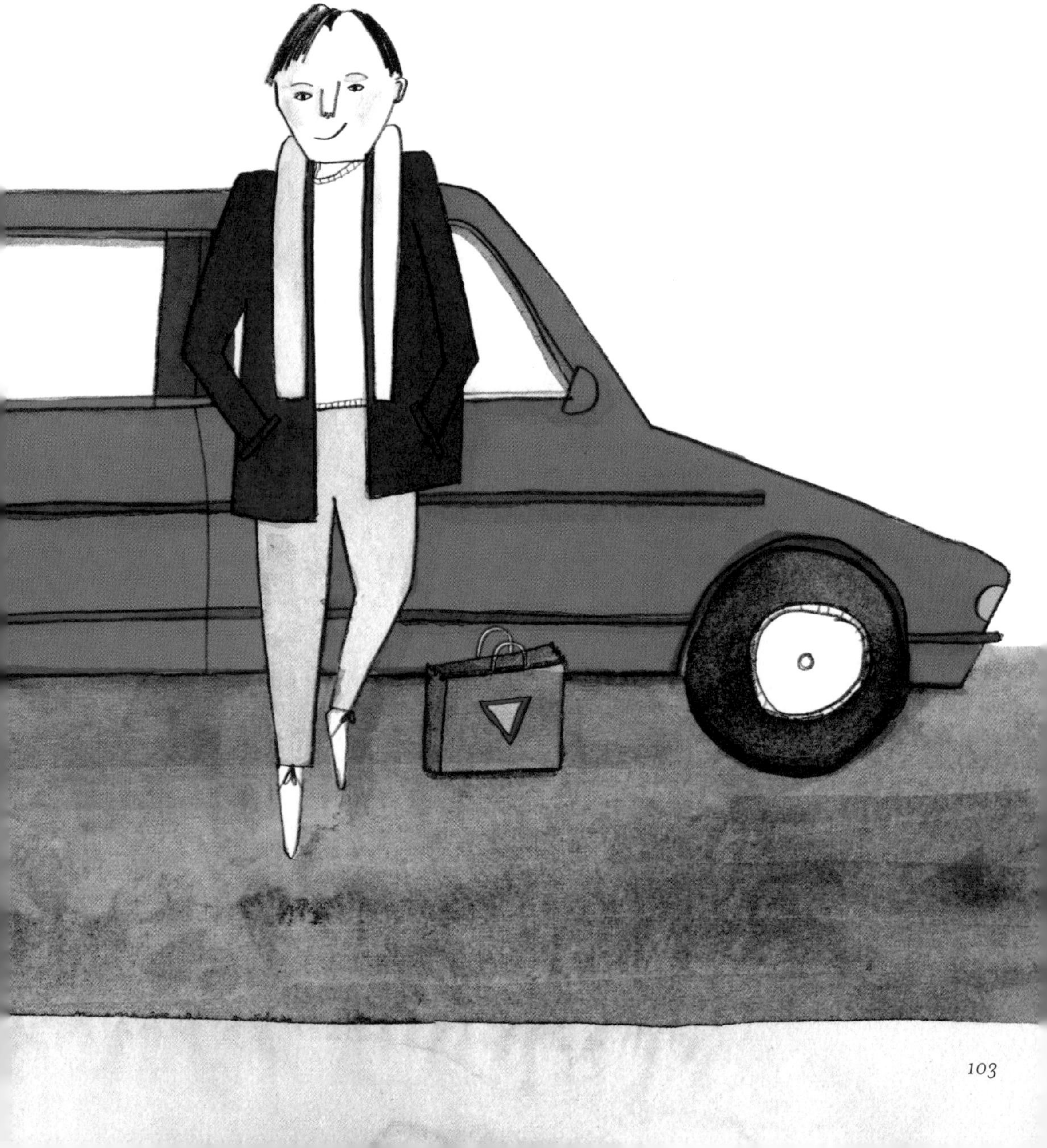

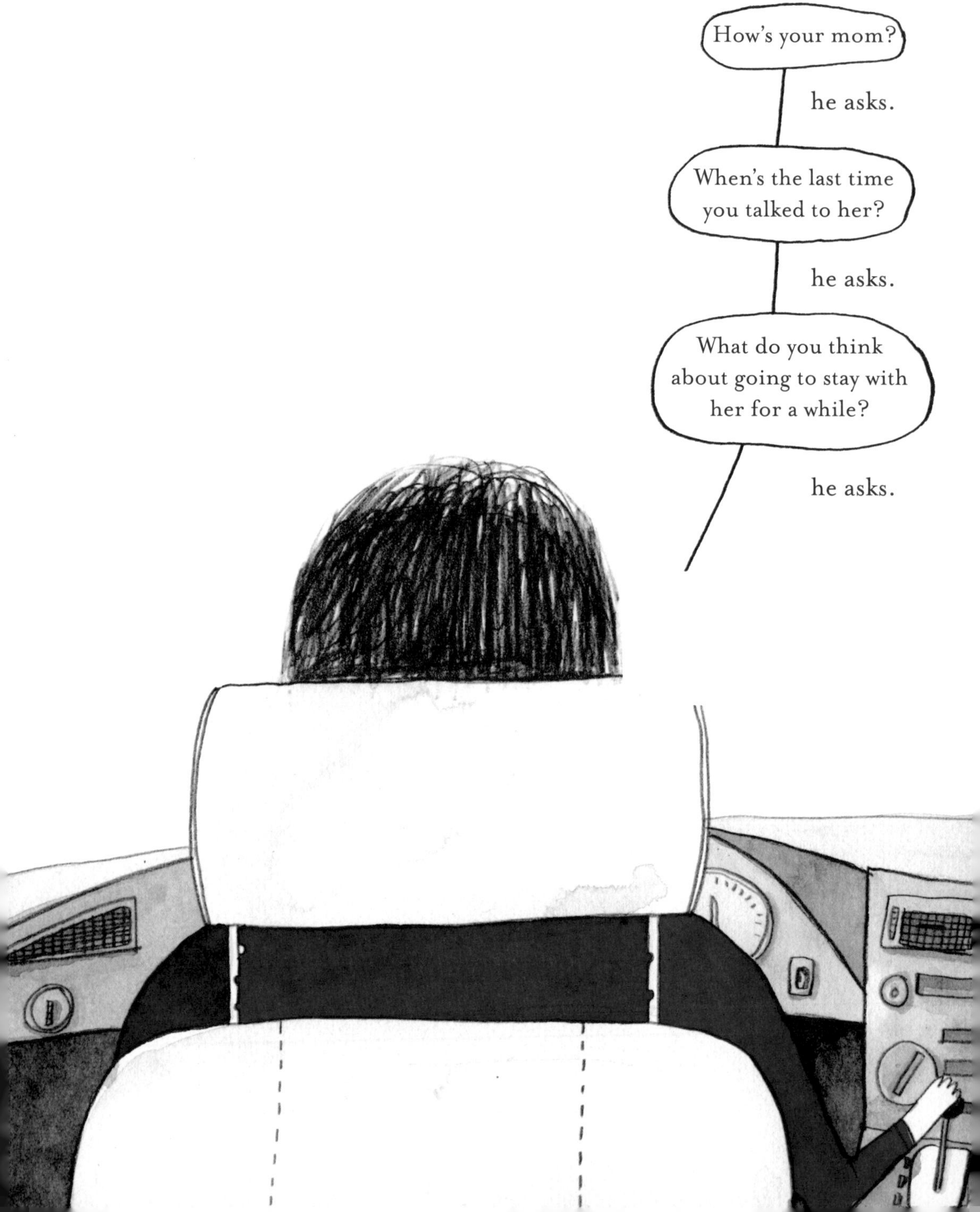
How's your mom?
he asks.
When's the last time you talked to her?
he asks.
What do you think about going to stay with her for a while?
he asks.

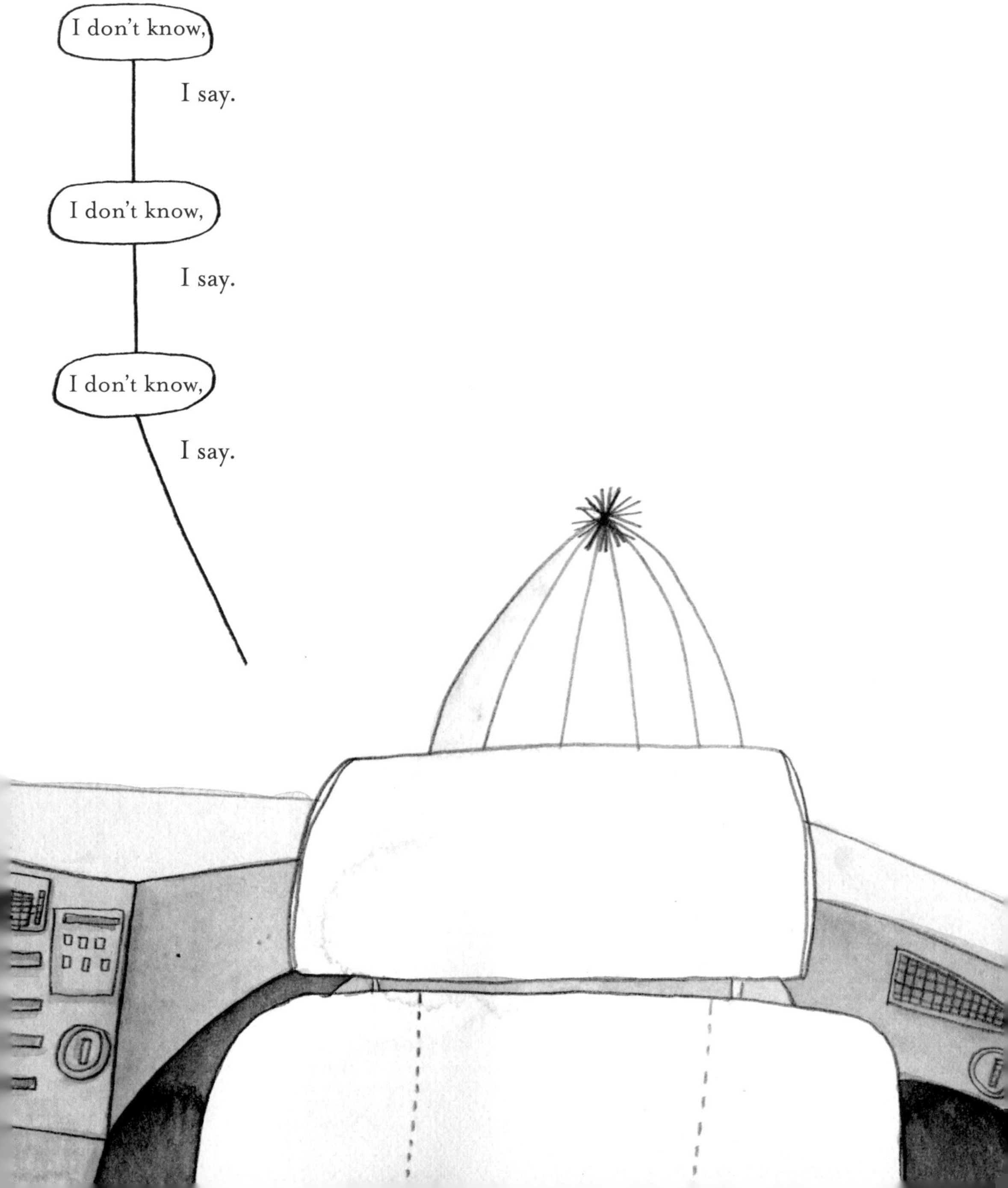
I don't know,
I say.
I don't know,
I say.
I don't know,
I say.

I'm feeling a bit weird about Masha and Natasha. I know we are over the whole math class thing, but I don't quite feel like things are back to normal. They are rarely in class and I miss them.

I run into them on the street in front of school.

"Are you guys coming in?" I say.

"Maybe later," says Masha.

As they round the corner, I yell,

Wait up!

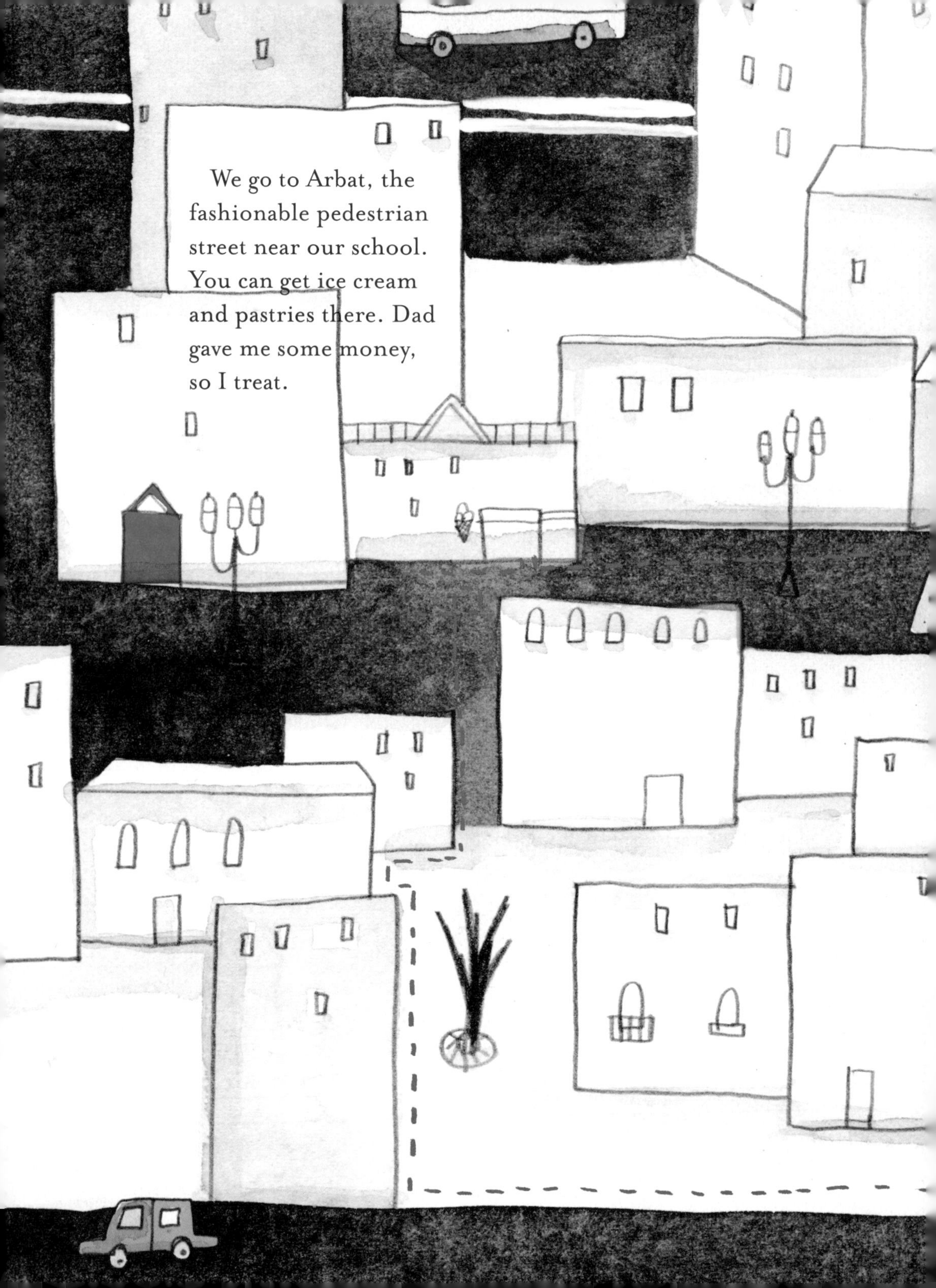

We go to Arbat, the fashionable pedestrian street near our school. You can get ice cream and pastries there. Dad gave me some money, so I treat.

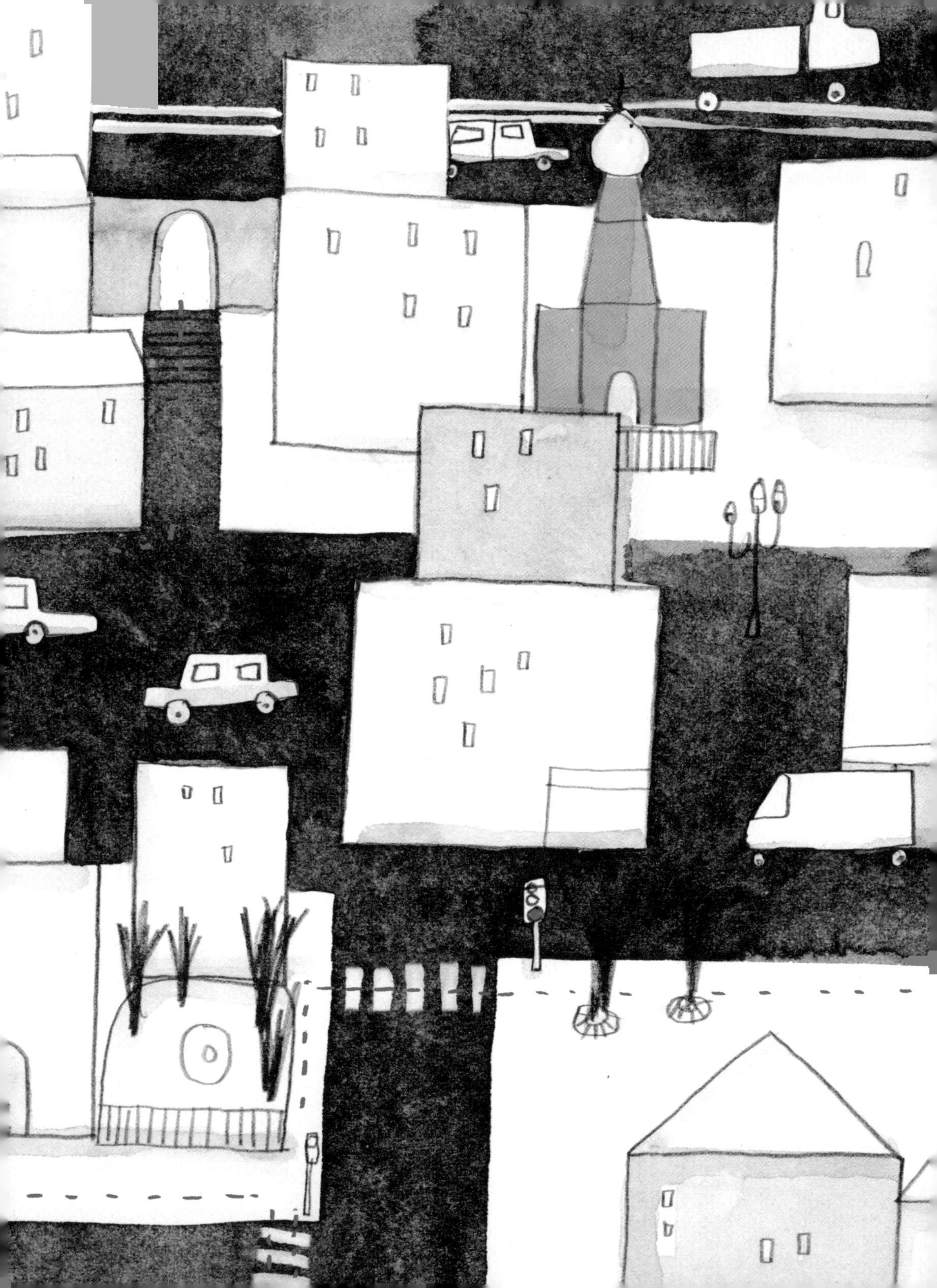

We find a bench and have a heart-to-heart.

Why wouldn't you guys talk to me when I got put in the other class?

I ask them.

We were worried you were going to get stuck up.

Are you in love with Petya?

they ask me.

You know, that Katya, she is a total delinquent. My brother told me. And Petya is an idiot if he does not see that you are a million times cooler,

says Masha.

How come you guys are never at school anymore?

I ask.

Masha is applying to 67 next year, and my mom is pulling me out so I can do the pre-college program. It's not like they are teaching us anything there anyway. Everyone knows you have to go to 67 or pre-college,

says Natasha.

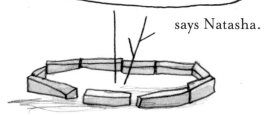

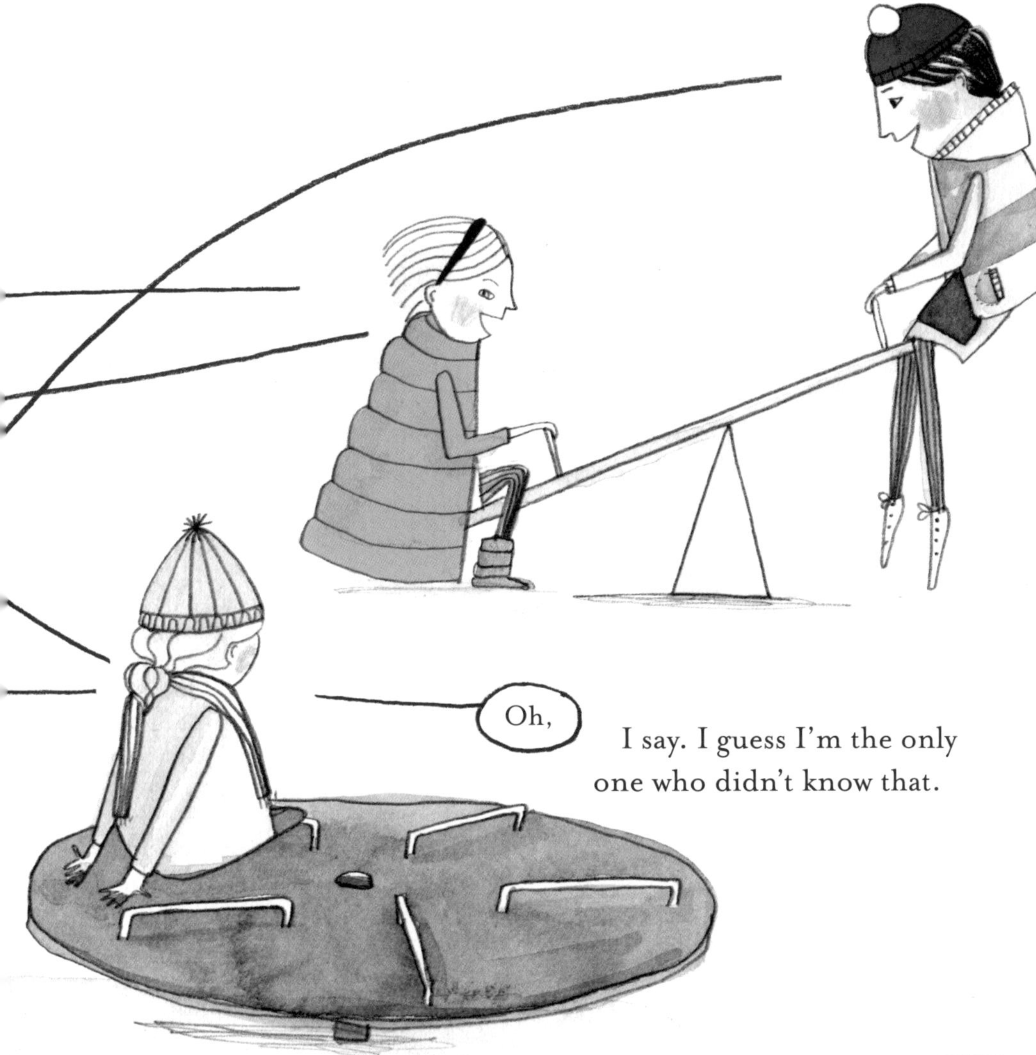
Oh,

I say. I guess I'm the only one who didn't know that.

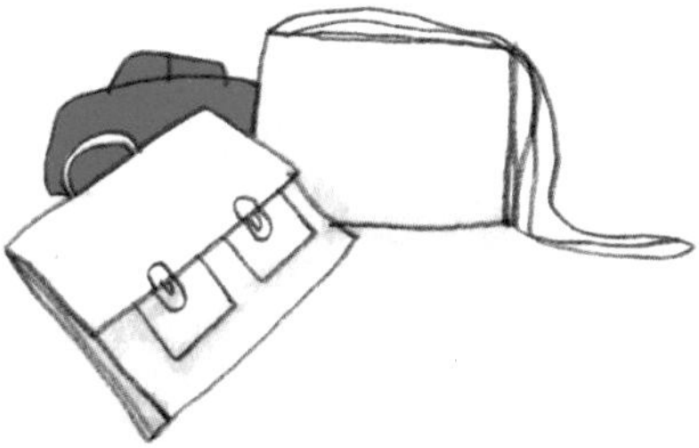

We keep wandering around. It's the first time I've felt happy in a long time. I am a little scared that I will run into someone I know and they will tell my grandparents I am not in school, but that feeling is so much smaller than the feeling of being happy with the girls. We are a team again!

Obviously they are right. Our school is a dump, and we all need to get out of here. I remember how much I loved visiting 67 when we saw Petya's play. Maybe if I get in I can be cool just like Katya, and he will love ME instead.

(What am I even talking about? Even their names match! PETYA? KATYA? There is no room for a Dasha — what a clunky name — in there. I am mad at my mom. Not only is she in America, BUT she also NAMED me this horrible name. I know for a fact my dad was voting for Natasha.)

I go to 67 with Masha to find out what I need to do to apply. There are three exams: two written (literature and algebra) and an oral (a foreign language — English for me and French for Masha). If you do any extracurricular activities, they say, these could help with your application.

Masha has her piano. I'll have to get a certificate from the art school! I'll have to study!

I work really hard for the next few weeks. I barely sleep or eat.

I decide that I don't need to go to regular school — I can study on my own. I need to save the rest of my energy for doing really well at art school so they'll give me a recommendation.

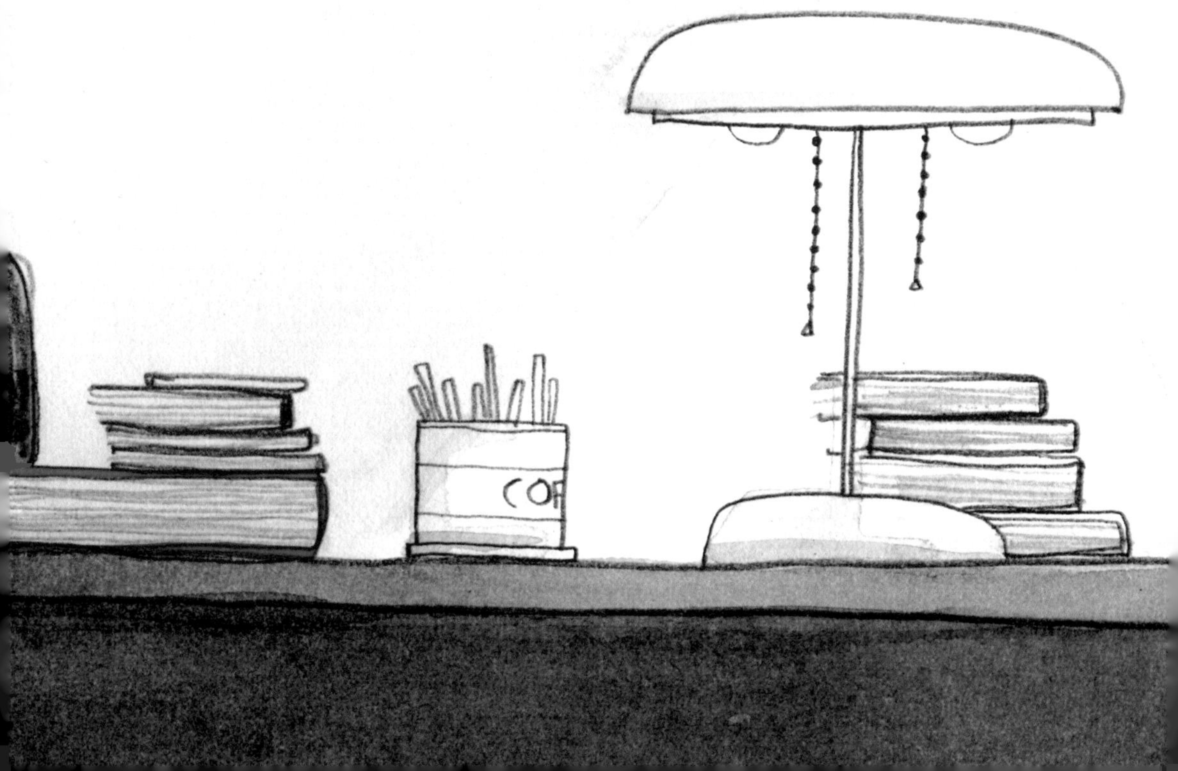
COF

During composition class, Maxim is sitting near me again. I am tired from staying up too late to study, and my drawing is not working out. Varya is sick at home and I miss her.

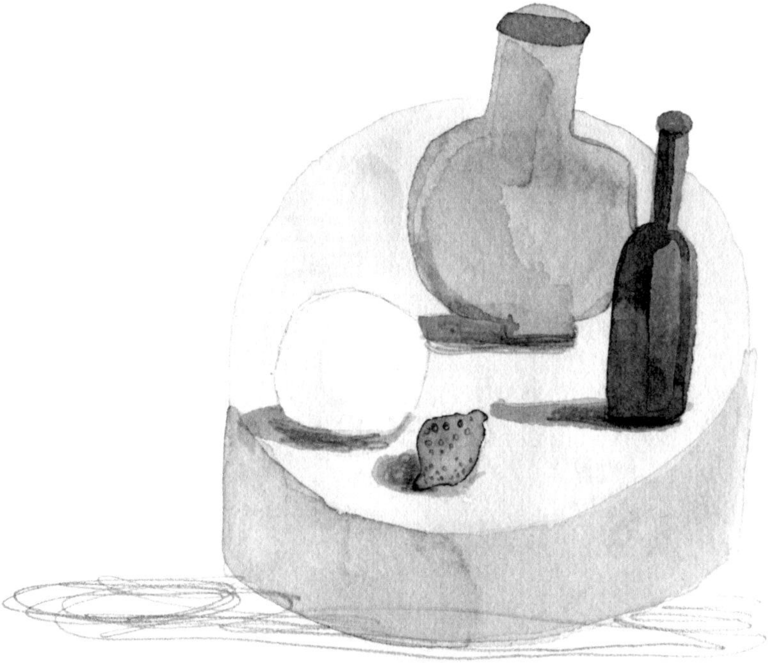

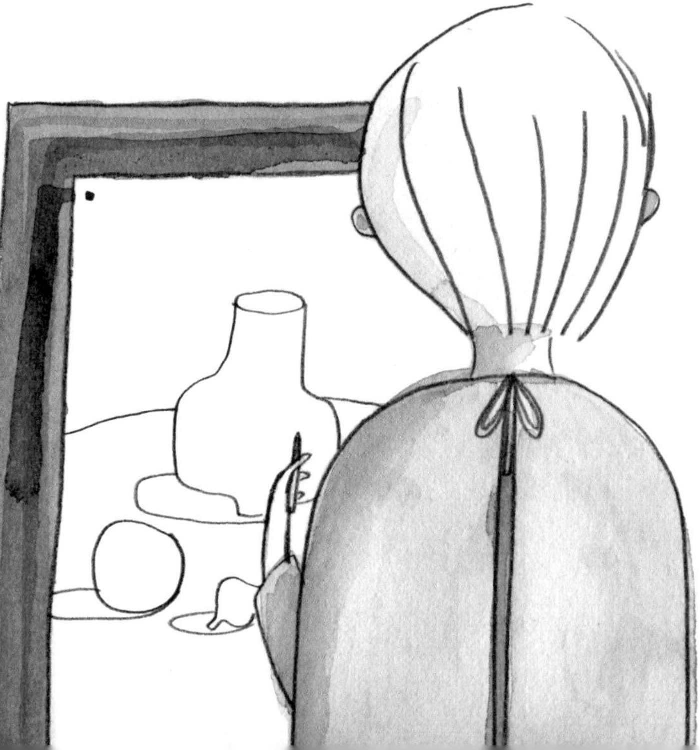

Have you considered…

I hear Maxim say.
I whip around.

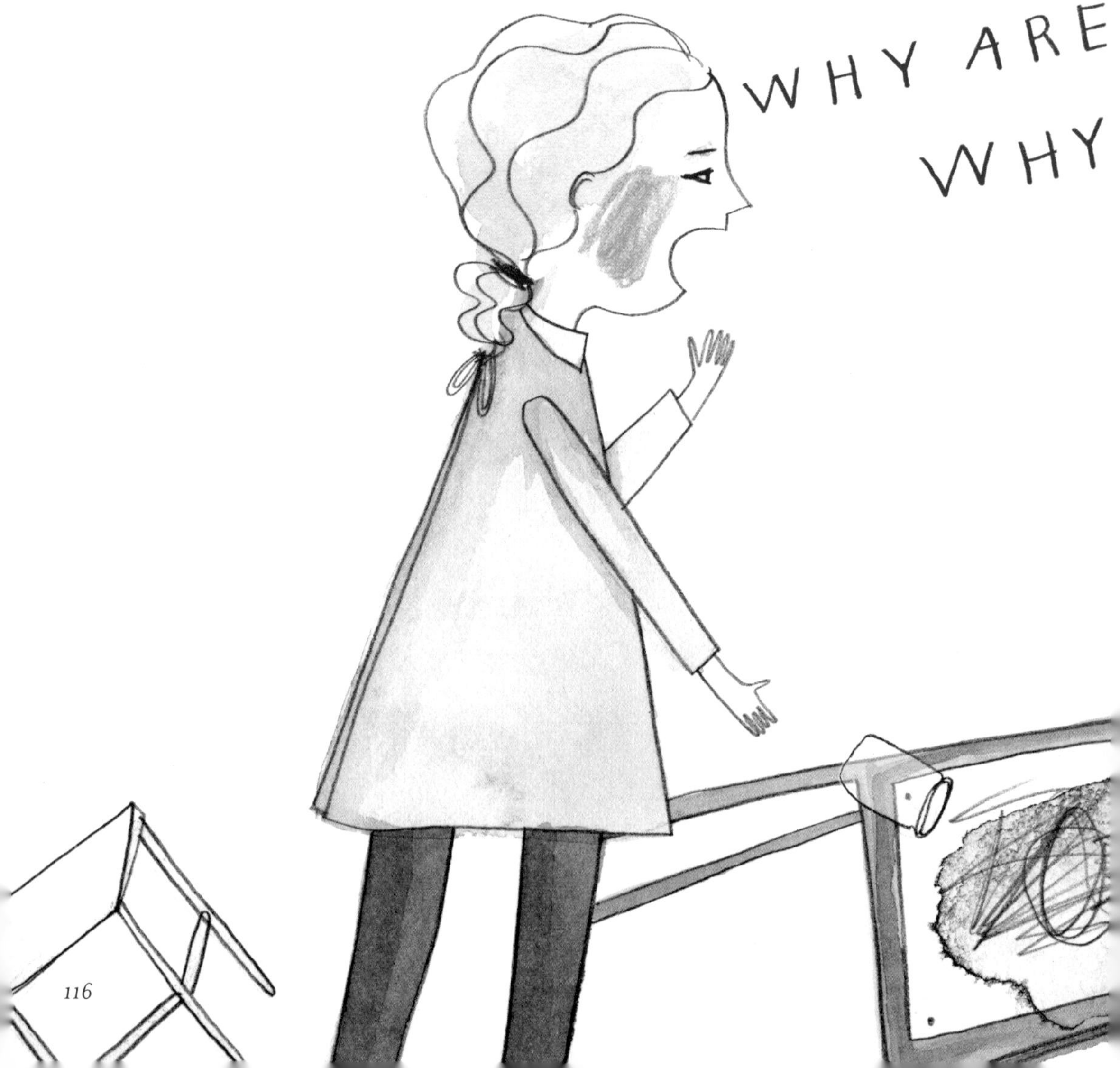
WHY ARE
WHY

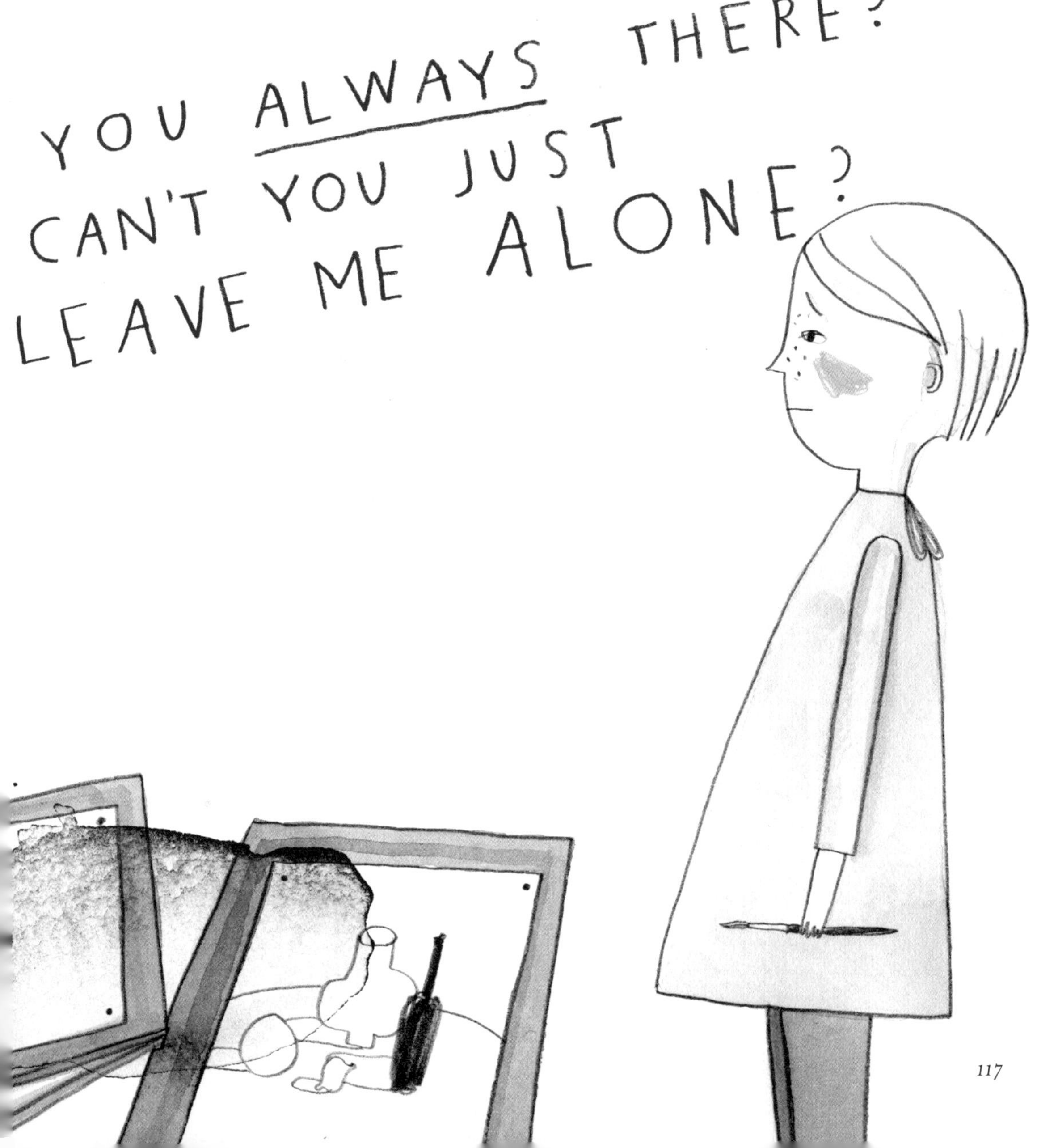
YOU ALWAYS THERE?
CAN'T YOU JUST
LEAVE ME ALONE?

To make matters worse, my grandfather
is waiting for me when I get home.
"You can't not go to school," he says.

YOU DON'T
YOU ARE

UNDERSTAND!

NOT EVEN MY

REAL

GRANDPA!

I say.

I pack my bag and go to stay at my aunt's.

APRIL

I am still there when Easter rolls around. It's really early this year and it's still very cold. Even though I only go to church when I am with my aunt, I really love Easter. You are supposed to observe Lent for forty days beforehand, and on Holy Saturday, you fast from noon until after the procession at midnight, so Varya and I are a bit woozy from hunger and everything is super funny.

As soon as we can, we run outside and stuff our faces with Cadbury eggs that my mom has sent.

It's crisp out and snowing very softly and I feel like anything can happen.

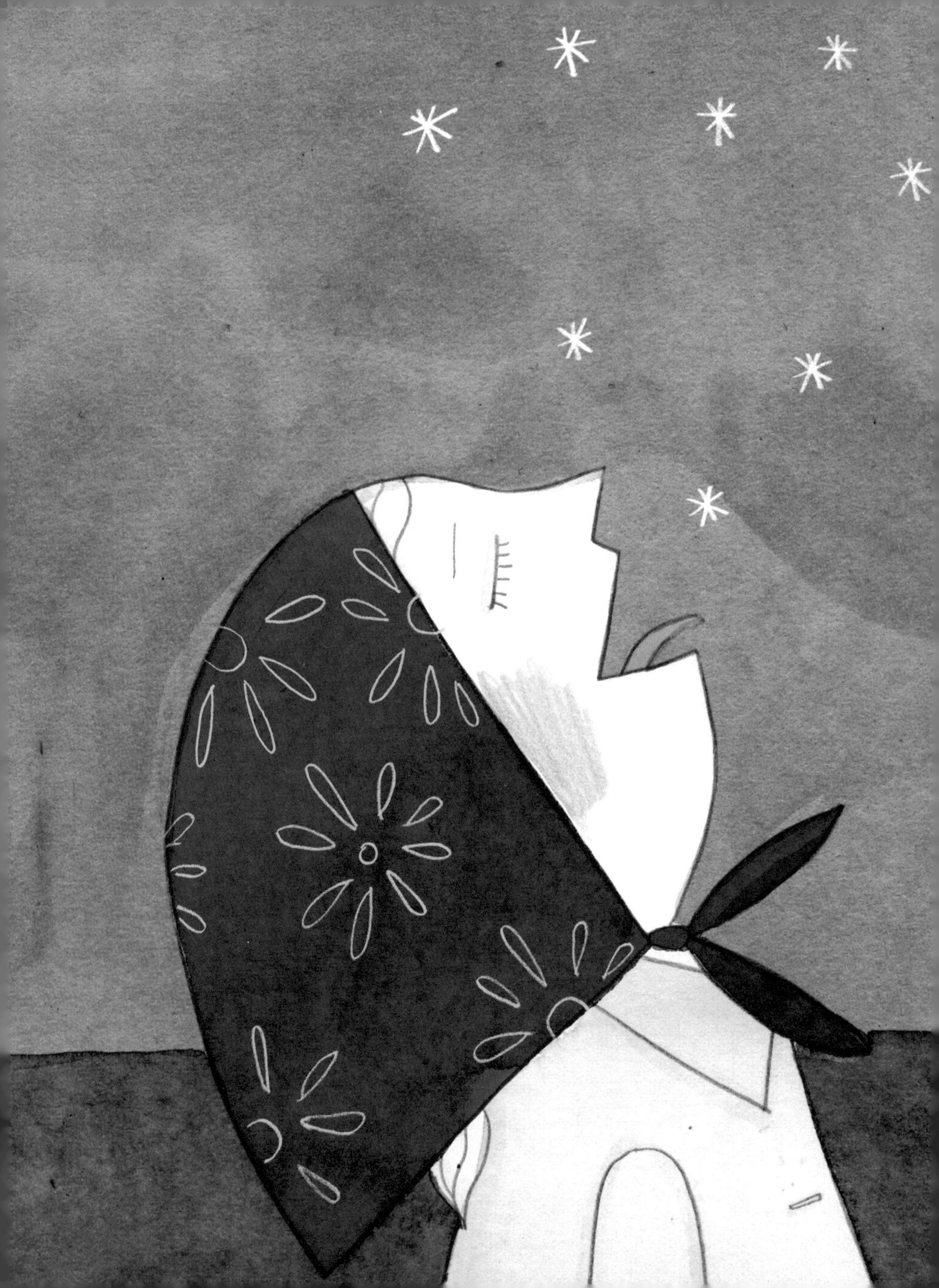

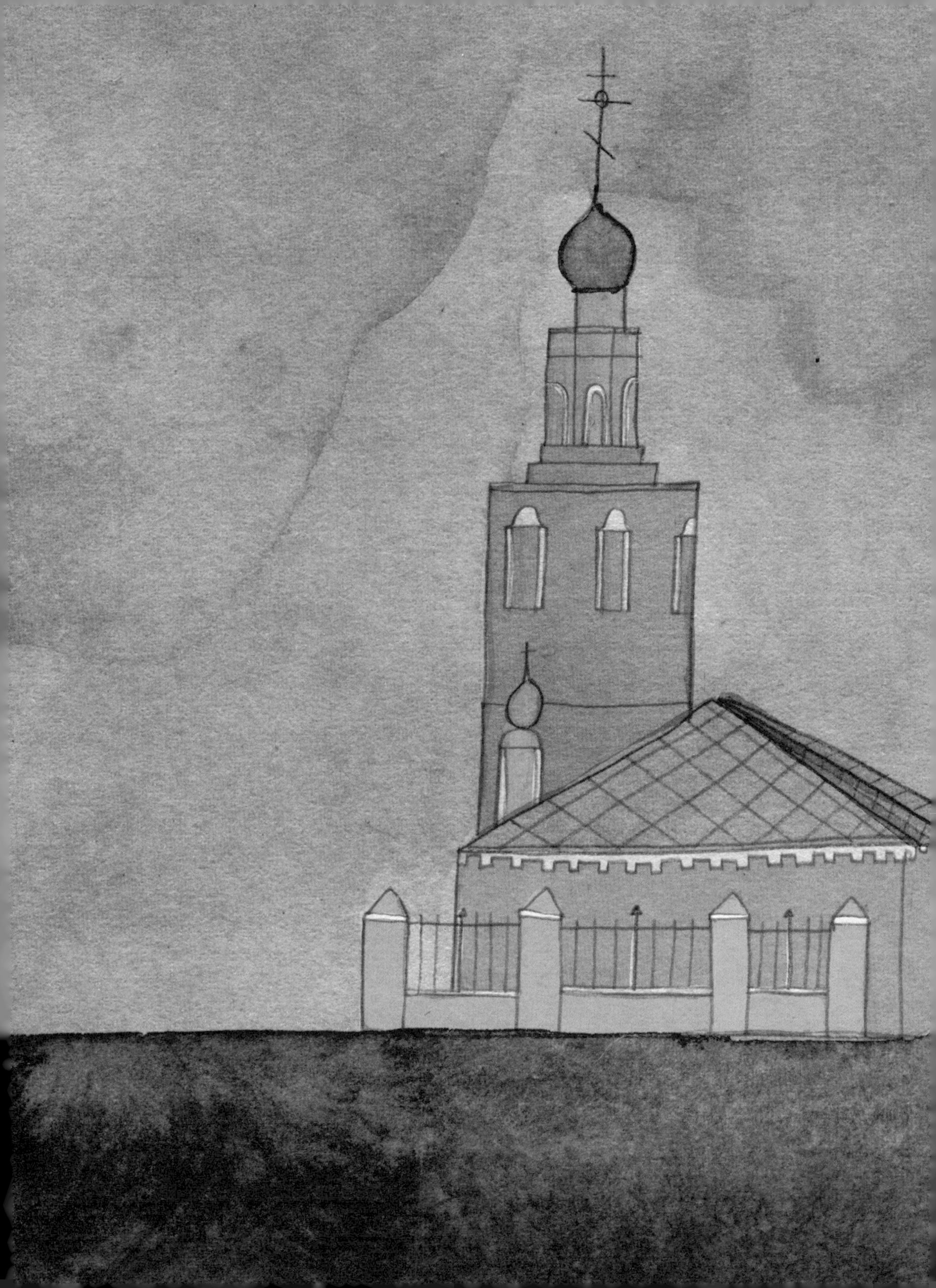

On Thursday, I go to take my last test for 67. I did the written lit and math tests earlier in the week, and I got a 4/5 and 5/5 on those. All of my staying up and studying has paid off! I feel pretty confident I am going to do just as well on the English.

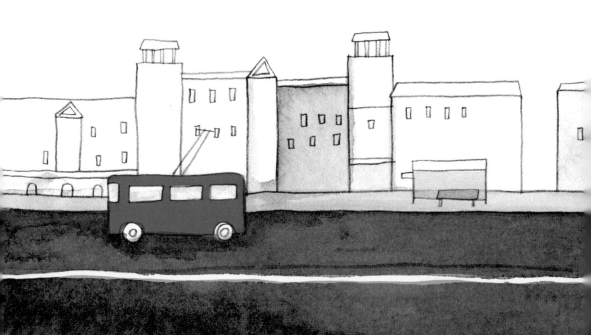

I am skipping from the bus. The magical feeling I got on Easter night has been inside me this whole time, and I carry it in me — contented and careful not to spill. Also, I just know I am going to see P today. I can feel it. I run to the school. Today is the day! I am going to tell him I love him. He has to know. And Masha is right — I AM awesome!

And then. When I turn the corner. I do see him.

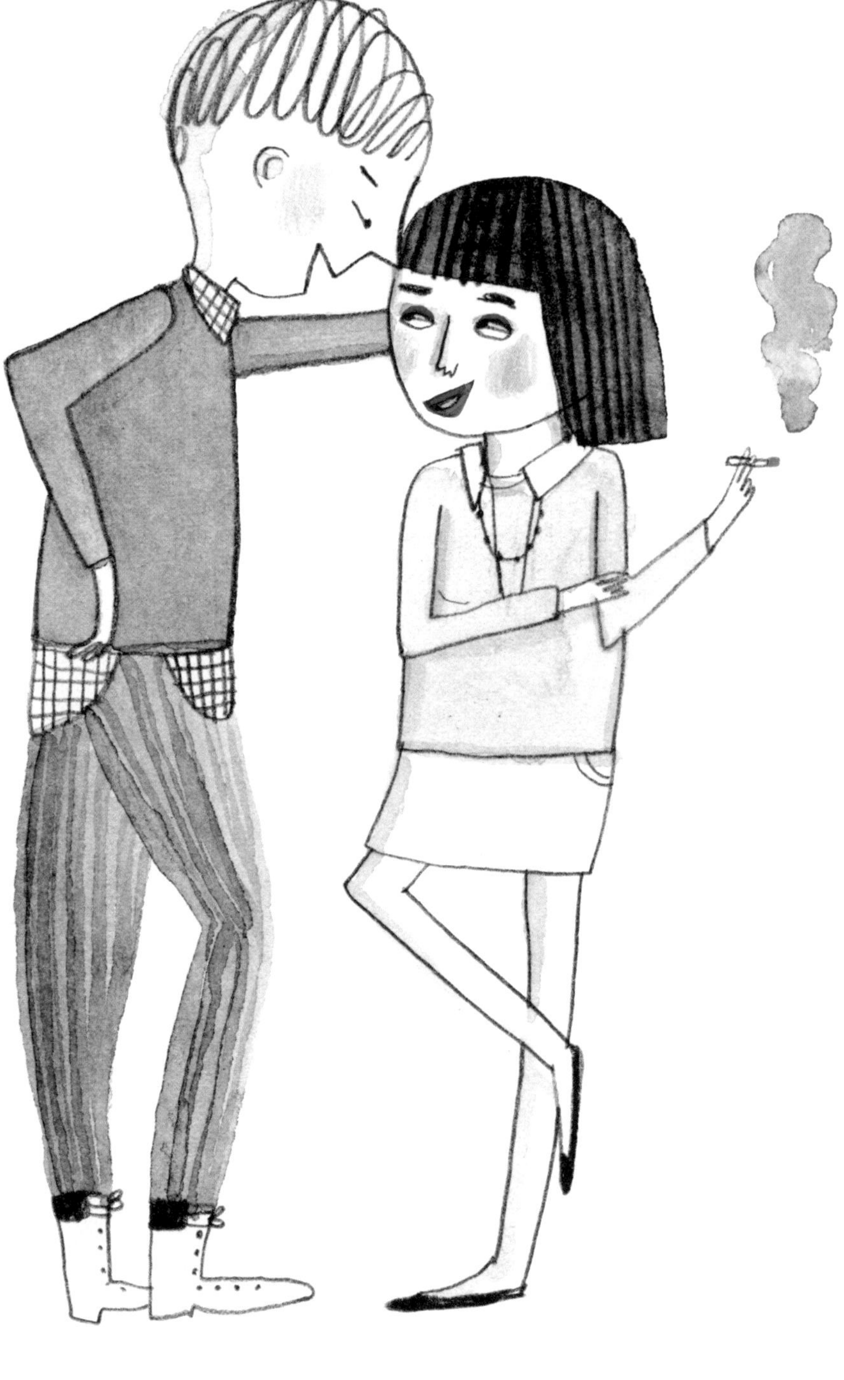

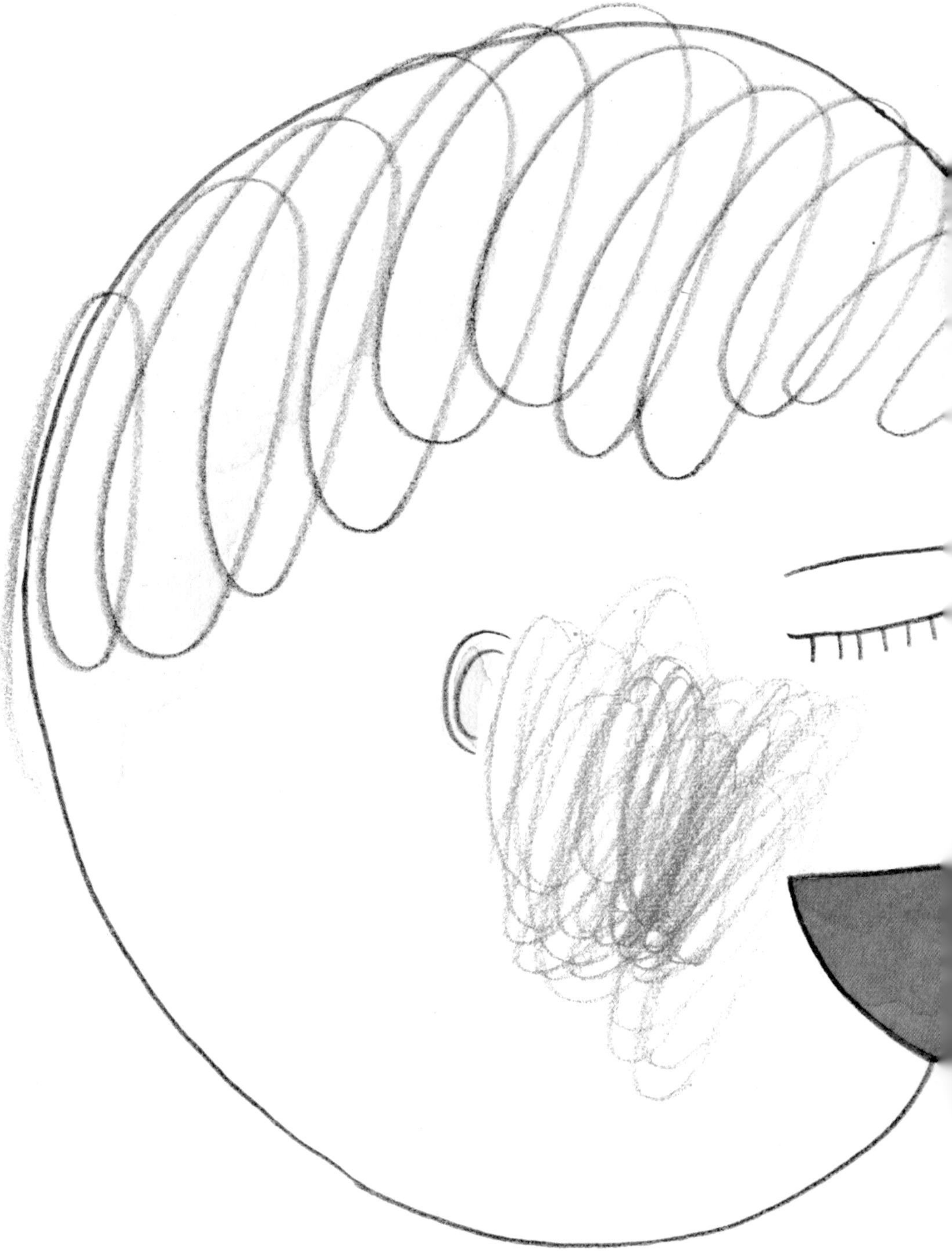

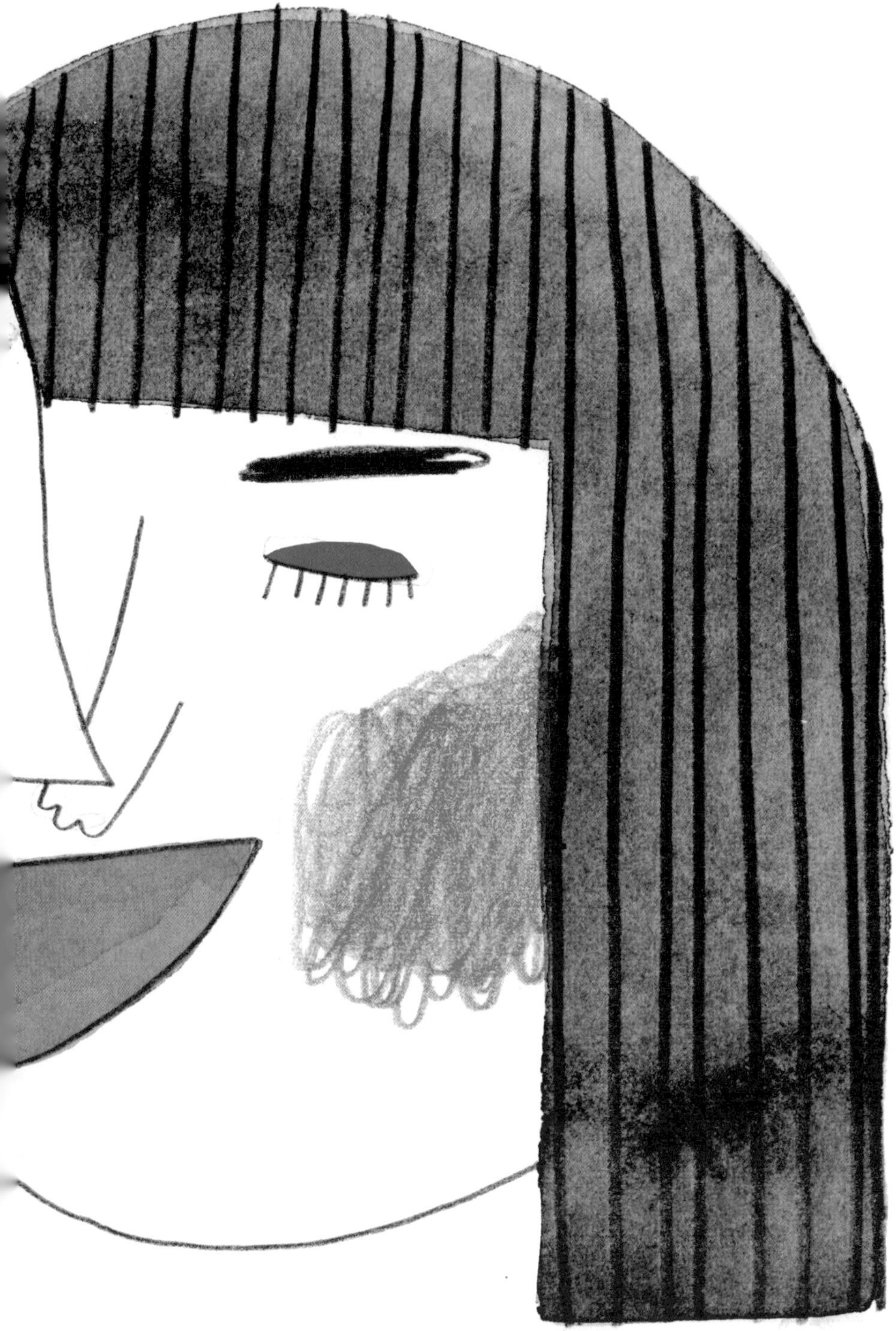

The topic that I pull for the exam is "what I did last summer." I am trying to write down notes for my exam, to prepare, but I have forgotten most of the English words I know. I keep saying "last summer" over and over, but nothing else comes. Slowly the room empties out, until I am the last one left.

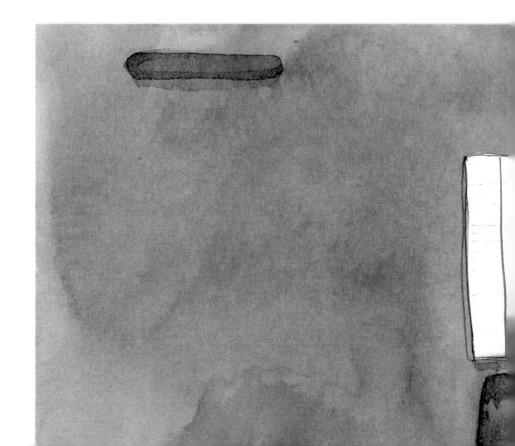

I remember nothing. The examiner seems extra mean — she keeps pushing me, overcorrecting every time I start to say something. I don't know if I start crying AT the exam or just as I shut the door, but once I start, I don't stop.

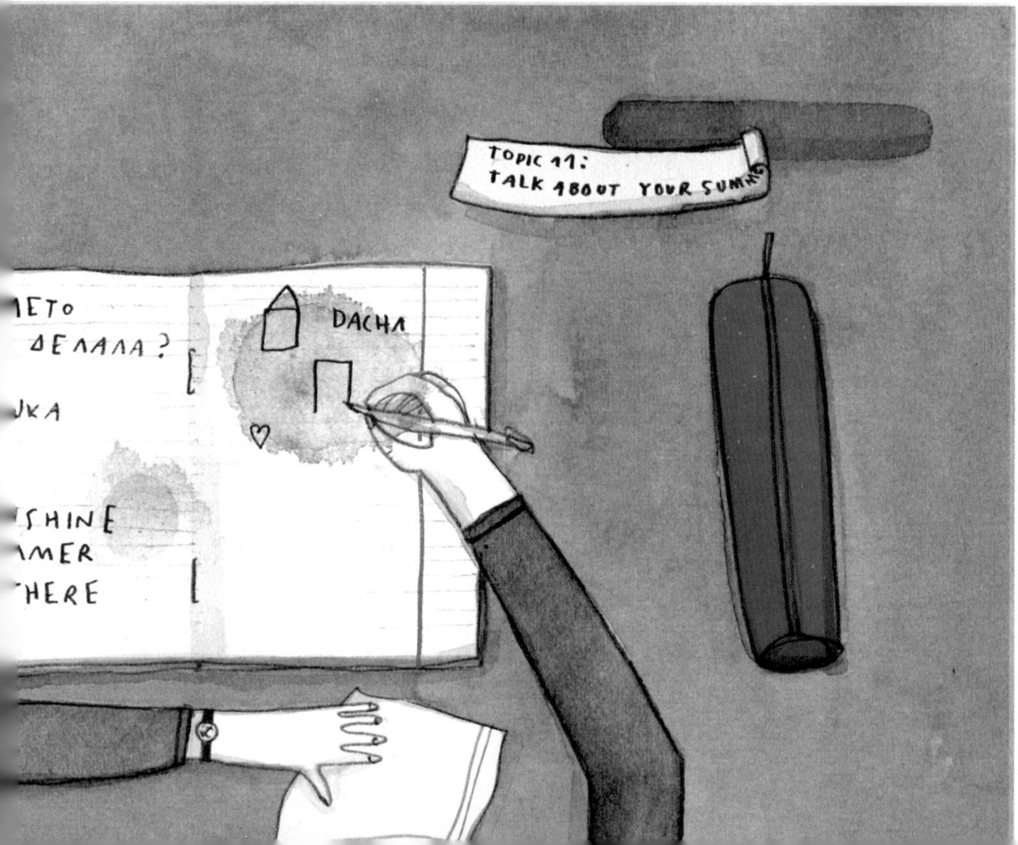

TOPIC 11:
TALK ABOUT YOUR
DACHA

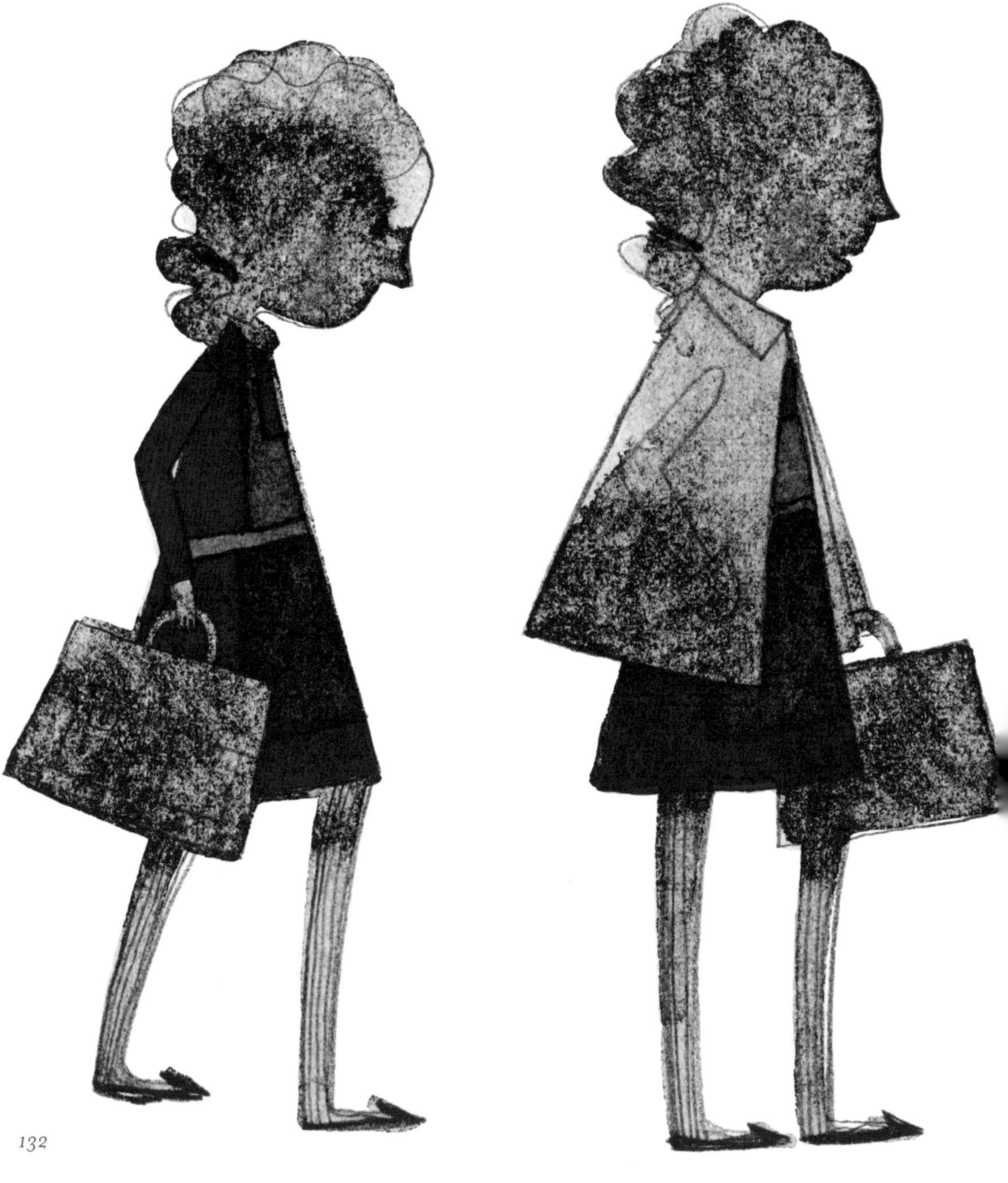

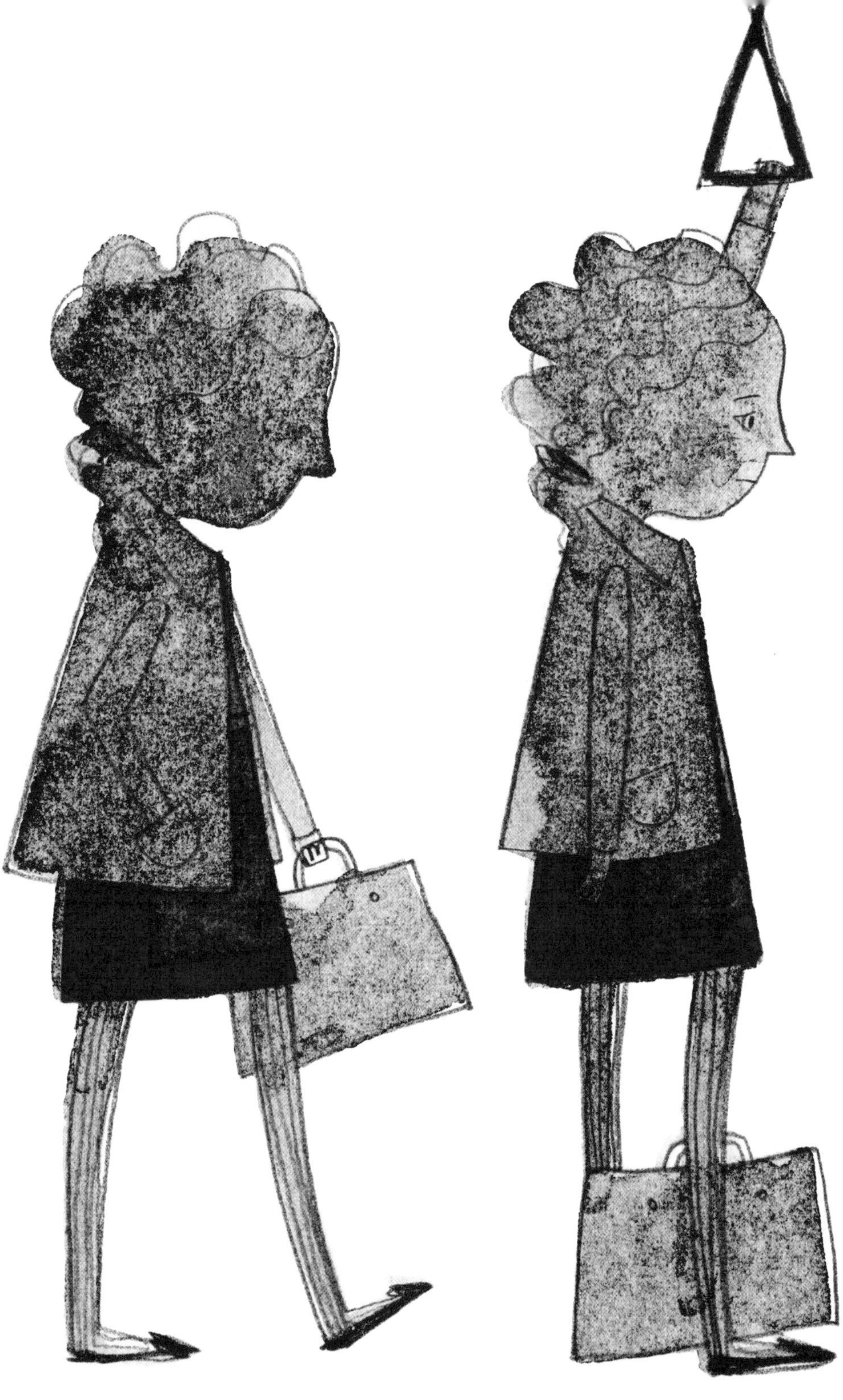

I cry running down the hallway of the school. I cry in the courtyard. I cry on my way to the bus. On the bus. Walking to our apartment from the stop. Going up in the elevator. And, finally, in front of the front door, where I buzz to be let in.

I tell my grandmother everything. I tell her about the failed exam, and Petya, and being so stupid and mean and uncool. She just keeps saying,

Oh, honey, I had no idea,

and holds my head on her lap and strokes my hair.

I am so impressed with you. All of that business with School 67. I know it doesn't feel like that now, but you did that all yourself! You submitted the application, and took the exams...

But I failed!
MY LIFE IS RUINED!

I sob.

Oh, baby girl, your life is just beginning. Nothing is ruined,

she says.

But Petya...

I whisper.

She strokes my hair more, in slow, even movements, until I fall asleep.

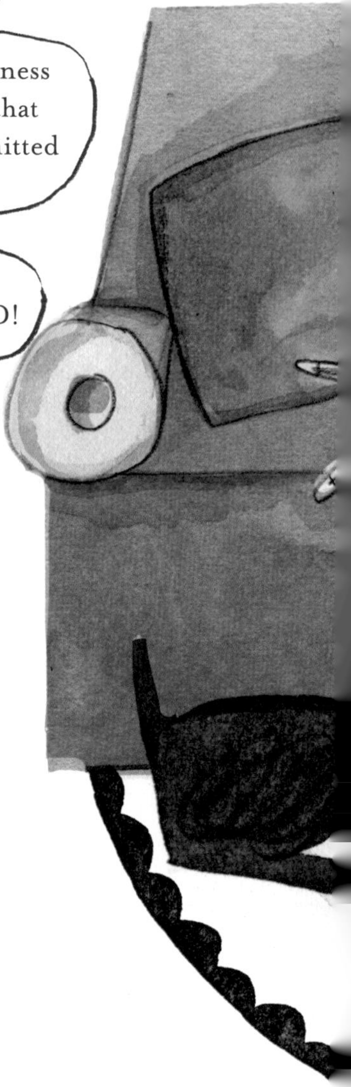

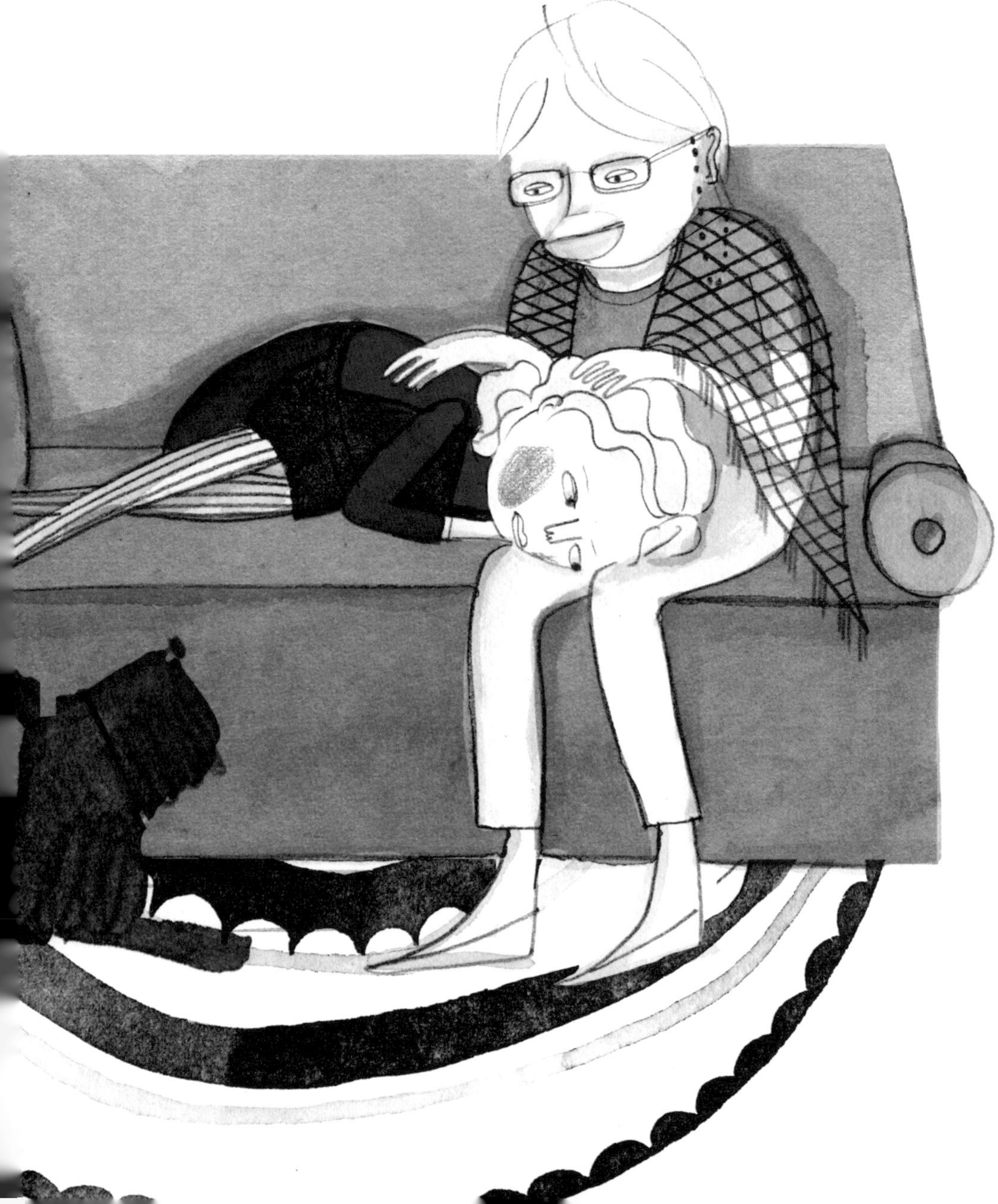

MAY

And then it's SPRING. The trees have that sticky halo around them — the see-through green. But really the way you KNOW is that you can walk home from school in just your uniform, without a jacket on!

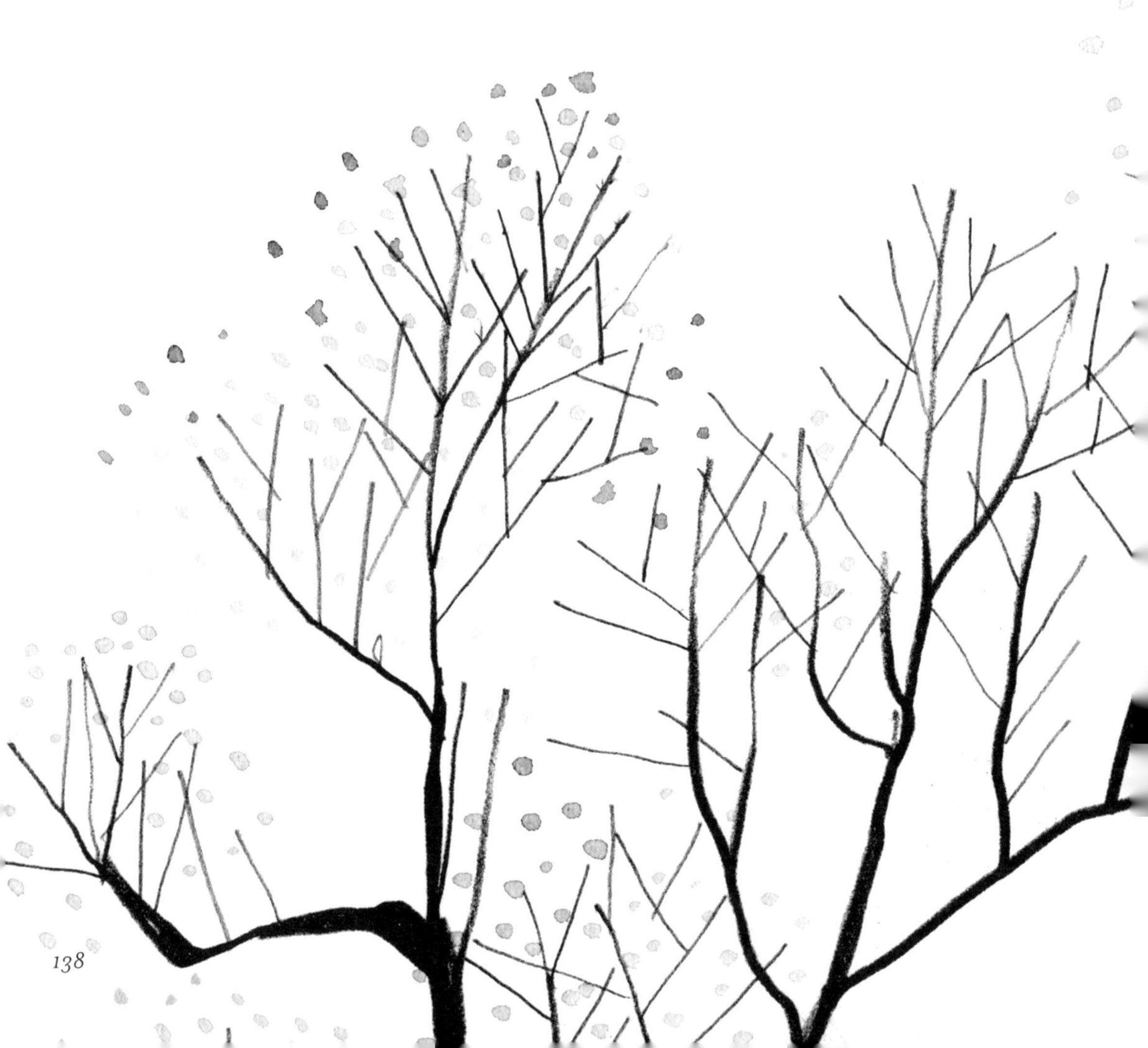

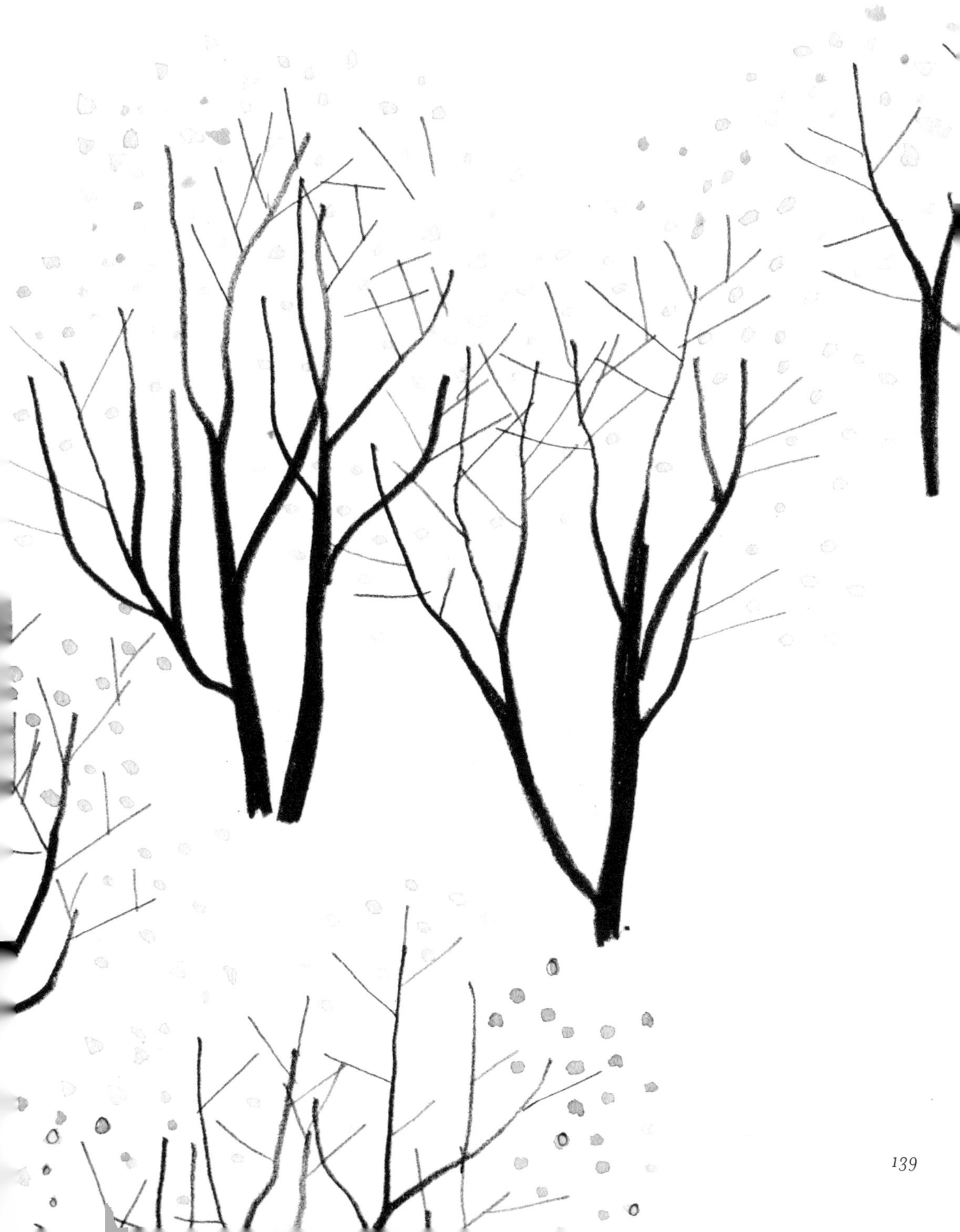

School is almost done for the year and
usually this is my favorite time. But THIS
YEAR it feels like everything is about to
change. Masha passed her French oral
so brilliantly that, even though her other marks were 4/5 and 3/5, she has been
accepted to 67 and will go there next year.
Natasha hasn't heard back from pre-college
yet, but I'm sure she'll get in, and, if not,
it will STILL be different without Masha.
It's complicated because I want the best
for my friend, but I also don't want her to
leave.

Masha swears she is not going to change.

You'll see, we'll still hang out every day after school!

Yeah, we'll see.

One thing that's changed already, though, is that I don't like Petya anymore!

I think I like Maxim!

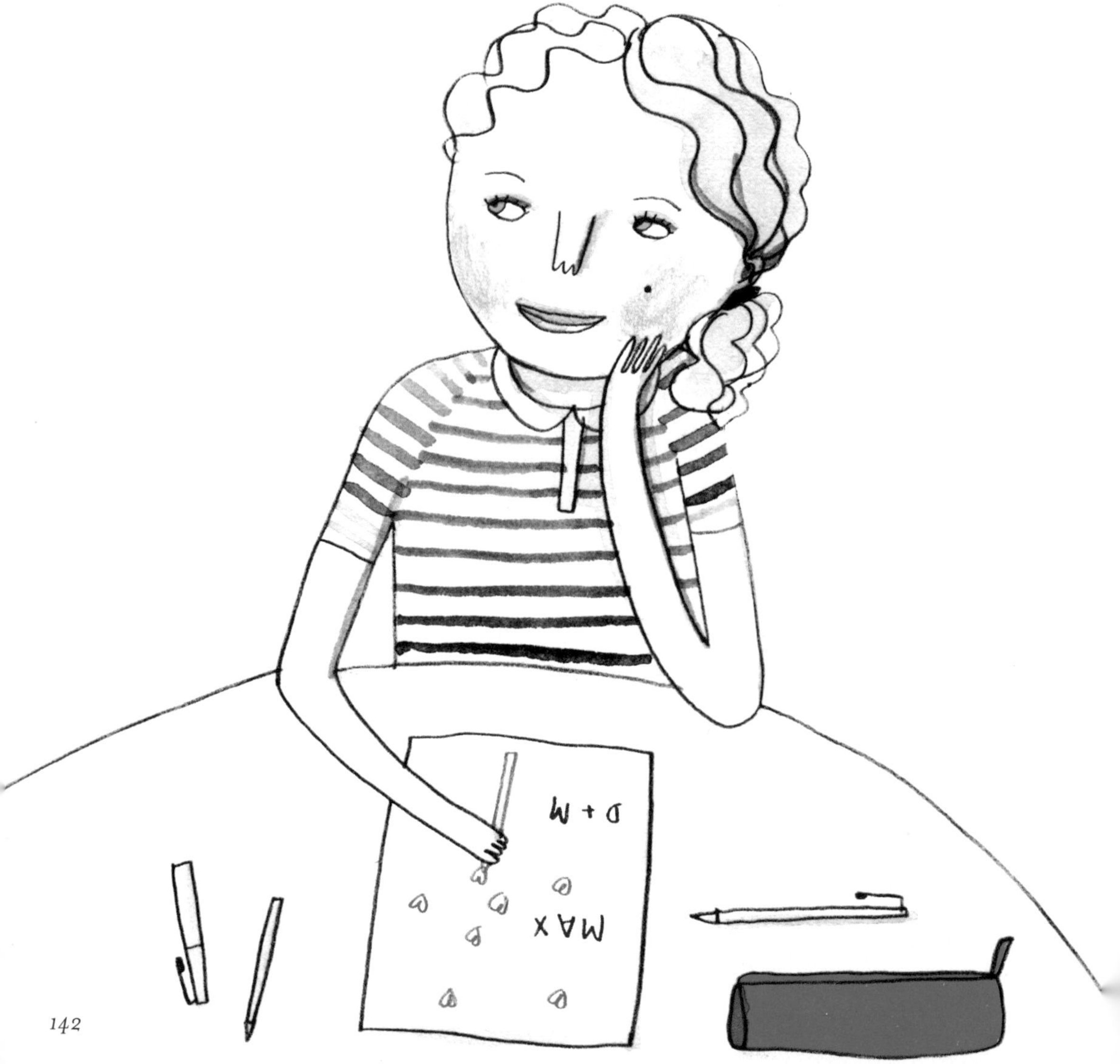
D + M
MAX

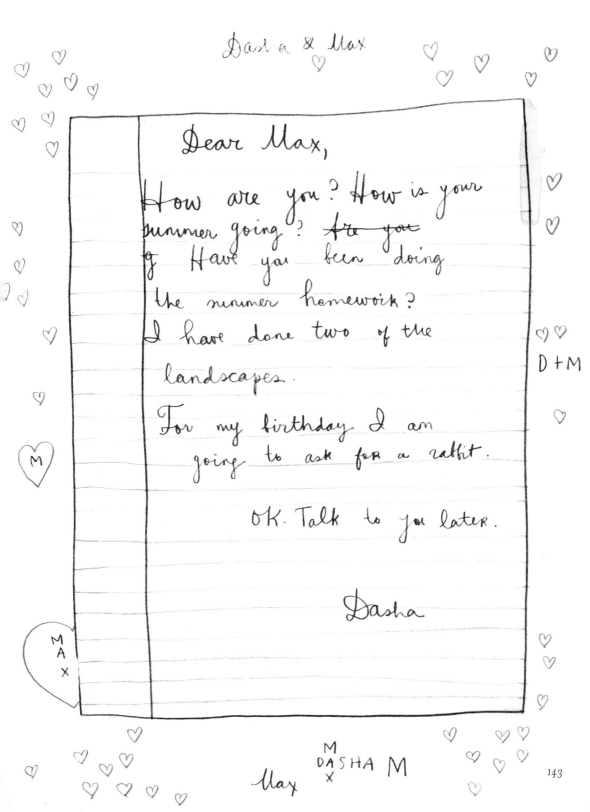

Dasha & Max

Dear Max,

How are you? How is your summer going? ~~Are you~~ ~~g~~ Have you been doing the summer homework?
I have done two of the landscapes.

For my birthday I am going to ask for a rabbit.

OK. Talk to you later.

Dasha

D + M

M

M
A
X

Max

M
DASHA M
X

143

JUNE

My mom comes home in the middle of the month.

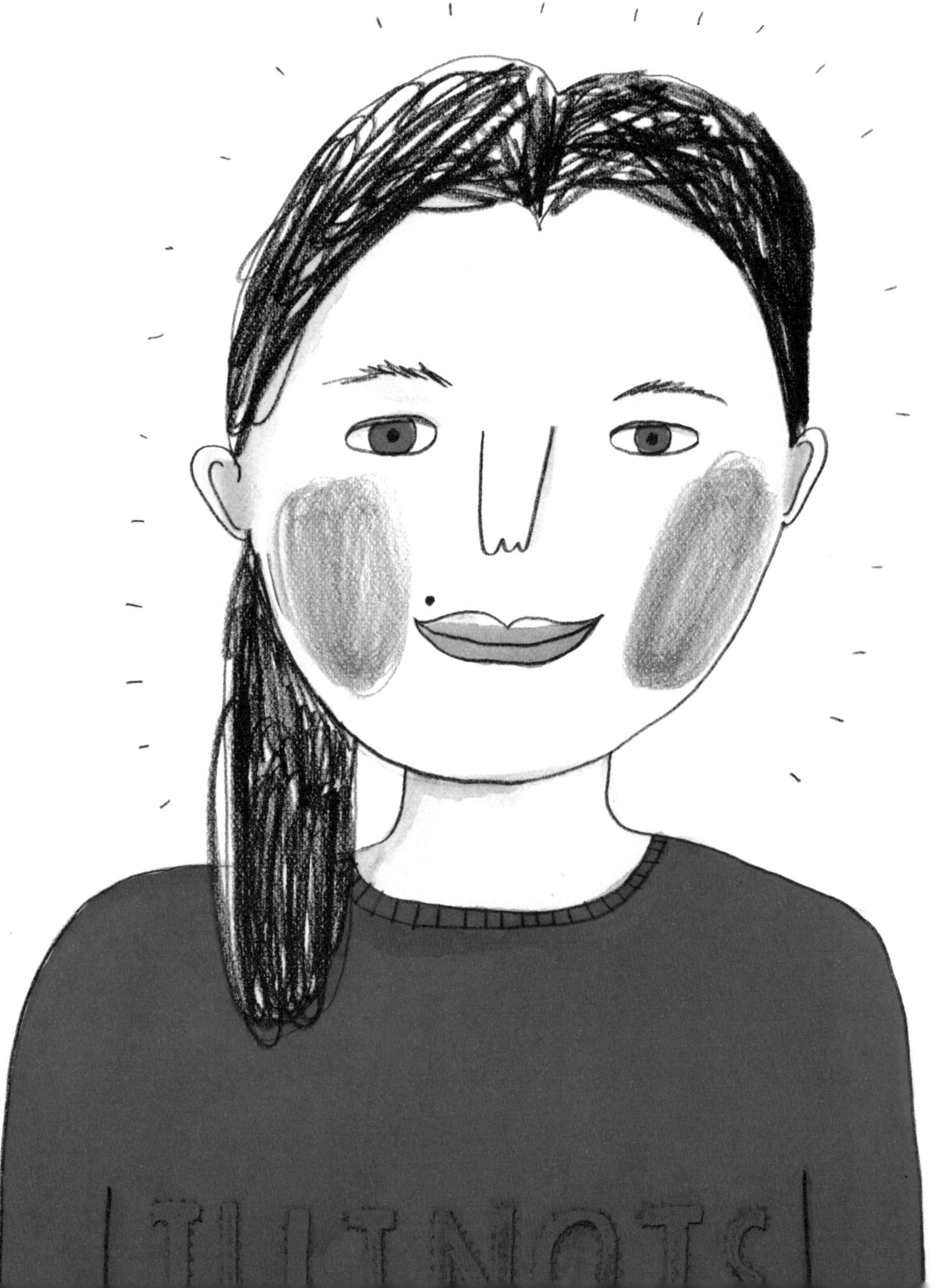

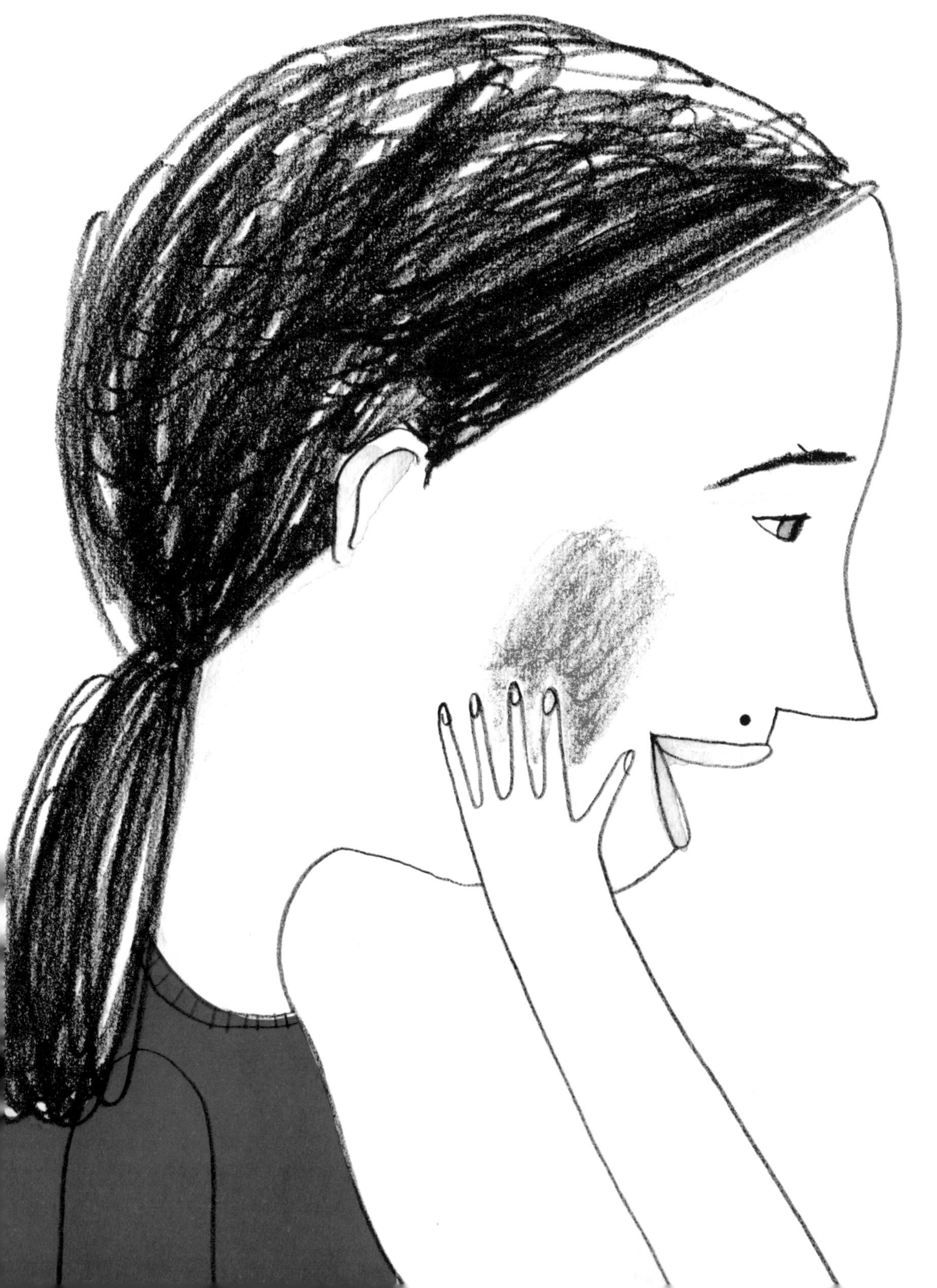

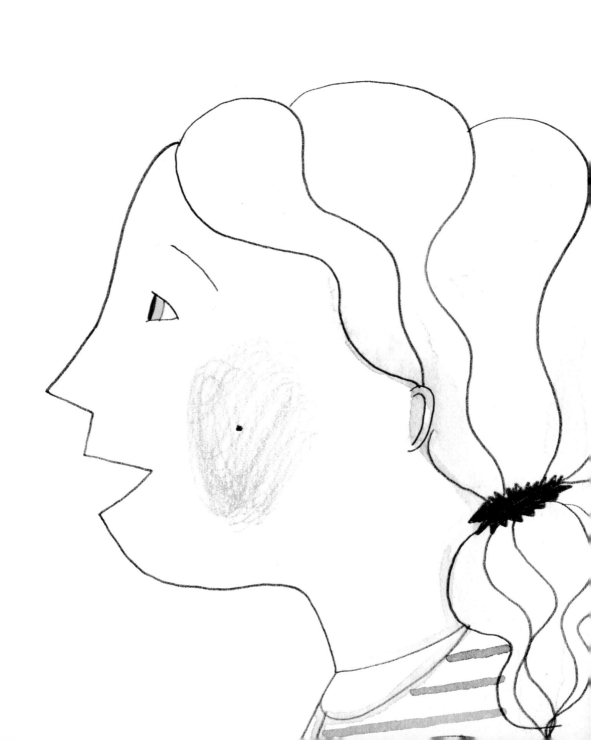

I am so happy to see her! She is the same. And seeing her is like finally taking a breath after holding it in for a year.

But also not the same. For example, she brought me presents and I am so happy that she remembered that my favorite color is pink, except that it isn't anymore. It's been lavender since September, but I don't want to hurt her feelings.

And in the morning she made me jam toast for breakfast — except I like Nutella now, since having it in Germany.

JULY

Mom's been telling me all about the place where she's been going to school. It's called Urbana and it's in Illinois, a couple of hours south of Chicago. I know Chicago because a) it used to be my dad's favorite band — I have the tape, and b) there is a saying, "You are not in Chicago, dearest" — which is used when someone has a request above their station.

She tells me about the town, the university, her classes, her new friends, the family she's been living with … and shows me pictures.

"This is going to be your room," she says.

WHAT ?!

I ask my grandmother.

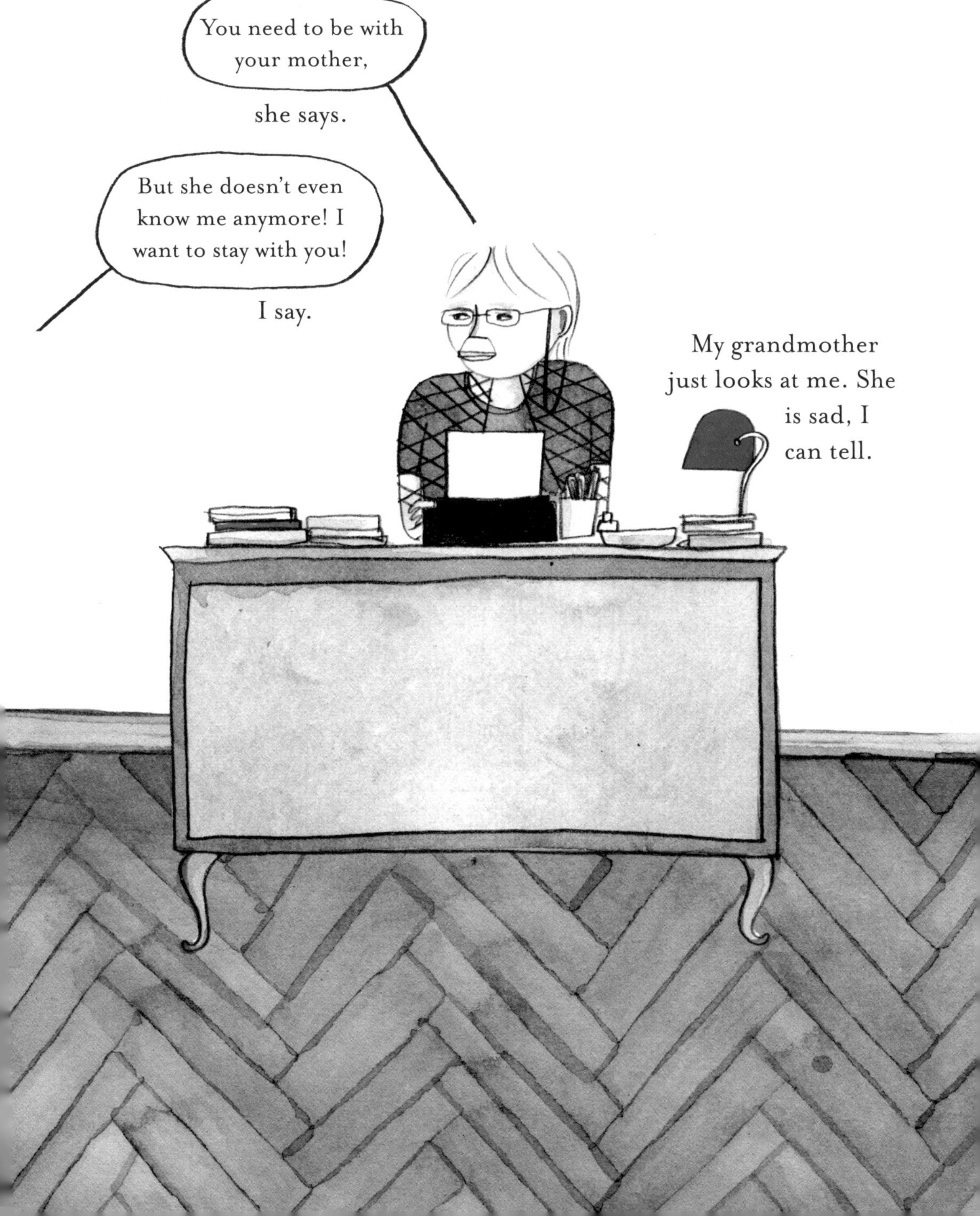
You need to be with your mother,
she says.
But she doesn't even know me anymore! I want to stay with you!
I say.
My grandmother just looks at me. She is sad, I can tell.

I am sad, too. I really don't want to go to America. Mom says it will only be for a year — until she finishes her master's degree. But it feels so far and for so long! I mean, the only things I even know about America are what I learned from *Gone with the Wind*, and also there was a girl who went there from our class back in the third grade — she wrote letters for a while and then we never heard from her again.

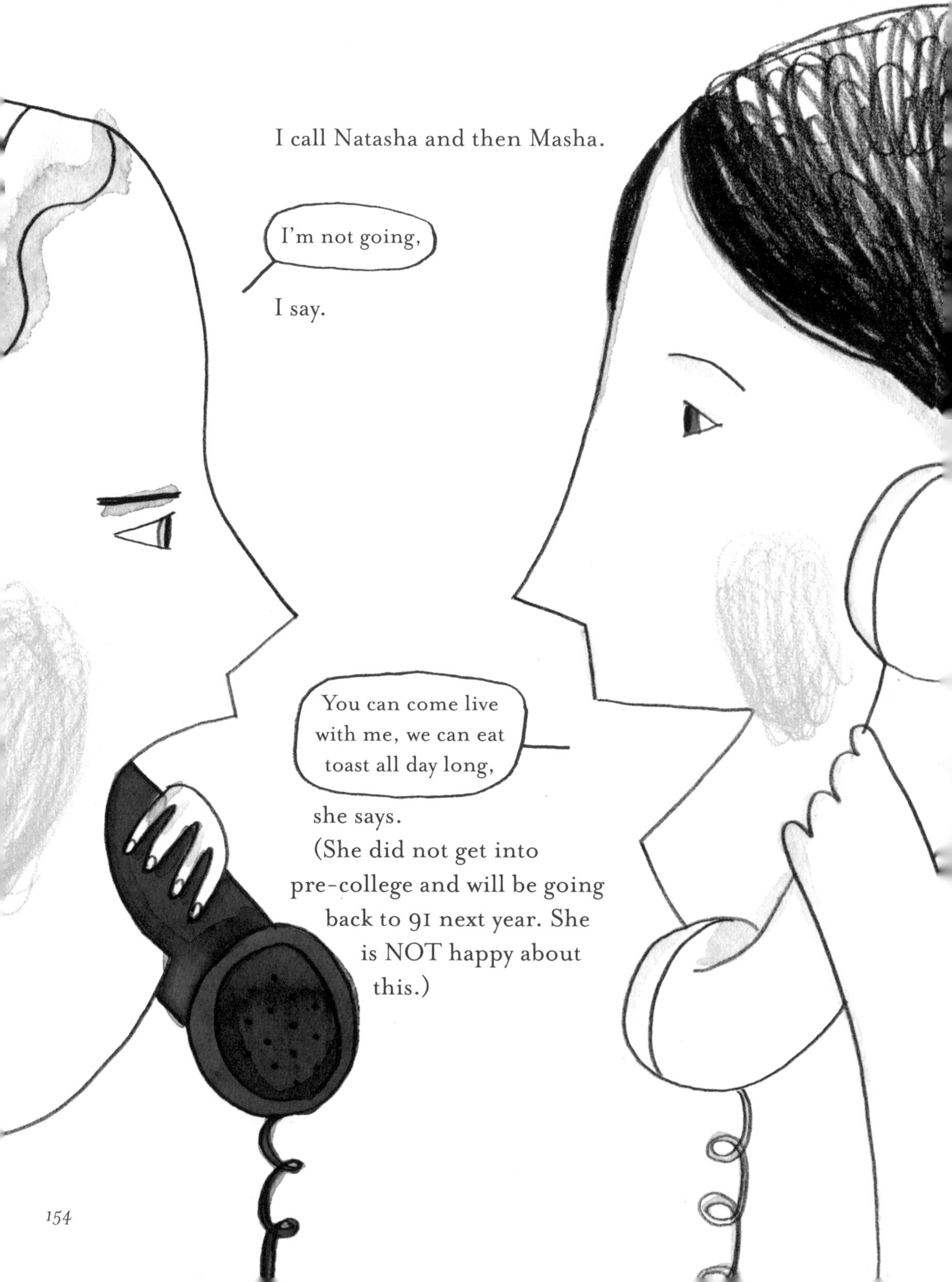

I call Natasha and then Masha.

I'm not going,

I say.

You can come live with me, we can eat toast all day long,

she says.
(She did not get into pre-college and will be going back to 91 next year. She is NOT happy about this.)

I really liked it in Paris. Maybe it will be more like that? Good chocolate,

says Masha.

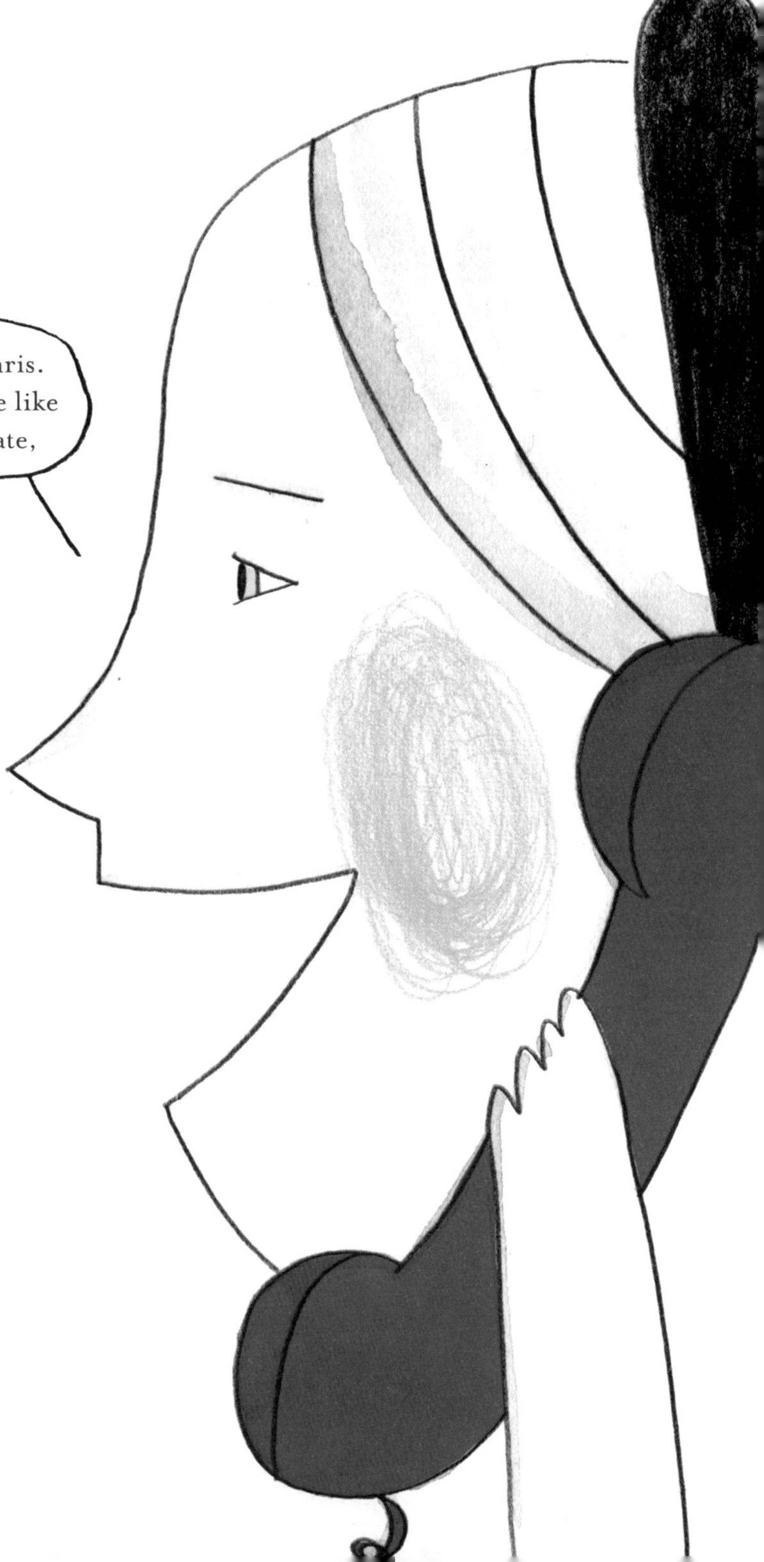

I cry and beg and plead, but in the end they say, "You'll like it there, you'll see. It's for your own good."

I'M NOT GOING!

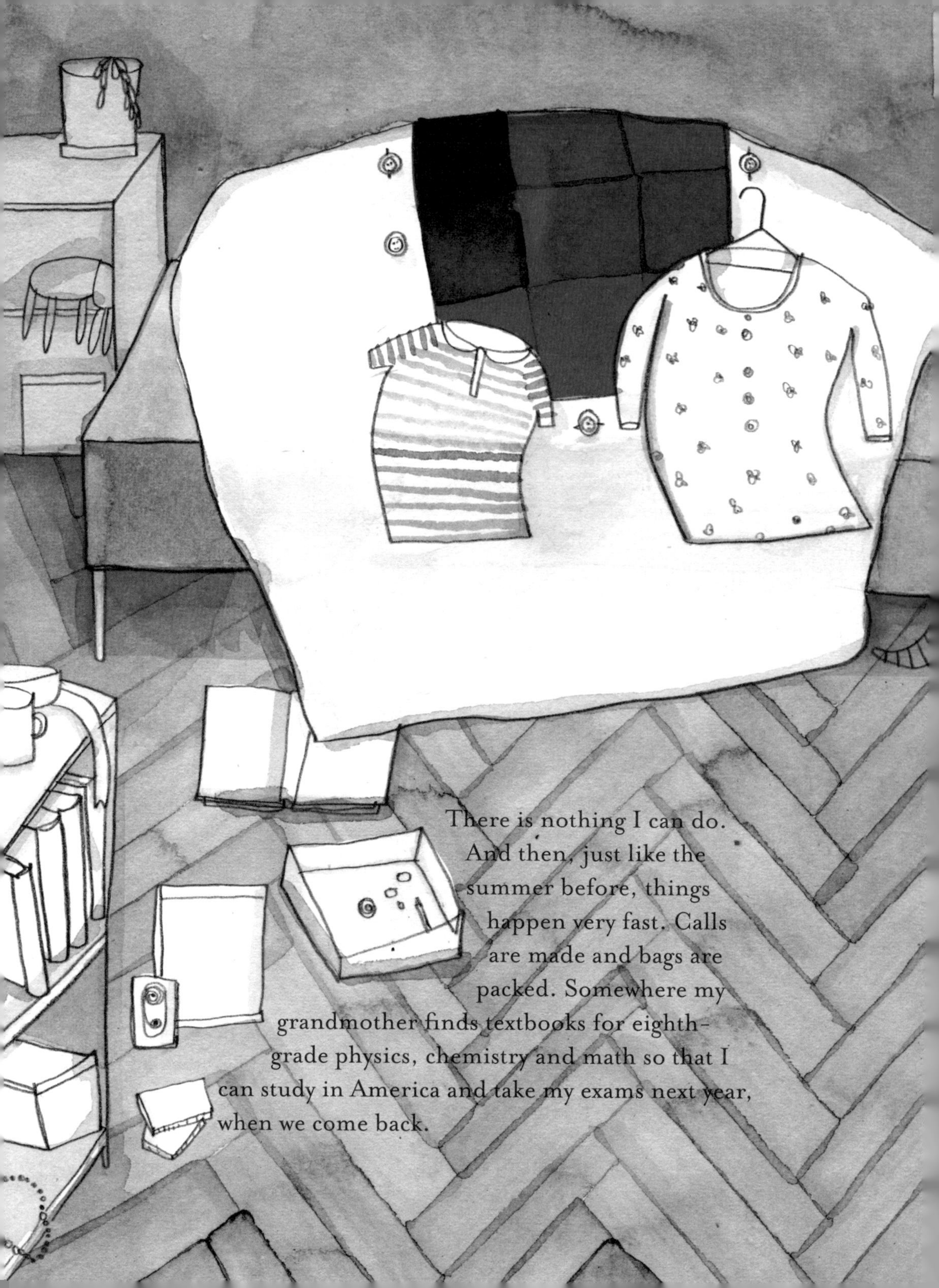

There is nothing I can do. And then, just like the summer before, things happen very fast. Calls are made and bags are packed. Somewhere my grandmother finds textbooks for eighth-grade physics, chemistry and math so that I can study in America and take my exams next year, when we come back.

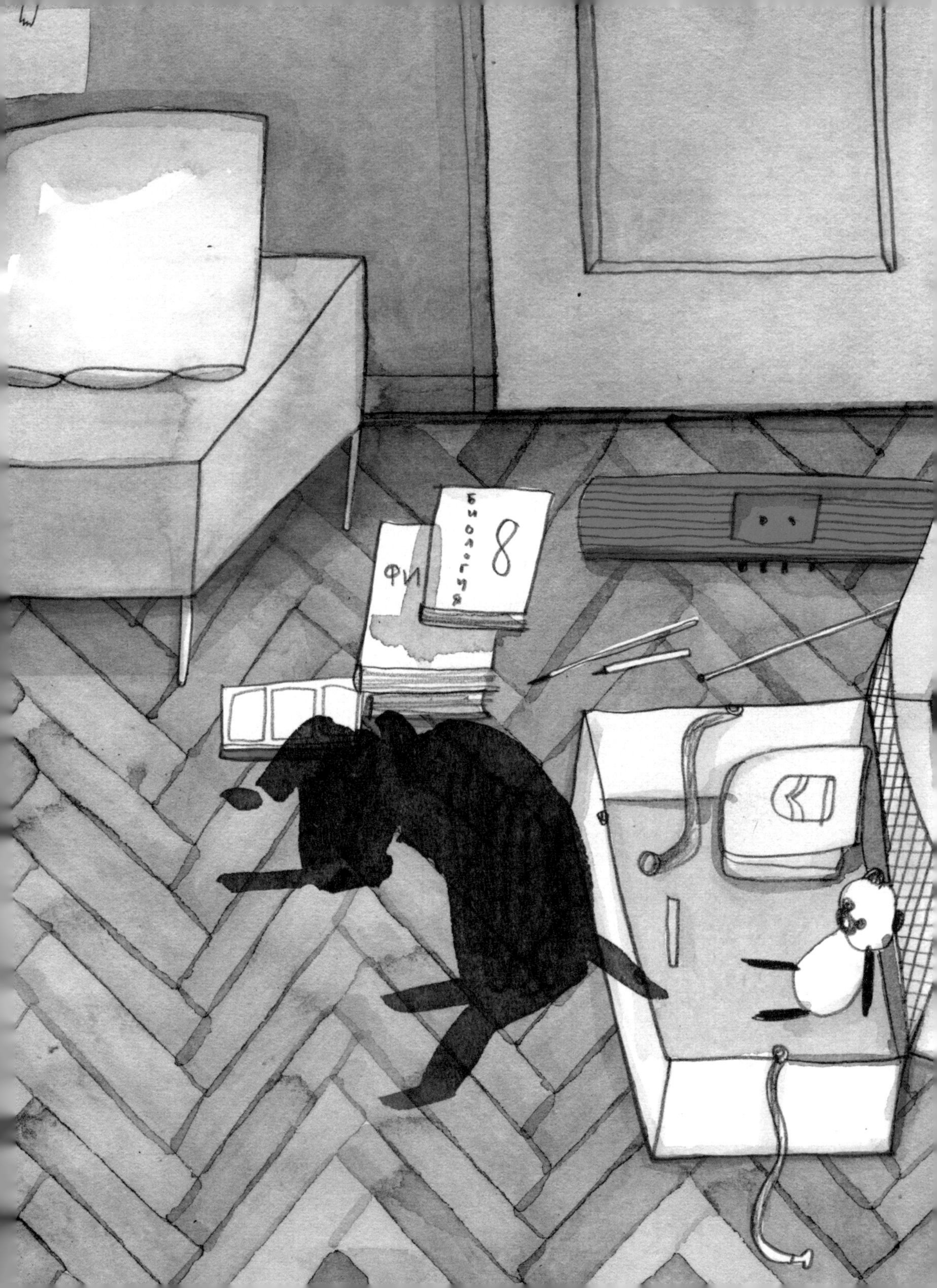
Биология
8
ФИ

AUGUST

It's an early-morning flight.

We have to get to the airport even earlier because there is a lot to do — a long line for check-in and then a long line for customs, and then for the passport control. I have my own passport.

We have a layover in Shannon, Ireland, and Mom buys me a pretty cup.

It's the longest I've ever been on a plane.

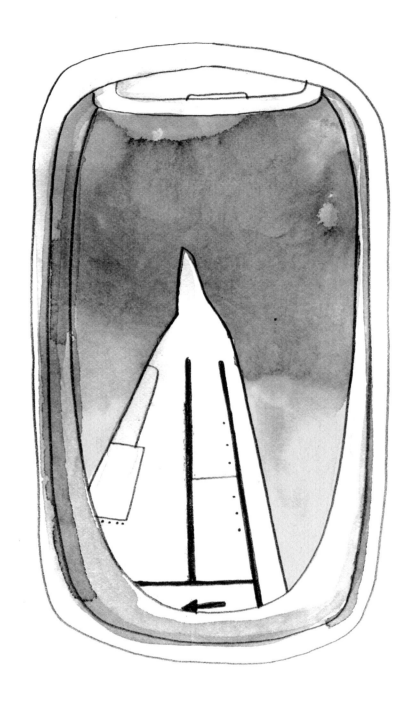

AME

When we land in Chicago, Dick and Frances, my mom's American family, are there to pick us up. It's a two-hour drive to Urbana.

There is almost nothing to see on the drive. Mostly it's farms.

"This is corn country," says Dick.

I don't like how flat everything is.

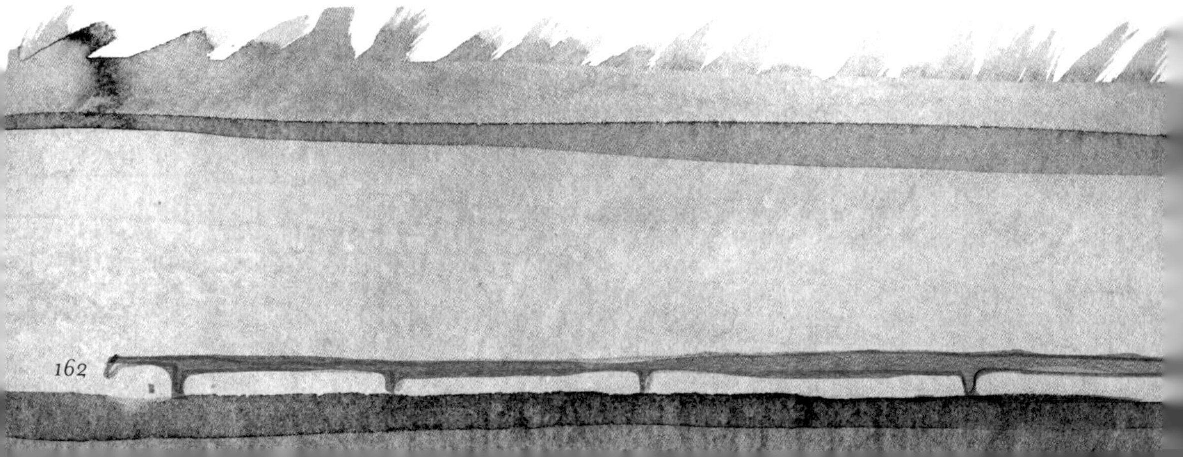

RICA

SOUTH
INTERSTATE
ILLINOIS
57

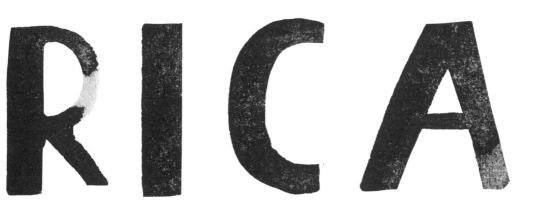

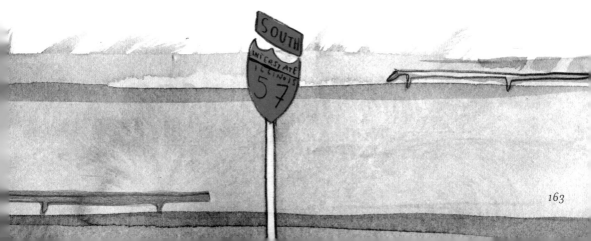

In Urbana, the houses are one or two stories with yards. There are so many cars everywhere and you have to drive to the store.

I see a lot of girls wearing short jean jackets with really long sleeves, and at least I'm glad I packed mine.

Frances tells me to call her Franny (like in *Franny and Zooey*!). We eat dinner at 6:00 every night, and I learn about things like Campbell's mushroom soup casserole and Dairy Queen hamburgers. (Hate the casserole, love the burgers.)

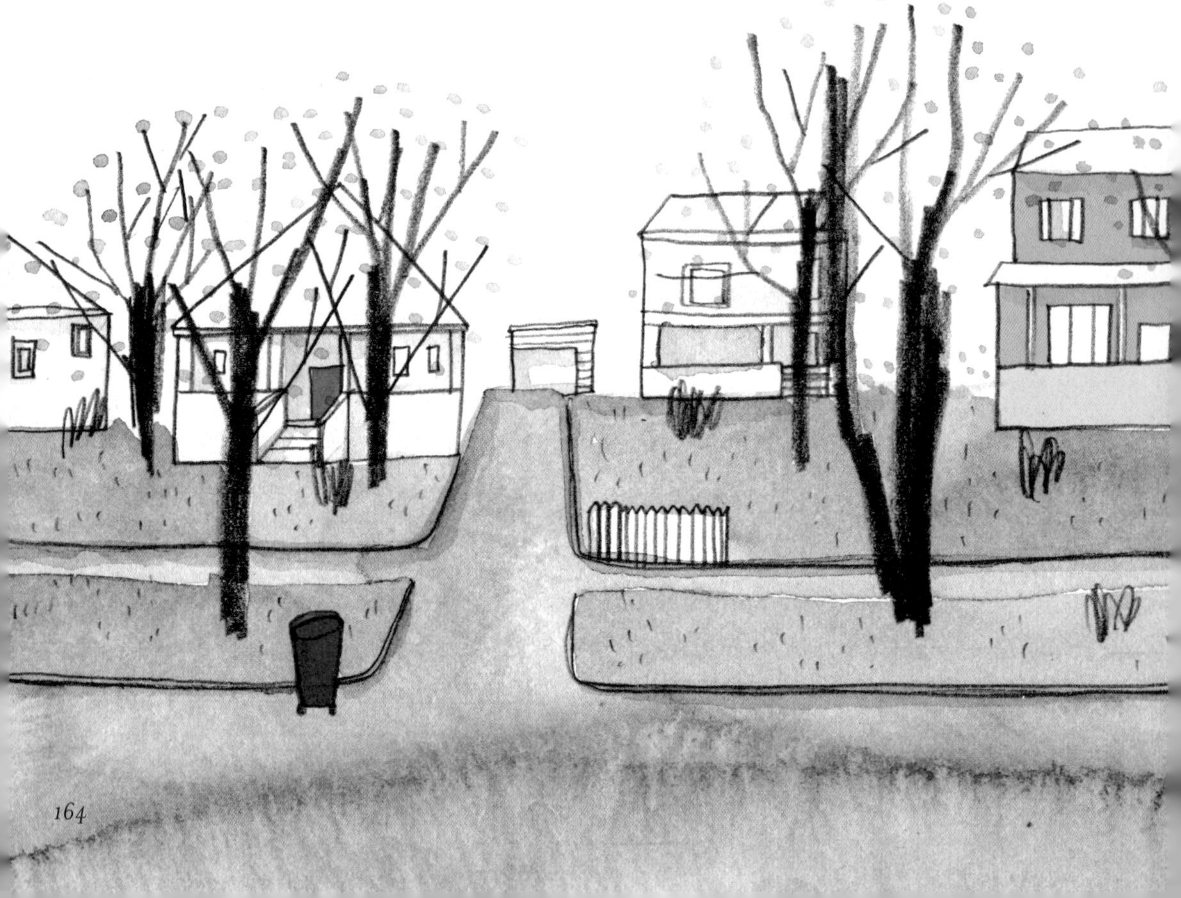

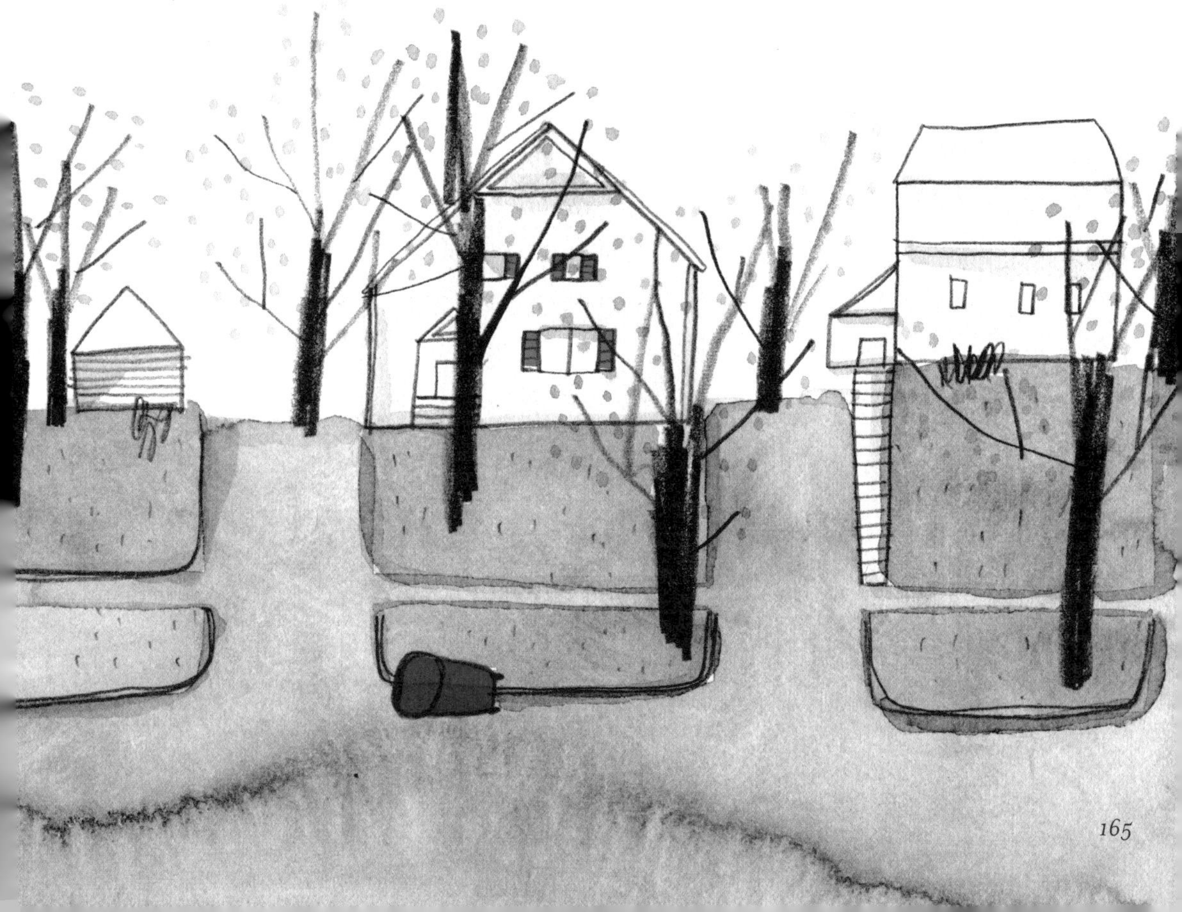

The second week we are there, Mom takes me to sign up for middle school. The school is so much bigger than my old one in Russia, even though it only goes from sixth to eighth grade. The principal of the school takes us around the building.

My mother goes into her office to talk in private for a second, and I wait in the hallway. A very blonde, small girl comes in and sits next to me.

"Hi," she says. "I'm Louisa. What's your name?"

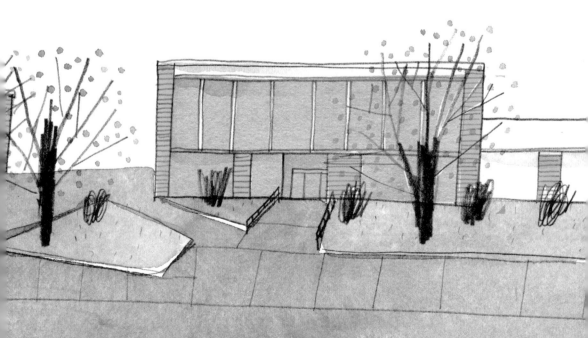

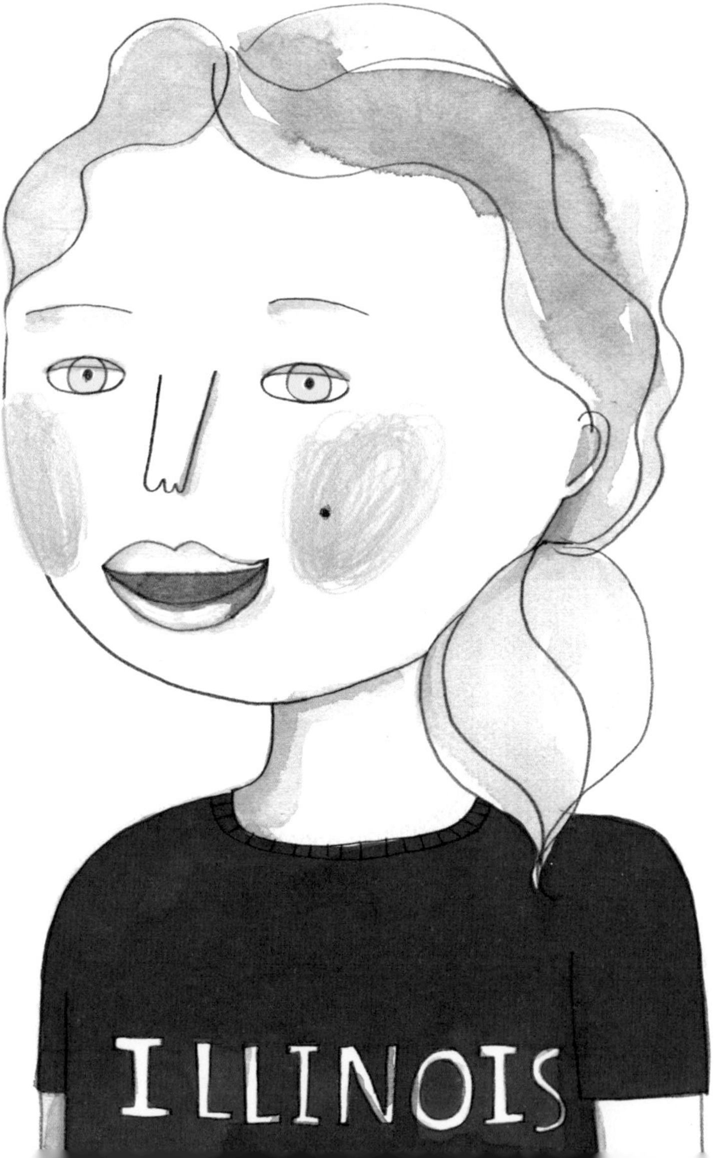
ILLINOIS